black
dove

also by carrigan richards

Standalone Novel
Pieces of Me

Elemental Enchanters Series
Under a Blood Moon (#1)
Under the Burning Stars (#2)
When Darkness Fell (#2.5)
Under the Winter Sun (#3)
Under an Onyx Sky (#4)

January Dreams Series
January Dreams
Silent Dreams
Shattered Dreams

black dove

Carrigan Richards

Carrigan Richards Publishing, LLC
PO Box 3782
Suwanee, GA 30024

Cover Design by: Lauren Perrin
www.laurenconnellydesign.com
Edited by Lindsey Alexander. www.theeditoriallist.com
Copy edited by Jennifer Watts
Proofread by The Literary Vixen

Library of Congress Cataloging-in-Publication Data is available.
ISBN-13: 979-8-9858225-2-6

Printed and bound in the USA

For Amber.

Dear Reader,

Please be aware that *Black Dove* contains content that may be triggering. For a list of content, please see the bottom of the next page.

Black Dove contains the following content: self-mutilation, physical abuse, alcohol addiction, death.

when a dove begins to associate
with crows, its feathers remain
white, but its heart grows black

German Proverb

alisa

Blood has such a pretty color. The deep red holds me in a trance as it rolls down my arm. Some of it sticks to the scissor blade and drips onto the carpet. Daddy will kill me if he finds out I stained the floor. But I can't stop staring at the color. I need to feel that rush again. I need to feel something.

I drag the blade across my arm again, always the same four spots, and watch the blood seep out. My pulse races and I feel the rush through my veins. It feels good. I feel alive.

And soon, I am far away. Laughing with my mom and dad. We are at the beach. I can feel the cool, grainy sand beneath my feet as the sun warms my skin. Seagulls squawk above eager for food. Waves crash softly against the shore. The salty, pungent ocean scent permeates the air. It's perfect. And everything feels good. It was the only beach trip we ever took.

When it's over, I clean my scissors and wipe the blood from my arm. I soak up the drops from the floor and flush the tissues in the toilet. Daddy will be home soon, and I need to start dinner.

I worked today. It was the usual. Customers complaining and reminding me of how insignificant I really am because I'm just a cashier. I've been sixteen since November, and this summer I started working at Piggly Wiggly, or The Pig as everyone calls it, to help Daddy with the bills. It's a small grocery store down the street.

My 1980 Ford Escort didn't want to start. Normally, I don't have issues in the summer, but today it gave me hell. It's usually the cold winter that makes the car less than reliable. Maybe it's the starter. Mom and Daddy bought it brand new a few months before I was born, and Mom drove it until she got sick with lymphoma. The AC doesn't work, and there's no radio. The seatbelts don't lock. The powder blue paint has started to chip, showing rust. Daddy gave it to me this year, and by some miracle, it made the trip from Kentucky to Alabama. Uncle Troy, Daddy's uncle, helped us move, and lets us stay at the house. We don't have much interaction with Uncle Troy, but I see him sometimes tending to the chicken houses or the cows.

The house is hot, stale, and suffocating. The only AC window unit is in the living room. I have a box fan beside my bed that helps, but the power is out again. We can't afford much more than that. Daddy works hard as a receiving clerk at the Wal-Mart distribution center, but it's not enough to pay the bills sometimes.

We recently moved back to Vinemont after Mom died. When I was ten, we moved to Kentucky to be closer to Mom's family. When she died in March, they didn't care much for Daddy and vice versa. They said he ruined her life. Got her pregnant, married her too young, and never took care of her.

But they're wrong. He always took care of us. He only gets angry when he's drinking and when I don't listen.

In the two months since we moved back, I haven't really left except to go to work because we live so far away from everything, and it reeks outside of cattle and chickens. I hate the smell. Uncle Troy had the house converted from a barn. Wood paneling covers the walls and ugly, thin carpet is laid throughout. There are only two bedrooms and two bathrooms. There is an empty metal barn outside next to a tool shed that's seconds away from falling apart.

I hate the house because it gives me the creeps and I swear it's haunted. Or maybe it's being out in the country that's eerie. Strange animal noises used to keep me up at night, but I'm used to them now. I still have to sleep with a night light because of how dark it gets.

Sweat drips down my tank top as I make my way toward the kitchen.

Every night, I cook for Daddy, as one of my chores. I started cooking when I was six, helping Mom in the kitchen and learning different techniques. After Mom got sick, and since Daddy was busy taking care of her, I took over and fell in love with it. It's methodical for me. I love creating recipes or following and revising them. Cooking calms me and lets me be myself. I love the sound of cracking open fresh garlic; the smell of flour and milk mixed to make biscuit dough; the first taste of a new recipe.

But I've not prepared anything like that in a long time. I wish I could cook all the time. Or bake. Mom and I used to bake a lot when we could afford it. I loved it. I miss it. I wish there was a home economics class at school so I could bake. I'm not good at anything, but I can cook meals and experiment with the different ingredients. If I have them. If I don't, sometimes I steal spices from work. I hate stealing, but cooking makes me feel good, and I want to feel good about myself.

Since we can't afford for me to experiment, Daddy and I live off mostly canned and boxed foods.

I pull out a pot and open a can of soup, pouring its simple chicken and noodle contents into it.

I let out a curse. The power is out, and I just wasted a can of soup.

As soon as I hear tires crunching on the gravel, my muscles tighten, and my alertness heightens. Daddy's home. Peering out the window in the dining room, I see his old blue truck coming down the long driveway. I dart into my bedroom and quickly throw a long-sleeved shirt on, pulling the sleeves over my hands.

I jump when he closes the truck door. As he walks onto the enclosed wooden porch, his footsteps echo from his heavy boots. The screen opens, then the front door. He slams it, making me jump again. My pulse quickens and my body starts shaking.

"Hi, Daddy," I say from the edge of the kitchen, watching him toss his keys into an ashtray on the bookshelf.

"Why don't the lights work?" he asks, removing his ball cap.

I clear my throat softly and stare at the soup wondering how I'm going to explain this to him. "The power got shut off."

"Fuck." Daddy looks around the dimming house. "What are you doing?" His face contorts into disgust as he stares at the cold, congealed contents of the pot.

"I was going to cook soup." My voice is barely above a whisper.

"The power is out. Don't you know you can't cook anything? Didn't you learn anything from your mom?" He heads toward the refrigerator and opens it. "Fuck." He slams the fridge.

No beer.

"We don't have anything else," I say, meeting his blue eyes. His dark brown hair has gotten longer, and his beard is growing out.

"And you just wasted the one thing we did have."

"I'm sorry." I bite my lip.

"How about this? How about your lazy ass work more and pay some of these bills?" I can smell Listerine on his breath, which means he's covering the smell of alcohol. I hate the smell of Listerine.

"Fine. At least they won't fire me for being drunk," I mumble under my breath.

"What did you say?" He moves closer, and I brace myself for what's to come. I deserve it. I shouldn't have said it.

I cringe as he makes his hand into a tight fist and punches me in the stomach. Falling to the floor, I let out a groan, and roll up into a ball.

"I'm sorry."

"I'm sick of your damn backtalk!" His booming voice makes me tremble.

"I'm sorry, Daddy."

"You should be. You deserved it. Don't bitch at me for not having food." He lets out a long sigh and runs his hand through his hair. "Dammit, Alisa. You know you do this to yourself. If you behaved better, this wouldn't happen."

I nod. "Yes, sir."

"I want this damn house cleaned when I get back," he says. Slamming the door, he walks out into the hot summer night leaving me.

When I am sure he's gone, I lean against the stove, shaking. Every muscle in my body aches. I feel like a truck hit me, but I get to my feet. He does this to teach me a lesson because he loves me. Mom always said he never meant it. Daddy apologized to her, and she always kissed me and hugged me and told me everything was fine.

I know he's still grieving over Mom. He works hard to provide for us, and I don't appreciate it enough. He'll get over this grief and once he does, he'll be a better person. He'll stop drinking and everything will be fine.

I should eat some of the soup, but I don't. The thought of eating doesn't sit well with me. I put it in a bowl and wrap some plastic over it, putting it into the fridge. Though, it will probably go bad because the fridge isn't on. I try to clean and tidy up the place as much as I can until I lose daylight. I return to my room, missing Mom and hating that she isn't here.

If only I hadn't given Mom that extra dose of morphine, she'd still be alive. It was too much. I shouldn't have listened to her when she asked for more. She had a strict schedule for the pain medication, and I chose to ignore what she was really asking me. She wasn't supposed to die. I just wanted to help her. She suffered enough.

"Alisa, I'm just in so much pain," she said, her body sunken into the bed as if it were swallowing her. "Just give me four. The pain will be gone."

"But Mom, you've already had your dosage."

"Baby, please. I need it to end. I promise, it's for the best."

I nodded, went to the bathroom, pulled out four pills from the bottle, and gave them to her. She took them all at once with some water.

Her cold, fragile hand held mine as tight as she could. "Just promise me that you will take care of your daddy. He needs you as much as you need him. Just do what he says."

"I will. But you'll get better soon."

"Don't forget about your dream, either."

As tears stream down my face, I clench my teeth. I hate crying. I hate the pain that eats my insides and I hate feeling so hopeless. I can never do the right thing and I hate myself for it. Hate brews inside me and turns to rage. I need to release it. The urge to hit something or break something takes over. I'm so tired of feeling this way. I need to feel alive. I want something to take away the pain.

Pulling out the bottom drawer of my chest, I frantically search through my sweaters, and let out a sigh of relief once I see it. I pull out the red cloth bag. There's only a little over four thousand dollars. Mom gave me what she had of her secret stash, and I've added to it since I started working. I want to go to culinary school once I graduate. Mom always told me I should and that I would do great. It's a small secret that I keep from Daddy. I hide the money under my sweaters again and close the drawer.

It won't always be like this.

I light some candles in order to see and take a very quick and very cold shower. My teeth chatter the entire time. I hate the cold. Once I turn off the water, I dry off and wrap the towel around me.

I dress in a pair of jogging pants and an oversized shirt that Daddy gave me when I was younger. It's still my favorite shirt because it reminds me of a time when things weren't so hard; back when Daddy and I used to build forts in the living room. Or go down to the local ice cream shop for a treat. Or when he took me with him on all sorts of errands, touting to everyone that I was his smart little girl.

Daddy won't be back for a while since he's gone off to the bar probably. I pull out my book from the library, hidden under my pillow so it doesn't get damaged, and crawl into bed.

I wince when I lean back against the headboard. Another bruise.

It hasn't been this bad since we moved away. Daddy's mom passed away when I was seven, and he started drinking and didn't stop. It got worse. Mom made him go through therapy and rehab, threatening to leave if he didn't. Both of them had good jobs, and they spent all of their savings on the rehab. It saved his life. It saved all our lives. Daddy was fine. Things were good. It wasn't all daisies and rainbows, but it was good.

When she fell ill, Daddy would hold her until she fell asleep. He'd wake up in the middle of the night and comfort her through her screams and cries. He helped her to the bathroom. Bathed her. I remember one night shortly before she passed, he was in the living room crying with a beer in his hand. He hadn't had a drop of alcohol in years.

"Daddy, are you okay?" I asked.

He looked up, closing a picture album. "Everything's fine sweetheart." He cleared his throat.

My eyes fell on the beer can, and he set it down on the table.

"Come here." He invited me to sit on his lap and he held me, his breath smelling of alcohol. "We're gonna be okay." He kept saying.

But everything's changed.

Tears threaten to come rushing out as I think about my seventeenth birthday coming up. The first one without my mom. Only a year and a half and I will be free. Even though I start school tomorrow, I'll ask work to add more hours to help. I can't sit here wallowing in my misery any longer. Daddy is struggling and is frustrated. He's right. I need to make money and support us more.

My eyes glance over my cassette tapes, wishing I could listen to music right now, instead of sitting in a sweltering, dark house alone. The Cure. Nirvana. Anything to kill the loud silence.

I know I won't sleep tonight. It's too hot.

Putting away my book, I blow out the candle and grab my little stuffed dog, Mr. Zebra. Mom gave it to me when I was five. It used to be white as snow, but now it's a dirty brownish color. I clutch it to my chest, hoping to soothe the sharp ache as I let the tears flow once more.

ben

I run every day. Five miles, no matter the weather. Then I practice for an hour on the court near my house. It's my favorite part of the day. I wake up and feel good when it's over. Gives me time to think about things, and no one bothers me.

Then the world wakes up. Demands have to be met. Everything has to be rushed. Everyone needs answers. The pressure builds, and some days it's too much. Some days I get the urge to do something for myself; something *I* want to do, not for anyone else. But it bites me in the ass.

Like now.

This isn't how I wanted to spend my last night before school starts. Arguing with Courtney, my girlfriend. We've only been back together for a little over a month, and we're already fighting. But this is what we do. I feel weird if we don't fight, like it isn't normal. It's almost comforting, honestly. Fighting makes me think at least she still cares.

We broke up in March because she slept with Tyler Long. For a month. I didn't find out until our spring break trip. It was the worst day of my life. I knew something was wrong when she was being overly sweet and didn't argue with me. We've been together since we were in seventh grade and experienced many firsts. I hated it when we broke up. For three months, I was lonely, miserable, and being alone doesn't suit me. Mom talked to me about how people make mistakes all the time, and forgiveness makes us better people. So, I forgave Courtney.

But, like always, she picks at every little thing and blows it up in my face. So what if I went to the Smashing Pumpkins concert with my best friend Zach Miller. It was awesome. They played a lot from their newest album, Mellon Collie and had three encores. We drove four hours to Atlanta and drove back. I'm exhausted, but it was worth it.

Courtney knew about it weeks in advance. I bought tickets right after we split up, but because I didn't go to her end of the summer party last night, she's pissed off like I ran over her damn cat.

Zach's the only one I can really talk about music with or go see all the great bands. Courtney hates my music. And I never hear the end of it.

"Are you even listening to me?" she yells, her blue eyes boring into mine. Her thick, platinum blond hair reaches her chest as she digs her fingers into her hips. Even though she's a little shorter than me, I know she could probably kick my ass with her strong cheerleader arms and legs. Her attitude is bigger than her heart.

That's not true. Courtney has a big heart. She just rarely shows it. I'm one of the few she allows to see it. She's fiercely loyal to her friends, and when her best friend, Micah lost her grandma, Courtney was there for her every step of the way. I don't see how Courtney ever has the time. She's always been there for me whenever I get into a fight with my dad.

"Why was some band so much more important than my party?"

I let out a sigh. *Because I'd rather enjoy a concert than listen to you bitch at me for not paying you enough attention*, I think. "You don't understand."

She raises an eyebrow, and any second lasers are going to shoot from her eyes. "I swear sometimes I wonder why I'm even with you."

"I wonder the same, Courtney," I snap. "Can we go one day without fighting about something?"

"Maybe if you learned how to be a better boyfriend. Start showing me that you care. It's always all about you. Your friends. Your concerts. Basketball."

"Here we go again," I mutter. She doesn't get it. Going out with my best friend to a concert was just what I needed last night—hell, all summer. I'd been home from basketball camp for a week, and Dad was already on my ass. Make sure you have perfect grades. Your game is perfect. Be the perfect boyfriend. It's like I can't breathe. I feel like a damn puppet sometimes. Nothing's ever good enough for him. Except my sister Hayden. She's perfect in his eyes.

I sigh. If I want things to work out with Courtney, I should apologize. She's right. I don't focus on her enough. Courtney's a great girl. She takes care of me, and I love her. I love that no matter what, she's always there. She would drop anything for me. Once when I had to pick up Hayden from school, but ended up having to stay after school, Courtney didn't even hesitate to offer to pick her up. It saved me from getting into trouble.

I know her parents don't make it easy, constantly making her feel inferior to her med student sister.

I stand from the chair at my desk and walk toward her. The closer I get, the softer her eyes become. "Court, I'm sorry I didn't go to the party. Zach had an extra ticket, and I'd been wanting to see that band for a while. If I'd known how much the party meant to you, I would've been there."

She curls her small body into mine. It perfectly fits, and I wrap my arms around her. "I forgive you. I just wanted one last night with you while my parents were gone."

"I know. I'm sorry. Why don't we go out Friday?"

Courtney rolls her eyes and lets out a groan. "I have to cheer Friday night."

"For who?"

"The football team. Duh."

"Vinemont still has a football team?" I tease, and she playfully hits me. It's been years since the football team at our school has made any positive headlines. It's become a running joke of how many games we lose. But basketball is what we're famous for. "What exactly do you do at those games? Cheer on the defense a lot?"

"You are bad." She laughs and tries to twist my nipple, but I catch her side, tickling her.

We land on the floor, wrestling. When we stop, she straddles me and kisses me long and deep. I know where this kiss will lead us, and while I want to go there, the image of her and Tyler together still pops up in my head.

I know the second I deny her, another fight will ensue, so I don't. Because we are *the* couple. The one who sets the bar for everyone else. The so-called "perfect couple" that everyone strives to be. We have to make it seem like we have no issues at all. And deep down, I hate it. Sure, I look like a king at school.

But I want something more. Something to ease the pressure. Something real.

When Courtney leaves, I crank up my music, thinking about how much I'm not ready for the summer to be over. Dread has been building inside me all week, but I'm a junior now, so only two more first days of school left.

Running my hands through my hair, I sigh, and there's a knock on my door. "Yeah?"

I turn down my blaring music as Mom comes in. Her blond hair is still pulled back in a short ponytail from her run. She always runs when she gets home from work. She used to run with Dad, but they've both been busy with work. The two of them have been acting weird lately, and I'm not sure what the deal is.

"Ben?"

"Yeah?"

"Did you and Courtney make up?"

I roll my eyes. How did Mom even know we were fighting? "Did she say something?"

She raises her eyebrow like I should know the answer. And I do. Mom and Courtney are close. Mom loves Courtney, and sometimes I think she treats Courtney better than her own daughter. "Ben, she called me shortly after you left for the concert in tears wondering why you didn't go to her party."

"Why does she call you? Why can't she call a girlfriend?"

"Why didn't you go?"

"Because I went to a concert with Zach. She and I already talked about it and made up."

"You two just got back together. You need to support her and not treat her so poorly."

"Are you kidding me? Why would you think I don't?"

"You are your father's son."

"What's that supposed to mean?" She always says this to me, like it's supposed to be an insult. I never understand why. Does she think I'm just like Dad? Am I rude like Dad? Selfish? Condescending? If she really thinks that, I need to reevaluate myself.

"Ben, don't raise your voice. Sometimes you can be selfish. That girl has been through a lot. Her parents are hard on her, and she really tries. You weren't here all those nights she came over crying in my arms because you broke her heart. She made a mistake, and she feels terrible."

Like always, Mom takes Courtney's side. Because Courtney cheating on me hurt Courtney more than me. And no one feels as terrible as her. Playing the victim because I broke up with her because she cheated on me. Mom plays right into her hand and acts like I'm the bad guy.

"I'll work on it." It's best not to argue with Mom. I'm pretty sure Mom loves Courtney so much because they had/have a similar upbringing. Parents constantly pressuring them to do better and limiting their social life. Courtney spends a lot of time being grounded, not that she ever sticks to the rules.

"I hope you do. Your father is bringing home dinner, so be sure you're ready by seven."

"Always am."

When she leaves, I crank up my stereo. I can't wait to have dinner with the two of them arguing. It's been like that for months. They still act like the perfect couple on the outside, but inside it's like they determined to tear each other apart. I briefly wonder if that's how Courtney and I will be.

An hour later, we sit down to chicken parmesan from the Italian restaurant in town. We live in a small town, one where everyone knows everyone, including their business. If you play like crap during a game, everyone will comment on it. I'll be glad when I leave. Hopefully, I'll get my basketball scholarship and be done with this place.

I sit next to Hayden, my little sister, and Mom and Dad sit opposite. They don't even look at each other.

Dad looks exhausted though. Dark circles weigh his brown eyes down. His dark hair seems grayer every time I see him. As always, he sits at the table in his white button-down shirt, tie undone. He works hard as a city councilman, constantly working. On the phone. Out for dinners. Events. Some sort of public something. It's a wonder we even still have dinner most every night.

"How was your last day of summer," he asks us.

"It was fine." I shrug.

"That's all?"

"I hung out with Courtney. Played basketball."

"Did you practice those free throws?"

"Yes," I groan. Because I've never known how to properly perform a free throw in my life. At least to his standards.

"Layups?"

"Just like you taught me the other day."

"Good. Because if you want to win this year, you really need to work on those. They were terrible last year, and we don't need a repeat of that embarrassment."

I clench my teeth. We lost the first game of the playoffs because I missed a layup. I'll never live it down. By Dad. By the town.

"How was your day, sweetheart?" Dad looks to Hayden.

She smiles and pulls her long, dark-blond hair behind her ears. She's thirteen years old which I can't believe. Just yesterday it seems like I was pushing her on the swings. Now, she wears too much makeup and has braces. I don't see how she manages to remain so positive. I should learn lessons. But Dad doesn't pressure her constantly about being perfect. In his eyes, she can do no wrong. Daddy's little girl at its best.

"Hayden don't play with your hair at the table," Mom says.

Hayden lets out a frustrated sigh. "My day was great. Janie and I swam most of the day."

"That's good." Dad smiles and winks at her.

"She didn't invite any boys, did she?" Mom asks.

Hayden rolls her eyes. "No. You can ask her mom. She was there with us."

It's messed up, and Hayden and I talk about this often. She wishes Mom liked her more, and I wish Dad liked me more, or at least respected us more.

A few minutes of silence pass, and the only sounds are the clinking of silverware to plates and the occasional clearing of throats.

Mom picks up her wine glass and swirls the dark red liquid. "Aren't you going to ask how my day was, Alex?" She stares right at Dad like she's going to set him on fire. I don't miss the bitterness in her voice.

"Vivian, you didn't ask how mine was."

"Oh, so now I have to ask you before you'll ask me?"

Dad sighs. I can see the vein in his forehead throbbing. Suddenly, I'm not hungry anymore. I'm so sick of their arguing. It's the same thing now. Why do we even have dinners anymore?

"May I please be excused?" Hayden asks in a timid voice. I hate that voice. It means she's scared, and I wish she didn't have to be. I wish Mom and Dad could see what they are doing to us.

But they don't.

I pat Hayden's knee to let her know it's okay. No matter what I have her back.

Mom takes a sip of her wine. "Finish your dinner."

"If she's done, she's done," Dad challenges her. "Go ahead, sweetheart."

Hayden hesitates.

"Why do you always undermine me? Just because you're the man of the house gives you the final word?"

"Vivian." He warns. "Hayden, you may be excused."

She gets up and leaves.

I scoot my chair back. "I'm leaving, too."

"Do the dishes." Dad tosses his napkin onto his plate and leaves the table.

Mom just sits with her wine glass, playing with her necklace, and staring at nothing.

"Are you okay?" I ask.

"I'm fine."

"Is there something going on?"

She sips her wine. "Do what your father says."

Rolling my eyes, I gather the dishes. I know from the dead look in her eyes, she's probably going to finish the bottle of wine tonight and go to bed early. Dad will probably stay in his office. I guess that's better than a yelling match all night. Setting the dishes in the sink, I let out a groan. I miss how things used to be. The way Mom used to smile at Dad or the way he'd kiss her temple. It hasn't been like that in months. Ever since Mom started having to work late.

I stop scrubbing the plate in my hand, and it drops loudly.

My heart's drumming against my chest. Mom is always working late. And lately she's been out of town for the weekends for work. Courtney was always busy on the weekends when she was cheating on me. She always had an excuse and was never at home.

Is that what's going on with my parents? Is Mom cheating on Dad?

alisa

The first day of eleventh grade makes me feel like I'm a kindergartener. I don't want to be here. I've been back two months and have yet to see my old friends Sarah and Ben. I thought about calling them, but would they even remember me? It's been six years since I left. Do they even still go here? Plus, I didn't want to explain why we moved back.

I watch from afar students chatting and laughing. I don't know anyone. Grasping my sleeves, I cross my arms in front of my chest.

It's so hot, the heat covers me like a veil. The long-sleeved shirt doesn't help, but I'm not about to show my scars and bruises to anyone. I keep my head down because I don't want anyone to notice me. Voices reverberate in the hallways. Locker doors slam. Shoes squeak on the shiny floors. I take a seat in the back of the room, crossing my arms. As I watch people file into the room, I see a girl with shoulder length reddish-brown hair with long streaks of black in the front. She looks very familiar. Her green eyes meet mine for a brief second, but she turns and sits in the row next to me a couple of desks up.

She looks like my old friend, Sarah, but she's changed a lot. She's head-to-toe in black. Nine Inch Nails shirt; baggy pants; heavy black eye makeup. The girl doesn't smile, but she has kind of an amused look on her face, almost like she's privy to some secret that no one else knows. She leans back in her chair and taps her pen on her notebook.

A tall, large guy comes in sporting a Type O Negative shirt with the same black, baggy jeans and sits in front of her. His dark hair is pulled back in a low ponytail, and he doesn't look at all friendly. His skin has an olive hue, and he has a full beard and mustache. He kisses her quickly and she laughs.

When he looks up, he locks eyes with me, but I turn away. Heat fills my cheeks. I know they're talking about me. I should be used to that, but it still bothers me. It was no different at my previous school. They all laughed and talked about the quiet, weird girl.

When the teacher comes into the room, he starts talking without missing a beat.

Throughout class, I feel the girl and guy's eyes on me.

I wonder if it is Sarah. Does she remember me at all? I never wanted to leave, but Mom insisted it was for the best. Sarah and Ben were all that I had to escape from my parents' fighting and yelling.

When we said goodbye, Sarah held onto me as tight as she could and made me a little box of knickknacks of our friendship. Ben hugged me and kissed me on the cheek. We kept in touch for the first year or so, then life got in the way.

We could never talk on the phone because long distance costs so much. In both of their letters, they spoke of how much they missed me and wished I would move back. Life in Kentucky was better for my parents. They had good jobs, and Daddy was sober. I only remember a couple of times when his anger got out of hand. He didn't start drinking again until Mom got sick.

The bell rings, and as I close my notebook, the girl makes her way to me with the guy following behind.

"Alisa?" Her eyes narrow.

I nod.

She drops her jaw. "Omigod! It's me, Sarah. Are you back for good?"

"Yeah." I blush. I don't like attention being drawn to me at all.

"Dude! That's awesome!" She turns to the guy. "Damon, this is my childhood friend, Alisa."

"Hey."

"Hi."

"Wow, it's been forever since I've talked to you," Sarah says. "How have you been? What brings you back?"

I hate answering that question. My throat tightens as I try not to choke up. I need my scissors. "Um, my mom died, so we moved back."

Her mouth hangs open again and she stares at me with wide eyes. "Alisa, I'm so sorry. That's terrible."

"Thanks."

"How did she die?"

The second worst question. Does it really matter how? She's dead and she's not coming back. "Cancer." It's the easiest explanation. No one wants to hear how it was my fault.

"Damn. I'm sorry."

An awkward moment passes.

"Well come on," she says and loops her arm with mine. "Let's go to the next class."

It feels good having Sarah walk beside me in the hallway. I missed her, and while she's different, she's still the same girl I remember. Still caring and vibrant. I didn't have any friends in Kentucky. Not like Sarah and Ben.

I want to ask about Ben, but I'm scared for some reason. She hasn't mentioned him at all.

"What all have I missed?" I ask.

"Oh man. Too much. We don't have enough time right now."

I bite my lip. "Does Ben still go here?" A tingling sensation races over my skin when I say his name, like it always did when we were young.

"Ben Lamar?" Damon asks, and I don't miss the disgust in his voice.

I nod.

"Oh wow," Sarah says, stunned, but quickly composes herself. "We haven't been friends since after you left. He started playing basketball, and now he's all high and mighty."

"And a total dick," Damon adds.

"Yeah. He's not pleasant anymore."

That doesn't sound like him at all, but I guess people change. "That sucks."

Sarah shrugs. "I don't care. He lives his life, and I live mine. Anyway, we should hang out after school and catch up."

I'm not supposed to do anything but go straight home after school or to work. But Daddy doesn't get home until six, and I'm off today so maybe I can hang out for a bit. I should look for a second job or ask for more hours. "Sure."

I feel less awkward as I make my way to my second class. It fades as soon as I walk inside the classroom. I'm one of the last ones there, and it's a lab. I hate group projects since I can never afford the materials. It's bad enough that all the other kids have nice clothes. All my jeans seem to conspire and make holes around the knees in every pair. It's embarrassing.

I find a table in the back next to a guy who's immersed in a book. "Um, is there someone sitting here?"

He doesn't look up but shakes his head. I sit down and wait for the teacher. Everyone's either talking to each other or in their own worlds. The awkwardness weighs on me. It doesn't help that everyone's already acclimated to the school and the other students. Being the new kid is one of the loneliest feelings.

When the teacher enters, she announces our project for the day, which happens to be a group assignment, and tells us to get started. Students shift, get up and collect beakers and other items. It's the first day of class and already a project.

I don't know where anything is, but it looks like my partner got everything.

"You're new, aren't you?" he asks.

I nod as I glance sideways. His messy dark brown hair and tanned skin make him attractive. He's wearing khaki shorts and a t-shirt, like most guys wear.

"I'm Zach."

"Alisa." I can feel the blood rush to my cheeks.

He starts filling beakers and reading the assignment.

"Do you need any help?" I ask. Talking to people makes me nervous, and I'm shy.

"No offense, but I could do this blindfolded, and I don't like having partners because they tend to make this last forever. I kinda like getting these things done so I can do other shit."

Clearing my throat, I push the tears back, and bite my lip to keep it from quivering. As usual, my partner doesn't want my help. In elementary school, kids would tell me not to do anything for the project because being as poor as I was, I couldn't make anything cool like they could for the assignment. Plus, I was never smart enough. It's like I'm diseased or something.

"It's not you," he says. "I promise."

I nod but refuse to meet his eyes.

"Where are you from?"

"Originally here. But my dad and I moved back a couple of months ago."

"You poor soul. From where?"

"Kentucky."

"Yikes. Not any better than here." He works on the assignment as he talks to me like it's the easiest thing in the world. At least he's not ignoring me. "I know I will be out of this place the day I turn eighteen."

Me, too. If everything works out. I know I promised Mom that I would take care of Daddy, but I'm not sure he needs me. I can't stay.

Zach slides his notebook to me. "Here are the notes. Just copy them."

"Are you sure?"

"Yeah. I wouldn't just do the assignment and not share with you. I'm not that much of a dick." He smirks.

I copy down the notes, which make no sense. I'm not sure how I'm going to learn this stuff if I don't know what it is. I slide back his notebook and go over the notes once more. The equations and words still look foreign to me. I hope the teacher doesn't ask questions.

Unfortunately, she does when everyone's done with the assignment. The whole time, my mouth is dry as I cross my arms gripping my shirt, not making eye contact, hoping like hell she doesn't call on me. The pounding in my ears is so loud it rings.

"Alisa Hopewell," she says and my heart stills for a moment. Heat races to my cheeks as I feel everyone staring at me. "What is the property for step four?"

I look at my notes, completely lost. I'm so antsy to find the answer that I'm not really reading my notes. Instead, it's all a jumbled mess of letters and numbers. If I don't say something, they're all going to laugh at me. Then I see Zach's finger pointing at a word.

"Chemical."

"Good," she says and moves on to the next question.

Relief pours over me. "Thanks," I whisper.

"No problem. You don't really know this stuff, do you?"

I shake my head. "No."

"Well, I can help you if you want."

"Really?"

"Yeah. I don't mind tutoring." He smiles. It's an attractive smile and kind. His clear blue eyes are sweet and gentle.

"Thanks."

"You said you moved back. You lived here before?"

"Yes." But I'm not a memorable person.

"Why in the world would you want to move back? I know it must have been your parents' decision. Mine decided they wanted a lot of land near the lake. Moved here when I was eleven."

"I moved away when I was ten."

"Just missed each other." He smiles again. "But you're here now. What brought you back?"

I look away. "My mom died."

He says nothing for what seems like forever. It's like my voice has stunned him into silence.

The bell rings and I gather my books.

Great. Now I'll always be the girl with no mother.

Just as I reach the doorway, Zach touches my shoulder, startling me.

"I'm really sorry to hear that."

Everyone's sorry. "Yeah." When I look up, I meet his eyes full of regret.

"Here's my number." He hands me a sliver of paper with a phone number on it. No one has ever given me their number like this. Well, one time, but it was because of a prank. I had a crush on a guy, and he and a few others decided it was funny to pretend he liked me. I fell for it, and they used it against me.

"If you ever want to talk, I mean. You don't have to."

I take the piece of paper and nod.

"See you later." He walks out the door.

I don't really know how to act or feel. I should've said 'thank you' or 'see you later.' But words don't ever come to me as quickly as they do for others. I wish I could be more confident. I want to be outgoing or carefree. I just can't.

ben

The first day of school sucks. I woke up late, so I wasn't able to run before school or shoot some hoops. My mind is in such a fog after last night. I couldn't sleep because I kept thinking about the possibility of Mom cheating on Dad. I barely spoke to Courtney when I first got here. My head is killing me, and I want to go home.

"Hey, man." Zach pats my shoulder when I reach my locker before lunch.

"Hey." Zach has been my best friend since we were kids. As soon as I joined the basketball team, he and I connected. He seems to get me more than most people.

"Where were you this morning?"

"Overslept."

"I managed without you." He jokes. "I'm still reeling from that concert."

I chuckle. "Me, too."

"How much shit did you get into with Courtney?"

I roll my eyes. "We made up."

"Damn, dude. I don't see how you deal with it."

"I just do."

"You know my thoughts on the whole thing."

That I do. He doesn't like Courtney. He thinks I shouldn't have gotten back together with her, but no matter what, he supports my decision. He told me he hated the way she treats me and that it isn't healthy that we always fight. We don't always fight. He just hears about the fights more than anything else because I'm venting.

"I guess if it's love, it's love," he says. "Hey, there's a new girl in chemistry. She's cute, man. Kinda shy. Her name's Alisa. She moved here from Kentucky."

My chest tightens. I haven't heard that name in years. I had a best friend named Alisa when I was younger. Who moved to Kentucky. "Alisa Hopewell?"

"Yeah. You met her?"

There's no way it's her. It has to be some other girl. Just a weird coincidence. I can trust Zach with the truth, but I don't want to tell him all of it. "I grew up with a girl named Alisa Hopewell."

"Oh yeah? Did y'all…—?"

"Dude, we were ten."

"Tell that to my sister. She's turned boy crazy all of a sudden."

"Your sister is twelve. It's a little more acceptable."

Zach shrugs. "I guess. I can't wait to scare off her little boyfriends though."

I shake my head. "Dick."

"What? You'd do the same for Hayden."

"So you gonna ask this girl out?" I blurt, even though the thought of him and her together makes me sick to my stomach.

Zach chuckles. "I just met her, man. But she does need tutoring, so I told her I'd help."

I can't imagine Alisa ever needing a tutor. There's no way it's her. Alisa always had straight As. She had to teach me a lot of subjects because I never understood them.

"You ready for the season?" Zach asks. He can tell I'm distracted by the questions he asks. He knows my answer.

"Ready as I'll ever be."

"We gonna blow this thing apart this year."

We still have two months, but it's hard not to get excited. The first two months of school are overrun by football. Then they usually start losing, and that's where we come in. We make the school look good. Basketball is the only thing we've won championships for, and we're determined to win it this year. Freshman year, we went to the state game. And lost. It was a huge blow to our egos. Our coach is on the verge of retiring, so we have to win. If we win, maybe he'll stay until we graduate.

"Yeah we are."

"You sure you're all right man?"

No. "I'm fine."

"You and Court at it again?"

"We're fine."

"Which translates to normal for y'all. All right. I'll catch ya later." He nods as Courtney makes her way toward me.

She's wearing a low-cut shirt that shows her cleavage with tight jeans and flip-flops. She looks hot, she always has. "Good morning, baby." She smiles and gives me a quick peck on the lips. The smell of apples wafts around us. She changes her scent every day since she has about fifty different types of body lotion.

"I'm starving."

We make our way to the lunchroom; images and thoughts are crowding my head. I want to go for a run and clear it all. The end of the day cannot come soon enough. I don't want to see Alisa. I don't want to deal with any of this.

alisa

After class, I wander through the halls to find the lunchroom. I hate this part of the day. I didn't bring a lunch or money for food. Daddy wouldn't want me on the lunch program because it would make him look bad. Maybe I can go hang out in the bathroom during the half hour.

With each step I take closer to the doors, a new wave of terror washes over me. I hate being the lonely girl at a table alone with no food. Teachers will wonder. They'll ask questions. Kids will laugh and talk. Glancing to my right, I see a bathroom and dart in that direction.

I collide with someone. Their hands catch my elbows.

When I look up, my heart stills, and I swear the rest of the world fades. I don't hear the chaos in the hallway or the chatter. He looks the same as I remember, just taller and definitely grown into a man with taut muscles. Hazel eyes that always reminded me of a sunburst of gold and brown with a touch of green surrounding. Short, brown hair like a military cut. He's lean and athletic and sexy. A crease forms between his light eyebrows as he stares at me. His eyes soften as though he recognizes me.

Someone clears a throat. "Excuse me," the girl next to him says. "Am I interrupting anything?" She stares at me like I'm a roach or something.

"Best to watch where you're walking," he says gruffly.

The walls spin as my ears ring. I have a terrible taste in my mouth, and I release myself from Ben. I know it's him, and I wonder if he really does recognize me.

"Sorry." I turn for the bathroom door.

When I find an empty stall, I slip inside and hide. All I hear is the throbbing of my heartbeat. My hands shake as I try to steady my breathing. I break out in a cold sweat, and I squeeze my eyes shut. I need to calm down. Resting my face against the cool tile of the wall, I slow my breathing. Just like Mom always taught me.

Ben circles my head. He doesn't seem to know me. He seems different, too. Is what Sarah said about him true? She warned me about him. But I wasn't expecting him to be so…mean. Does he hate me for leaving? Does he hate me for not keeping in touch better?

Everything has changed. I knew it would, but there was some part of me that hoped it didn't. I wanted to find my old friends or something from the past to console me. Instead, I'm left with the same ache and emptiness I first felt when Mom died five months ago. I miss her so much. She made everything better. I need solace. Something to calm me down. I wish I had my scissors.

I pull up the sleeve to my shirt and stare at the fresh scars on my arms. It calms me, if only for a little bit.

ben

It *is* her. I can't believe I saw her. I could never forget those dark, expressive, beautiful eyes. Her long, brown hair comes just past her shoulders, just like it did when we were younger. Her skin still has that angelic pale color with tiny freckles across flushed cheeks. Always flushed cheeks.

Alisa Hopewell was my best friend when we were kids. I knew she had some issues with her parents; or rather, her parents had issues. I remember one night, they got into a huge argument. She got scared so she ran to my house in the pouring rain. I let her sleep in my bed, and she told me she hadn't slept so well in a long time.

When she left town, I was heartbroken. I hoped things would get better for her and her family. But when I saw her just now, she looked sad. Different. Still beautiful though. Something was wrong, but I saw this light in her eyes that made my heart hammer. Just like it still is. My heart hasn't beat like this since I don't know when.

And now she's back. When did she come back? Is she here for good? Does Sarah know? The past feels like a whole other lifetime to me.

"Hello, Ben?" Courtney nudges me. We're sitting at lunch, and all I can think about is Alisa.

"What?" I snap, immediately regretting my tone.

She crinkles her forehead and stares at me like I'm crazy. "What is your problem? I'm trying to talk to you. Could you at least listen?"

I sigh. "Sorry. What were you saying?"

"I was saying that Rebecca and Jared want to go with us Saturday to the movies."

"Okay. Great."

"What's wrong?"

"Nothing."

"Whatever. Something's wrong. What are you thinking about?"

"Why'd you call my mom about me not going to your party?"

Surprise crosses her face. "I was upset."

"Can't you call your friends? Why do you have to tell my mom?"

"Since when does it matter? You've never cared before. If you hadn't hurt my feelings, I wouldn't have called your mom."

"Is this how it's going to be? Anytime we fight, you'll call her?"

She furrows her eyebrows. "Why are you so upset? Did your dad yell at you this morning or something?"

"No."

I really don't know why I'm upset. Seeing Alisa has stirred something inside, and I'm not sure what it is.

"You were even mean to that girl in the hallway. Not that I blame you—she looked like a real weirdo."

My eyes meet Courtney's. Was I really mean to Alisa? *Damn.* The littlest thing seems to set me off these days. "I didn't sleep well last night." I soften my tone. I don't feel like fighting.

She frowns. "Me either."

"Why not?" Was she up all night talking to Tyler?

Courtney shrugs and looks away.

"Mom and I got into a fight. I didn't even do anything. She saw my cheerleading outfit and got pissed. Like she knows I made the team this year."

Dammit. I feel like a dick. Her mom hates that Courtney is a cheerleader. She thinks the only good thing Courtney has going for her is the fact that she's dating me. It's messed up.

I squeeze her hand, still feeling guilty.

I really need to learn to trust her, but it's hard. Mom told me, before I got back with Courtney, that forgiveness makes you strong, and while Courtney did break my heart when she hooked up with Tyler, forgiving her would help her to do good things and to be a better person. Courtney is sorry for what she did, and I know she feels terrible. She constantly asks if I'm okay, and she writes me long apologetic notes.

Ever since I got back with Courtney, there are moments when I cringe and ask myself why I reconciled this. I wonder why she wants to be with me so much. Is it really because she loves me, or is it because she enjoys how we look walking down the halls together? Or is it to placate her mom? Especially since I haven't exactly been the greatest boyfriend lately.

Now that I've seen Alisa, she's all I can think about. She was my best friend, but she was more. I wanted there to be more with us. Guilt starts to settle in from the fact that I stopped writing to her after about a year. Dad started riding me harder about basketball so finding the time to write was difficult. Mom said I needed to let Alisa go. Let her live her life. So that's what I did.

But seeing the sad and hollow look in Alisa's eyes makes me think she isn't living much of a life. And I hate not knowing her all these years. I'm not sure how I can even talk to her without Courtney breathing down my neck. I know how Courtney looked at Alisa, and I already know she thinks she's better than Alisa.

But she doesn't know the girl who left town with my heart and has now returned.

alisa

The sweltering August afternoon is nice since the school keeps the temperatures like Antarctica. I look for Sarah in the empty parking lot. When I spot her, she waves, meeting me halfway.

"You ready to go?" she asks.

"Where are we going?"

"My house. My mom hasn't seen in you in forever, and I know she'd love to see you."

"If she's not having a party," Damon whispers under his breath.

Sarah playfully hits his chest.

I nod. "Are there a lot of people?"

As if she can see the stark fear on my face, she frowns. "Um. There can be sometimes, but not until later."

I know this will not help my nerves, but it's better than being at home alone. But I know I have to be home by five. "I can't be long."

"That's fine."

"Um. Could I ride with y'all?" Daddy checks the mileage in my car so he knows I'm not going where I shouldn't. "My car likes to break down." Which isn't a complete lie.

Sarah chuckles. "Sure. I'll take you back to get your car later."

Nodding, I follow her to a beat-up maroon Chevy Cavalier. Damon sits in the driver's seat, inhaling a drag from his cigarette with the windows rolled down as Type O Negative blares from the speakers. I squeeze in the back, put my seatbelt on and bite my lip. Knots twist inside my stomach. I try to drown in the music, but it hurts my ears. It's so loud I think the speakers might blow any second.

Damon peels out of the space and speeds down the road. No one talks on the way. We just sit in silence listening to the song. Its explicitly sexual lyrics make me blush. It's not something I care to listen to when I just met Damon.

Sarah takes a cigarette from Damon's pack and lights it. It's weird. She used to wear princess dresses and ribbons in her hair. I kind of miss that. I feel like I don't know her anymore. But at the same time, it's almost like we didn't miss a beat in all these years.

We round a corner and Damon jerks to a stop, shutting off the engine.

When I get out, I look around. The neighborhood looks like a dump; most yards are full of old rusty cars with no wheels. There's a toilet outside the house across the street, and the screen door is hanging from the top hinge. The house next to it appears abandoned with graffiti written all over it.

None of this looks familiar. But I recognize the little yellow house that Damon parked in front of.

Sarah takes my hand and drags me toward her house. It hasn't changed much, except the paint has chipped in a lot of places. We used to play a lot in her backyard, but now it's overgrown with kudzu and bushes.

Inside it's dark and dingy. A pile of mail sits on the coffee table with several fast-food drink cups. Cigarette ashes and butts fill an ashtray. A large TV with a wooden frame around it sits on the floor and a VCR rests on top.

"Mom," she calls, and disappears down the hallway. Damon goes into the kitchen which still looks like the same 70s kitchen. The appliances are yellow, and the cabinets are a fake wooden laminate. Damon takes a beer from the fridge, sits down on the couch, and turns on the TV.

"Alisa." Mrs. Downs pulls me into a tight hug. Her blond hair is short, like a pixie cut. Wrinkles surround her brown eyes, but her smile is still the warm and kind smile I remember. She's dressed in her yellow Busy Bee Café outfit and wears bright makeup like it's still 1980. "Oh, my second daughter is back. Sarah told me about your mama. I am so sorry to hear that. How is your daddy? Poor thing, I bet he's just brokenhearted."

"Mom." Sarah draws out the word in an annoyed tone.

Mrs. Downs releases me but keeps me at arm's length. "You look exhausted, sweet pea. Are you hungry? You need to put some meat on your bones."

"Yeah. She hasn't changed at all." Sarah teases her mom and looks at me.

I smile a little. I always liked Mrs. Downs. She's a little eccentric, but she's kind.

When she lets go, I notice her hands shaking. She's very thin, and I wonder if she's gotten better. I remember Mrs.

Downs always being gone or on drugs. The men she dated were always getting her into something.

"I have to go to work, but if you kids need anything, just call. Damon, honey, do you want me to bring back some pancakes?"

"Nah, I'm good. Thanks."

"Okay. Well, you kids have fun. And Alisa, it is so good to see you, sweet pea." She hugs Sarah and kisses her temple. "Love you kids."

"Love you, too," Sarah says, and her mom walks out. She shakes her head. "She was so high."

At least she told her she loved her. I wonder how Sarah knew she was high. I didn't notice anything off about her.

Sarah pulls a beer from the fridge offering it to me.

I shake my head.

She shrugs and opens it for herself. "Not a drinker?"

I shake my head again. Doesn't she remember what it did to my father? His drinking started when he was young. Helped take the edge off, but it made him think he can't live without it.

Sarah pulls a chair out from the old brown table and offers me the one next to her. "It's been forever since I've seen you." She picks at the black nail polish on her nails.

"I know."

"That sucks about your mom, man. Lotta kids at school don't have a mom or dad. Some are fosters."

"Where is Tonya?" She's Sarah's older sister.

She takes a long sip. "It's just Mom and me. Dad left, and Tonya got out a long time ago."

I swallow the lump in my throat. "I'm sorry." From the sound of it, she doesn't talk to Tonya anymore. They used to be close.

"I take care of Mom."

I nod. "How is she?"

Sarah lifts a shoulder. "She'll get better one day. Today's just not that day. I want her to, you know? I've already lost my dad and sister. I can't lose my mom."

A bulge lodges in my throat. I lost my mom five months ago. The last memory I have of her is drooling in a bed, unconscious from copious amounts of morphine with no hair, and her skin had turned an awful shade of yellow. She was nothing more than a skeleton with a thin coat of skin over the bones. Unmoving and every so often moaning. That image is burned into my memory forever.

"Oh man. I'm sorry. I didn't mean to say that."

"You're fine." I lost my mom, not my entire family.

"How's your dad?"

"He really misses Mom." I clear my throat. I'm not going to cry.

"Yeah, I bet."

Feeling the need to run away and hide, I rub my arms, needing that high. I hate talking about Mom.

"Sorry. Everyone's families are fucked up. Damon is great. He'll do anything for me, and he protects me. He lives with his brother and his wife. She's pregnant and Damon feels so left out. Not that Derrick or his wife make him feel that way. He just feels like the third wheel. Their parents were involved in an accident."

My heart drops. "That's awful."

Sarah nods.

"How old was Damon?" I lower my voice, feeling awkward that he can hear us.

"I was twelve," Damon says as he crosses into the kitchen. He leans against the counter, one hand in his pocket, and the other holding his beer.

"I'm sorry."

He waves his hand. "Sarah's told me about you and how close y'all used to be. My brother is ten years older and sort of raised me."

"Oh."

"But Sarah and I plan to get out of here when we're eighteen. Atlanta. We're going to work for a year, save up, and she's going to art school."

Sarah drains the rest of her beer. I hope she doesn't get wasted. "That's the dream. I'm so glad you've come back. I really missed you. It's been hard without you."

Guilt settles over me, even though I know it wasn't my fault for leaving. "I'm sorry. I missed you, too. Things were okay when I moved, but I didn't have any friends in Kentucky."

"That's because it's too cold there. Makes people cold."

I laugh because it's true.

"I'll let you two catch up. I'm going to play some Mario." Damon kisses the top of Sarah's head and throws out his bottle. A few minutes later, I hear the unmistakable sounds of the Mario Brothers game on the Nintendo. Every few minutes, we hear him curse because he died. I remember playing the first Mario game with Sarah and Ben. We spent hours trying to figure it out and getting frustrated every time we died. I'm glad that Sarah remembers me and still thinks of me as a friend. What happened to Ben?

"You still think about him, don't you?" she asks.

"Who?"

She cocks an eyebrow. "Ben."

Not at all. I shrug and look away.

"Be careful with that one. He'll turn on you in a second. Him and his friends are always messing with people."

"What happened to him?"

"Made the team. Became their star. Started dating She Devil. Left me in the dust," she says, not hiding her resentment.

Would he have done the same to me if I stayed? It doesn't matter. He deserted Sarah, and she was his friend too. "I saw her today. She Devil. She doesn't like me."

"Because you don't wear Birkenstocks and Tommy Hilfiger. Speaking of, aren't you burning up in that?" She points to my long-sleeved shirt and heat rises to my cheeks.

Yes, I'm sweltering. "I'm fine." I pull the sleeves over my hands. It's nice to have someone to talk to, but I hate it when people comment on my long sleeves. "I'm just cold a lot."

"Yeah. Except it's a freaking sauna in here." She gets up and opens a kitchen window. "I'd offer to go outside, but those asshole mosquitoes eat me alive."

I chuckle. "Me, too."

"Sorry. I know I'm probably a lot different to you now. I promise, I'm still the same girl. If you want to keep hanging out with me. God, I sound pathetic."

"No, you're fine. It's nice having you back. I didn't think you or Ben would remember me."

She snickers a little. "Are you kidding? Hell yeah I remember you. I've told Damon about you a lot."

"When did you meet?"

"Eighth grade. He moved in with his brother, and we became friends, started going out in ninth. He's my rock," she says, and I can see the pure love in her eyes.

I smile. What I would give to have that. I'll never have that because I'm not good enough. Guys only go after girls who are worthy. Who are pretty. Who don't constantly screw things up. Who don't kill their mothers.

"What time do you have to be home?" she asks.

"Five."

"We'd better get you home."

Home is the last place I want to be, but I have to go back. I have to cook dinner, and I can't have Daddy worrying over me. Besides that, I don't want to get into trouble. I need to stop being a troublemaker for Daddy.

ben

Math is easy. It's logical. It challenges me. It's the universal language. Girls, however, speak their own language, and it's not universal. Maybe to them. I swear I can't catch a break with Courtney breathing down my neck every five seconds. She's great when she's great, but other times she drives me crazy.

Like tonight. I was trying to help her with math, but she blew up in my face and left. Maybe I'm not the greatest teacher in the world, but I am trying to help her. It's difficult when she gets huffy within five seconds of me trying to explain a problem. She sure as hell didn't have to act like a child and call me a jerk. Hell, maybe I am. I'll give her time to cool off, then I'll call and apologize for whatever I did. I'm used to that routine by now. Sucks that I'm always the one apologizing, but it's easier to go along with her than argue.

Alisa keeps floating through my head, which is bad. Ever since I saw her, she's been like an itch that I can't scratch. Like a song in my head that I'm dying to listen to but can't.

There's a knock on my door. "Yeah?"

I turn down my blaring music as Mom comes in. "What happened with Courtney?" she asks.

Dammit. Is this becoming a trend now? Why can't people leave me alone? "I was trying to help her with calculus, and she just exploded in my face."

She crosses her arms. "Were you condescending?"

"Why would you think that?" I ask, immediately defensive.

"You are your father's son."

"Why do you always say that?"

"You can sound like you're above others."

That isn't true. At least I don't think it is. It doesn't help when Courtney wanted to talk about cheerleading issues instead of learning math. So yeah, I probably got annoyed with her when she kept telling me she didn't understand what I said. True. I hate drama and there is no shortage of drama on the cheerleading squad. A lot of times I laugh, which pisses her off even more.

"I'll try better next time."

"Just call her and apologize. Everything will be fine. And keep the music down. It's late." Mom absently plays with her pearls, which means something is up. "Also, I have to go to Tampa this weekend for work. Make sure your father gets dinner for you three."

"Tampa?" Hayden pouts from the hallway. She bursts through the door with a look of horror. "You never said a word about going to Tampa."

"I'm sorry. It was a last-minute thing."

Hayden scoffs. "You were supposed to take me and Janie to the mall."

Mom rolls her eyes. "Get your daddy to take you. Or Ben."

Oh shit. "No. I'm not taking two thirteen-year-olds to the mall."

"Well they can't go by themselves, Ben. Just take them for a couple of hours. Bring Courtney."

"A couple of hours? You realize the mall is an hour away, right?"

Mom lets out a frustrated groan. "Just take her." She leaves my room, leaving Hayden glaring at me with her arms crossed.

"You owe me," I tell her.

"Just don't make us listen to your crappy music the whole way there."

"Whatever."

When she closes my door, I release a breath. Tampa? Since when does Mom have to travel for work so much? That familiar gut feeling settles. I know she's lying. Is that why she wanted me to forgive Courtney so much? Because she's doing the same thing to Dad? I'm reaching, I know.

Does Dad even care that she's taking all these "business" trips? What is happening to my family? Why are we falling apart?

alisa

When Sarah drops me off at my car, I pray like hell it works. It comes to life and I breathe a sigh of relief. The last thing I need is not making my curfew.

Once I'm home, I flip the light switches and they work. Daddy paid the bill today. I hurry to the kitchen and try to figure out what to cook. There's not much in the cabinets. I let out a sigh and lean against the stove. I was supposed to go to work to see if I could add hours, but I didn't. Instead, I was selfish and went out with Sarah. I need to help Daddy more. The hospital bills from Mom hurt a lot. That's just like me. Never thinking of anyone else but me. Maybe I should give him my savings.

When I hear his truck over the gravel, my body stiffens. I close my eyes, hoping for a quiet night. Hoping for him to be in a better mood.

When I see Daddy carrying a fast food and a brown paper bag, I relax a little.

"Hi Daddy," I say.

"Hey. I got us dinner. I know we'll need to go get groceries soon." He reaches inside the brown paper bag and pulls out a pink stuffed dog. "I got you this. I'm sorry about last night. I got out of control, and it won't happen again."

I grab the dog and bite my lip. "Thanks," I mumble.

"You're a good kid. Just need to be more mindful."

"Yes, sir."

"Let's eat," he says, holding up the McDonald's bag.

I take some plates out of the cabinet and hand one to him. Then we move into the living room. He sits in his recliner, and I sink into the couch. We eat in silence as we watch TV. We don't have cable, so we stick to the local channels.

The silence is nice. The burger and fries fill me up. I haven't eaten much in a couple of days. Staring at the pink dog, I remember all the stuffed animals Daddy got me growing up. He gets them out of a claw machine. He would get Mom jewelry.

Nights like these are welcoming. But they're becoming less and less frequent, especially since Mom died. Daddy's just grieving. That's all it is. He'll stop drinking when he's done. We'll get through this, and things will be better.

"I start second shift tomorrow," he says. "You think you can handle the chores until I get home?"

"Yes." Second shift. Means he'll be working four to midnight. I'll hardly see him.

"Good. Make sure there's dinner for me and the house is cleaned."

"Yes, sir."

"It's getting late."

I nod and collect the trash from our dinner and head to my room. Tonight was good. Maybe it'll be like this from now on. I have to keep being good and not screw up. I have to do what he says. I can do that. I can be daddy's little girl again. Life will be better.

ben

My run this morning didn't help. The thoughts about whatever's going on with my parents still crowd my mind. And Alisa. Her name is like a basketball constantly bouncing around inside my head. Driving me crazy. I'm eager to get to school so I can see her. I want to talk to her and see how she's been. But I can't. I have to stay far away from her. I have a good thing with Courtney, and I can't ruin it. I don't need any distractions, and Alisa has been one big distraction since Zach first mentioned her. It's been messing with me, and I can't have that. Maybe he should ask her out.

Besides, if Alisa really wanted to be friends, she would've kept writing. That isn't fair. It wasn't just her fault. I stopped writing, too.

"You must have a gift." Zach leans against my locker.

"What are you talking about?"

"I made it easy. I gave the girl my number. No call. No phone number back. I'm attractive, right?"

I shake my head. "You're very attractive."

"I don't get it."

"Maybe she has a boyfriend." That thought makes me jealous.

"Dammit. No wonder she acted so aloof."

I chuckle. Not exactly sure why I find that humorous. In the time I've known Zach, he's never had a girlfriend, though not from lack of trying. Girls are fickle. There's no telling what any of them are thinking.

"On that note, I'll see you later." Zach leaves right on cue as Courtney makes her way toward me.

"Hi baby." She gives me a kiss on the cheek. Not the lips.

"You okay?"

She nods. "Yeah. I'm fine. Why?"

"I'm sorry about last night. I didn't mean to be a jerk."

"It's okay. I hate math and no offense, you're a terrible teacher."

"Fair enough."

She clears her throat. Which means she has to ask me something she doesn't want to. "I think I'm going to get someone else to tutor me."

"Who?" My insides twist with jealousy. Courtney's getting a tutor. Alisa's getting a tutor. And neither one is me. I'm starting to hate the word.

"I don't know yet." She looks away, and I know damn well she's lying.

Whatever. "If that's what you want," I say, but it feels like we're not talking about math.

Her pager beeps, but I can't see the number.

"I'll see you at lunch." She reaches on her tiptoes and kisses my cheek, then leaves. I swear if Tyler is paging her or calling her again, I'm going to be pissed.

I look up, and my pulse accelerates when I see her. There's a funny taste in my mouth, and it's hot as hell in this hallway. Those stunning brown eyes are staring right at me. She is so beautiful, like an angel delivering my own calmness. God, I've missed her.

I need to keep walking. I can't be drawn to her. Just as I take a step, some jackass bumps into her, forcing her to fall to the ground. I lunge toward her, but I don't make it in time to save her. I can't explain the anger in my veins, but I am pissed. The guy laughs and walks on. I should punch him out, but I don't want to be like my dad. I help her into a sitting position, but she draws away like I'm a disease. I can't help but feel hurt. It's like every female doesn't want to be around me.

Am I really that awful?

alisa

"Alisa?"

He says my name, and I feel like I might turn to mush. His voice is different now. It's deep and smooth, and I can easily get lost in it. When I meet his hazel eyes, my heart flutters at the caring way he looks at me. I missed him more than I thought I did.

"Are you okay?" He holds out his hand, and I stare at it. I don't like touching people or having anyone touch me. I don't deserve his kindness at all.

I nod, unable to say anything. My knee slammed into the floor when the guy pushed me, and now it's throbbing. I'm not sure why he did it, but I'm used to it. Kids in Kentucky used to shove me into lockers or pull my hair. It's because I'm a freak and I'm poor.

I get on my hands and knees, careful not to put weight on the bruised one, and next thing I know, Ben's hands are on my arms helping me stand. He touched me and it didn't hurt. My throat tightens, then I breathe in his scent.

He smells like freshly fallen snow and crisp winter air. Its coolness calms me for a moment. I haven't felt this relaxed in a long time.

"I should punch him in the face."

"It's okay."

"I can't believe it's you. Are you back for good? When did you get back?" he asks. He still rambles when he's nervous. It's nice to know some things haven't changed.

"Yeah. Back for good. How have you been?"

"Good."

I can feel several eyes on us, and I realize he's still touching me. I jerk away from him, and the bystanders start whispering and laughing. I know they're talking about me. The freak. Ben was touching a freak. My palms are sweaty, and there's a lump in my throat that I can't swallow. There are too many people. I can't breathe.

"Are you okay?" Ben asks, his forehead wrinkles in concern. "You look like you might pass out."

I shake my head, but I mean to nod, and the crazy motion makes me dizzier. I look around us at the people whispering, talking about me. It's too much.

Ben moves into my view, forcing me to look at him. "Alisa, take a deep breath."

Staring into his eyes, I do what he says. My pulse slows down to a normal pace, and I breathe out. I feel less nauseated, and I notice he's touching my arm again. Isn't he worried about what people might think? I gently pull away from him and stare at the ground.

"It's really good to see you," he says, scratching the back of his head. He looks nervous, almost like he's doing something he shouldn't.

The bell rings and people hustle to their classes. "Want me to walk you to your class?"

Heat rises to my cheeks, and I bite my lip. "Sure." I can't believe he offered. Guys like him don't offer to walk me to class, let alone talk to me. He's so much taller than me, and I'm not used to that. When we were younger, he was taller, but not like this. He has muscles and hair on his arms. It's weird. "I hear you play basketball now." I glance at him, and he smiles, a genuine, relaxed smile that reaches his eyes.

"Yeah. I love it."

"When is your first game?"

"Not until November."

"What do you do until then?"

"Practice. I'm probably more obsessed with it than most people. Courtney hates it."

My stomach sinks. "Courtney?" But I know who he's talking about.

He hesitates. "She's…my girlfriend. The girl you saw yesterday."

Oh. *Her.* I wonder why he doesn't want to tell me.

"Why'd you move back?"

"Mom died," I say with more force than I intend.

"Oh, shit. I'm so sorry."

We're quiet for a few seconds.

"It's good seeing you. Maybe I'll see you around," he says and walks away, leaving a blast of cold air in his wake.

I'm not sure what to think. Sarah's warning parades around in my mind. Why is he being so hot and cold? He was never like that before. Maybe I need forget about him. I never thought he'd like me as more than a friend, but now it seems like he doesn't like me at all.

ben

It's too dangerous talking to Alisa. When she told me her mom died, I wanted to hug her. The need to comfort her became too strong. I had to leave. I can't imagine what she's going through, but I can't be her friend. What would people think? Not only that Courtney would never allow it.

Courtney waits outside the classroom as usual, but today she has an amused scowl on her face.

"Hey." I lean in for a kiss, but she backs up.

"Hey? That's all you have to say?"

"What is it?" I play the naïve card. It's better this way.

"Who's the girl you walked to class with?"

I roll my eyes. "Some guy pushed into her, and she fell. I was helping her up. She kinda looked like she was going to have a panic attack, so I made sure she was going to be okay."

"That's all?" she asks. She wants more because some asshole told her there was more. Or maybe her imagination has come up with a story. She's the one who cheated but is so quick to assume I'm going to cheat on her.

"Yes. I swear." No way I'm going to tell her I actually know the girl.

"They said you stood there talking to her, smiling and flirting."

"You're seriously going to accuse me of cheating?" I cross my arms in front of my chest.

She clenches her teeth, and her face turns red. Shit. Now I've really pissed her off. "You are such a jerk, Ben. I told you I was sorry and that it meant nothing. I was drunk."

For a month?

"If you wanted to get back together with me just so you could hurt me—"

"Courtney, that's not it. I didn't flirt with the girl. I helped her up and left. That was it. End of story." I'm definitely not going to tell her that she was my best friend when I was younger or that I had a crush on her. That won't go over well. Secrets begin to pile. They're harmless since nothing will come of Alisa and me. Alisa wouldn't have anything to do with me.

Finally, she nods and lets out a breath. "Sorry I freaked out. I'm just hormonal."

Of course, you are. That's your excuse for everything. "It's okay." Placing my hand on the small of her back, we head to lunch.

"I love you," she says. "I just get crazy."

"I love you, too. You have to learn to trust me, Courtney. And I have to learn to trust you again."

"Wait," she says, stopping us both. "You don't trust me?"

"Who paged you this morning?"

"No one."

Dammit. "Tyler?"

She doesn't answer. Instead, tears pool her eyes.

Shit. I can't stand to see a girl cry. I don't care who it is. Sometimes I think Courtney plays this game because she knows it makes me feel bad.

"What is it?"

"Why can't you trust me? Why do you think I'd do that to you again? It didn't mean anything. I made a mistake. I thought we were over this. My sister paged me, okay?"

I soften. Why couldn't she have just told me? Pulling her into a hug, I breathe in her pear scent and tell her the words she wants to hear. "I'm sorry. Yes, I trust you."

"Are you sure?"

"Yes."

"I would never hurt you, Ben. I love you."

"I love you, too."

I'm sure I'm partly to blame for her running to Tyler anyway. Basketball consumed me, and I let it. I hardly took her on dates. I took her for granted. But she's been there for me. She's listened to me vent about Dad hounding me, which I know can't be easy since it's a lot. She's helped pick me up when I play like shit. Especially when I blew the game last year. Courtney consoled me to no end. Baked cookies. Rented movies to help cheer me up. Helped relieve a lot of stress.

We both need to let the Tyler thing go. For good. Maybe that is why I keep thinking of Alisa. Maybe I want to even the score with Courtney.

But I really don't. That isn't who I am. And Alisa isn't a means for revenge.

alisa

"What's this I hear about you and Ben Lamar flirting in the hallway?" Sarah has a strange look in her eyes when she and Damon sit down at the lunch table. Seeing the food on their trays makes my stomach growl.

"What?"

"Yeah, everyone's talking about it."

"H-he walked me to class. That's all."

Her face twists into confusion. "Ben?"

I shrug. "He talked for a second then left after I told him about my mom." Like he had a plane to catch. "What is up with him?"

Damon rolls his eyes. "He's a dick."

"Pretty much. I can't stand him."

Hearing this hurts me. "What happened to you two?"

Sarah shrugged. "He wasn't the same after you left. Basketball controlled him, and because he's so good, he became popular. Popularity made him into this selfish jerk.

I'm not saying this to ruin your outlook on him or anything. Be careful with him, okay?"

"I don't think he wants anything to do with me."

"Probably because of She Devil."

"Why do you call her that?"

"I'm sure she's the biggest reason why Ben is who he is now. They're the popular couple. So perfect." She rolls her eyes and pretends to gag. "Until she cheated on him and yet he forgave her."

"It proves he has no backbone," Damon says, and it offends me a little.

"Why would he forgive her?"

"Who knows? People hurt others all the time and get away with it."

I can't help but think she's talking about her father as well.

"How are you not hungry?" Sarah asks.

I'm starving. "I'm just not," I tell her, and she exchanges a look with Damon.

"I hate this food, but I'm always hungry. I can get you something to eat. I'm on that free lunch program thing. Mom can't afford much. Wanna come over this afternoon?"

"I have to work."

"Yeah, me too, but I'm gonna call out."

I've never called out of work before. Wouldn't I get into trouble? Daddy would never know. "What do you tell them?"

Sarah shrugs. "I'm sick. They won't care."

"How about tomorrow?"

"That works, too."

"Are you ever going to go back to work?" Damon teases her.

"I hate that place."

"I know. You tell me all the time."

Sarah laughs.

"What do you know about Zach?" I ask them.

"Zach Miller?" Damon asks.

"Yeah."

They exchange another look. "He's on the basketball team and friends with Ben."

I didn't see that coming. Is this some game Ben's playing with me?

"Why?"

"He offered to tutor me."

Damon lifts an eyebrow, then shrugs. "He's quiet. I don't really know him."

"He's Ben's best friend. Do you really need to know more?"

"He may not be a bad guy. He seems to keep to himself mostly."

"What's he going to tutor you on?"

"Chemistry."

Sarah whistles. "Yeah. I suck at that."

"He's helped me the last couple of days."

"That's nice of him. Just tread lightly."

Damon kisses her forehead and wraps an arm around her neck, pulling her close to him.

Why does she keep saying that? Does she think I'm such a fragile weakling? Or did something happen to her?

School ends and I make my way slowly through the crowded hallway to hide in the bathroom. I wait until the halls are clear before I leave. I hate crowds. I hate being pushed around because I'm small or because I'm a freak.

Once the halls are empty, I make my way to the parking lot. I hear shoes squeaking and a ball bouncing as I pass by the gym. Ben's voice carries into the hallway, and like a magnet, I'm drawn to it. I only want to see him play. Then I'll leave.

I walk inside and see Ben and Zach playing one-on-one. The bleachers are locked tight against the wall, and banners hang from the rafters. Division champs for the last five years, and only one state championship back in the eighties. The school logo of an eagle with its wings spread gripping a basketball is plastered across the wall.

Ben nails a layup, and the ball swooshes into the basket. Zach jogs over and gives him a high five.

It has been so long since I've seen Ben, but that innocent boyish grin on his face still makes my heart swell.

He heads toward the benches and grabs a towel. Ben looks up and our eyes meet.

Feeling the heat rise to my cheeks and the back of my neck, I chew on my lip. "You're good." I make my way toward him.

His lips curl into a half smile. "Thanks. Gives me something to focus on instead of." He shakes his head and wipes the sweat from his face.

"Hey, Alisa." Zach joins us.

"Hi."

"When do you want to work on chemistry?"

His question takes me off guard, and I don't miss Ben giving him a side glance.

"Um. I don't know."

Zach gives a small laugh. "Okay. Well, I'm ready when you are."

Blood rushes to my cheeks, and I look away.

"You wanna hang out for a bit and watch me kick Ben's ass?"

I open my mouth to say something, but the door to the gym opens. A dark-skinned girl with an athletic build walks in. Her shoulder length black hair is straight, and her skin is flawless. Are all the popular girls pretty? Staring at Ben like she's judging him, she makes her way toward a pom pom and a bag someone left behind.

Ben lets out a curse, obviously embarrassed that someone sees us talking. "You should go. Coach gets mad if people distract us during practice."

Zach looks at him, surprised.

The girl leaves.

"Yeah." My heart sinks, and I turn for the door, wanting to get out of here as fast as I can. Sarah was right.

ben

I'm burning up. I can't catch my breath. And it isn't from basketball practice. Grabbing my water bottle, I chug the entire thing. I can't relax.

"What the hell was that?" Zach asks.

I check the ball to him. "Don't worry about it."

"You didn't have to be a dick to her." He checks the ball back to me.

I go left, but he stops me.

"Just stay out of it."

I lunge right, but he's too fast.

"Is she off limits or something? Are you jealous? What's up?"

Clenching my teeth, I knock into him harder than I mean. When I go for a layup, he blocks the ball.

Damn. I can't get around him.

"You can do whatever you want. I don't know her anymore."

"What is with you?"

"Jesus. Are you my mom?" I wish he'd stop asking me questions about Alisa. Kim is probably already blabbing to Courtney about her and me talking.

The idea of Zach asking Alisa out doesn't sit well with me. Why should it matter? Why do I even care? I shake my head. I'm with Courtney anyway.

"Just wanna make sure you aren't going to beat my ass."

I look at him like he's crazy. "I don't care, man. Go for it. Now, can we please practice?"

"Oh, you wanna get creamed?" He checks me the ball.

"Bring it."

But the rest of the time we practice, I miss every single free throw. Zach kills me with the points. My defense is way off. It's like I've never played basketball in my life.

After taking a quick shower, I drive home in time to witness Mom and Hayden arguing about something. Sounds like something about a boy. Both are shouting, and I head upstairs. Someone is always fighting in this house. There's always too much tension, and I feel like I have to walk on eggshells because at any given second, someone is going to snap. It never used to be like this. I want to find out what's going on between Mom and Dad. Are they getting a divorce? Are they just going to live in this nightmare?

I can't take much more. I need some reprieve. Alisa comes to mind, and I feel guilty that she's taken residence in my head. I need to stop thinking about her. It's been so long. How do I even know she really wants to be my friend? Who knows what Sarah told her about us? I wasn't exactly the nicest person to Sarah, and I regret it because I lost two really good friends.

But why should I care? I have an amazing girlfriend. A great friend. Basketball. What more could I want? Other than my family to stop arguing.

Now that Alisa's back, I feel like I'm being tested. I don't know what to do.

Dinner sucks as usual. Mom and Dad put Hayden and me in the middle while they continue fighting. I'm so tired of everything. I want to sleep.

My pager goes off, and my heart leaps with the thought of Alisa paging me for some reason, but it's Courtney.

"What have I told you about wearing your pager at the table?" Dad stares at me.

"Sorry. I forgot."

"Watch the attitude, son."

"I learned from the best," I mumble under my breath.

He drops his fork against the plate. The clang of metal on china echoes through the dining room.

Out of the corner of my eye, I see Hayden jump, and I feel guilty. This one's on me.

"Alex, for god's sake. Stop it," Mom says, practically baring her teeth.

"I told him not to bring his pager to the table, yet, he does it anyway. This is family time. But you know what pisses me off? The fact that you had plans with your daughter this weekend, yet you're insistent on going to Tampa."

"Daddy, it's o—"

He puts his hand up, stopping Hayden. "We are a family, dammit. We need to start acting like one. Do you think we can all do that?"

No one answers.

We sit for several minutes in silence until Dad finishes his food. Both Hayden and I are afraid to say anything. When he's done, he gets up and retires to watch television. Hayden bolts upstairs and, as I stack the dishes from the table, I watch Mom calmly drinking her wine.

She looks up at me with wrinkled eyebrows. "What?"

"I hope you're happy, Mom." Taking the dishes into the kitchen, I leave her alone at the table with her wine.

When I go upstairs, I knock on Hayden's door. She opens it, annoyed when she sees me. "What?" Alanis Morissette blares from her room, which makes me cringe. Alanis whines about living and learning or something. Her voice grates on my every nerve.

"Are you okay?"

She lets out a groan. "I'm fine. What do you want?"

"Why are you mad at me?"

"You had to set him off."

"I'm sorry. It just pisses me off. I don't get what's going on."

"They hate each other." She crosses her arms in front of her chest.

"Yeah."

"By the way, Janie's sister heard that Alisa was back. Have you talked to her? How is she?"

"How the hell would I know?"

Hayden steps back, offended. It's like no matter how hard I try, something or someone is shoving her in my face. Can't a guy get a break?

"Geez, excuse me, buttmunch. I figured since you two were such great friends that maybe you'd have talked to her."

"Whatever."

She slams the door in my face. When I get to my room, my pager goes off again.

Picking up the phone, I dial Courtney's number and pray like hell she doesn't yell tonight. I can't take much more fighting.

Lying on my bed, pinching the bridge of my nose, I wait for her to answer.

"Who is this girl, Ben? Why do I keep hearing about you talking to her?"

I release a sigh. "She's no one. Just needed to ask Zach a question about chemistry is all."

"I'm sorry. It bothers me that you're talking to some girl all the time."

"It's not all the time. She's nothing, I promise. Just stop listening to Kim. You know she feeds you drama."

"You promise you don't like her? I don't want you to start liking someone else because of what I did."

"That's not going to happen. I promise."

"I'm sorry I sound like a crazy jealous girlfriend."

"You shouldn't even be jealous of her."

"I know. Have you seen the way she dresses? I feel like giving her some of my clothes."

I shake my head. "That's so wrong."

"Want me to come sneak into your room and stay tonight?"

I smile, knowing full and well that's exactly what she's going to do. She's done this a few times. Mom and Dad are too busy doing whatever to care. "Yeah."

But as soon as I hang up, Alisa pops in my head. It annoys me.

I can't do this to Courtney. I need to forget Alisa. We can't be friends. It's not fair to Courtney. I love her. This girl has been absent from my head for six years. All of a sudden, she's everywhere, and I wish I could forget about her permanently.

alisa

"I'm so glad you're here, Alisa." My manager, Seth greets me, panicked. He whisks me into the back to get my till. He's always freaking out about something, and everything has to be done that second. No wonder his brown hair is balding, and he has a large belly. He stresses out way too much. Sometimes I can't help but feed off that anxiety. He's really nice, but stern. Some of the other cashiers joke that he needs to get laid. "We are slammed right now. Beth called in and Stacy had to leave early."

He doesn't even let me count my till. He's ready for me to be out on the floor. The rush hour lasts until about 6:30, and I'm tired. It's constant customer after customer. I'm always jealous of the food and amount they buy. Some of them have food stamps and buy whole buggy-fulls of food. Why can't we have that?

When it's slower at night, I wish I could work on homework, but that's a definite no. As much as I hate working, it helps get my mind off Mom and things at home.

Tonight is especially slow. It's hard to look busy when I've cleaned my area five hundred times. The candy aisle is stocked and organized. My bags are fully stocked. My belt is clean. I flip through a magazine, barely listening to Sheila gab about her latest boyfriend.

"I gotta take a smoke break." She flips off her light. She really needs to stop smoking so much. And frequenting the tanning salon.

"Slow night?" a guy asks, and when I look up, I freeze. Zach. Blood creeps up my cheeks.

"Yeah."

He sets a few items down on the belt and gives a playful smile.

As I scan, I can't help but chuckle at his items, and I'm not entirely sure why. Coke. Snickers. Chips. Twizzlers. "Dinner?"

"I needed some fuel for studying."

I nod but feel a tad jealous that he's able to spend money on such frivolous items.

"Why didn't you tell me you and Ben used to be friends?"

I shrug. "Didn't come up. Why?"

"He's my best friend. I don't know. It's weird. He seems like he doesn't want to talk about you."

That stings, but why would Ben talk about me? "Oh. We haven't talked in years. Maybe he feels like he doesn't know anything about me to talk about."

"Pretty sure I can guess why."

I meet his blue eyes, confused.

"His girlfriend is a controlling bitch. He doesn't see how manipulative she is."

"Oh."

"Sorry. She drives me crazy. Just steer clear of her."

"I'll do my best." I'm getting tired of all the warnings.

I'm not sure why he's telling me these things. I don't want to talk about Ben with him. It makes me feel strange for some reason.

"I can't imagine you two being friends, though."

I frown and look away. I know why he says that. It's because I look like poor trash, and Ben's rich and popular. He's always been rich, but the popular thing is new to me. Pulling my sleeves over my hands, I withdraw. "Your total is $7.76."

He hands me a ten-dollar bill. "I don't mean it in a bad way. I just meant he seems to like shallow, vapid girls. Like Courtney."

I take his money and enter it into the register. "And how do you know I'm not shallow and vapid?" The drawer opens and I count out his change.

He cocks his head at me. "You're not shallow. You're kind and smart. Need a little help with chemistry, though," he teases, making me smile a little.

"You like movies?"

"What?"

"Movies. There's a place that shows movies on a screen."

I roll my eyes. "Yes."

"We should go see one sometime. I hear *Phenomenon* is good. The one with John Travolta."

Why is Zach even talking to me? I know once he realizes who I really am, he'll want nothing to do with me. And Daddy always said no boys.

"You shouldn't have boys distracting you. You have a hard-enough time concentrating on school. If I so much as sniff a boy around here, he better be ready to meet the business end of a shotgun."

"Is that a yes? No?"

I bite my lip. "Maybe. I'll let you know."

"Okay. See you later."

"What is wrong with you?" Sheila nudges me as soon as Zach leaves. "That handsome boy just asked you out."

"I said maybe."

Sheila shakes her head. "You're just gonna let that boy leave?"

"I'm not allowed to date."

She scrunches her face into a look of bewilderment. "Neither was I, sugar. But sometimes you gotta break the rules. Who cares? Live a little."

But I'm scared. I'm scared it'll all be some big joke. Why does Zach even want to go out with me? What could he possibly see in me?

Once my shift is over, I drive home and cook hamburgers for Daddy and me. For some reason, Tuesday nights have always been for hamburgers. Mom would cook them on the little grill we kept on the back porch, no matter the weather. She always knew how to make them so perfect and juicy. The last time she made hamburgers, Daddy was upset. I remember hearing glasses break in the kitchen, and when I ran from my room to see, Mom smiled at me.

"What's wrong?" I asked.

"Baby girl, everything is okay."

But the kitchen was a mess. Broken glass mixed with lettuce and tomato on the floor. She kept trying to block my view.

"Everything is fine."

But there were tears in her eyes, and her cheek was red.

She hugged me. "Go back to your room, sweetie. I'll call you when dinner is ready."

Something pops, bringing me back to the present. Grease. I left the hamburgers cooking a little too long.

Crap.

Removing them from the heat, I hope Daddy will be okay with them. After I make him a plate and put it in the fridge, I eat as much of a burger as I can, then I try to do homework.

Zach and Ben are firmly lodged in my thoughts, though. What does Zach want from me? And why is Ben being so mean to me? Does he hate me? I don't know what I expected when I returned, but I didn't expect this. The questions looping through my mind are exhausting.

Something prods me awake. I raise my head realizing I fell asleep on my open math book. Daddy stands over me, his breath reeking of Listerine.

"Why the hell are you sleeping at the table?" Daddy opens the refrigerator.

"I must have passed out doing homework."

He inspects my blank notebook page, beer in hand. He shakes his head. "Doesn't look like you did anything."

I want to cry. I don't understand math, and I have fifty problems due tomorrow. It's one in the morning. I'm exhausted. How am I supposed to go to college if I can't even do math? How am I supposed to even graduate high school, which is a requirement for culinary school? I have no time for a tutor. Am I doomed to stay here with Daddy forever?

"What the fuck is this?" Daddy yells, startling me. He shoves the plate of burger patties under my nose and grips the back of my neck, forcing me to look. "You burned dinner? Can't you do one thing right? I'm tired and work hard, but you don't seem to give a shit."

My chin quivers. I can't even cook a burger. What am I good for? "I can cook another." Which is what I should've done earlier.

"Don't waste food. Just get out of my sight."

Swallowing hard, I gather my books and go to my room, knowing it won't be a good night. Daddy will get drunker. He'll throw things. He'll yell. He'll cry. There's nothing I can do to comfort him through the pain. There's nothing I can do at all.

Mom always knew how. I remember she would hold him until he fell asleep. She did the same for me. I can't comfort anyone.

Staring at the cover of my math book, I gnaw on my lip. I can't do this. I can't do anything right. I need something. I need to reach that high. Stealing into the bathroom, I close the door and pull out my scissors. My pulse quickens. It's the only thing that brings me relief.

alisa

When I wake up, I find Daddy passed out in the recliner, clutching a picture of Mom. Beer cans clutter the coffee table. As quietly as I can, I gather the empty cans and throw them away. It wasn't until three that he settled down. Exhaustion clings to me, and there's an ache in my stomach that never goes away.

I tiptoe out of the house and try to start my car. It doesn't turn over. Clenching my teeth, I force the oncoming tears to disappear. I have to take the bus.

The bus is crowded, but everyone's pretty quiet, thankfully.

Sarah, Damon, and I sit together in English class. We mostly write notes to each other, and it feels like I never left. We laugh at Mr. Frank waddle to the dry erase board and scribble sentences. No one can make out his handwriting.

My stomach twists as I walk into chemistry and see Zach. I want to take Sheila's advice. But for some dumb reason, I can't get Ben out of my head. Ben will never like me more than a friend, and I guess I have some stupid wish that he will.

"Well if it isn't my favorite cashier," Zach says once I take my seat. "Those snacks you sold me last night fueled me enough to get all my homework done."

"You know I don't provide them, right?"

"No, but if you hadn't been there, I wouldn't have been able to purchase them."

"Someone else would have."

He smiles. "Yeah, but they wouldn't have been as cool."

"Glad I could be there for you."

"Me, too. If there's anything I can do for you, just let me know."

I need help with school. "Thanks."

"You okay?"

No. "I'm fine."

Class starts and as usual, I'm lost, but Zach helps me. I don't know why he's helping me, but I'm grateful. When it's over, Zach walks with me, chatting about how school is a waste of time and that he can't wait for basketball.

"You'll come to the games, right?" he asks.

I've never been to a sports game in my life. I've watched a lot on TV with Daddy, but that's it. "Um. Maybe." As we walk, we come near Ben at his locker. Ben stares at me then shakes his head and walks away.

"Do you have a boyfriend?" Zach asks.

His question catches me off guard. "No."

He nods. "Should I leave you alone?"

"No. I'm sorry. I didn't get much sleep last night."

"Everything okay?"

Not at all. "Yeah. Work and school keep me busy."

"I can imagine. I don't know how you do it."

We reach my locker, and my brain is in such a fog that I can't remember the combination. I'm trying hard, but it's not coming to me. Why can't I remember the simplest thing? Why can't I do anything right?

"Alisa?"

"What?" I accidentally snap at Zach, and immediately feel guilty.

"I'll...talk to you later."

Leaning against my locker, I watch him disappear through the crowd. Why can't I be a normal kid?

When school ends, I pass by the gym and see Zach and Ben practicing again. As much as I want to go inside, I don't.

"Excuse me."

My heart jumps to my throat as I turn around. I'm face to face with Courtney Andrews. She slinks toward me like a cat about to attack a mouse. She's very pretty, not a single blemish on her face, and she smells like some sort of manufactured apples. She's perfect. Thin, tanned. Every girl wants to be her, I'm sure. She's wearing a perfectly pristine white shirt and jeans with no holes. Her shoes look brand new.

"Yeah?" I say.

She narrows her blue eyes. "Weren't you the one Ben talked to the other day?"

If you want to call it talking. "I just asked him a question."

"Hmph. I just wanted to meet you." She lifts an eyebrow and looks me over, giving a disgusted expression at my holey jeans and ratty flannel shirt.

The dark-skinned girl from yesterday catches up to Courtney. I hold my stomach as the nausea settles inside. The walls start to close in, and I feel like I'm going to pass out.

I turn around, wanting to get away as fast as I can.

I overhear her say to her friend, "She was standing outside the door like some stalker." And they both laugh.

I reach the parking lot in time to see Sarah. She and Damon offer me a ride, but we go to Sarah's house. I don't feel like going to work, so I call out for the first time ever. Mrs. Downs is at work, and we end up playing Mario Brothers 3.

"Ugh, what is her problem?" Sarah asks, after I told them about Courtney.

"How could Ben be with someone like her?"

"Because she's perfect, and he's just as mean."

No argument there.

"Zach seems to like you."

I shrug. "Why? What's his angle?"

"He may not have one," Damon says. "Maybe he really likes you."

"Maybe we could go on a double date?" Sarah asks.

"Did you just—"

"Shut up." Sarah elbows Damon. "No, I don't like double dating, but we could get to know the guy better."

I shake my head. "He won't want to go out with me. Not after today."

"You don't know that. Call him."

The door opens and there's a lot of noise coming in. I flinch as a few guys walk in with cases of beer and put it into the fridge. I get up and move against the couch. There are too many people in the house. Loud, shouting voices.

Mrs. Downs comes in with a tall, skinny man, his arm hanging around her neck.

"Mom, seriously? Tonight?" Sarah meets her mom in the kitchen. "It's a school night." Some of the people laugh.

Damon stands near me watching everyone around us like he's planning on what to do if something happens to Sarah or me.

"Oh honey, it's okay. These are some of the regulars from the café. We won't be up too late."

The voices amplify, and I bolt for the door. A couple of guys covered in tattoos and piercings stare at me as they smoke cigarettes. I lower my head so that my hair hides my face, hoping Sarah or Damon come out soon.

I bite my lip and make my way toward Damon's car.

"Where ya goin' honey?" one of the guys asks as he follows me.

Crossing my arms, I ignore him.

The front door swings open as Damon drags Sarah from the house and across the yard to his car.

"I suggest you leave her alone," Damon tells the guy. I've never had a guy do that.

Sarah guides me into the car, and Damon slides in the driver's seat. Seconds later, we're speeding through the dark country roads toward my house.

"I'm so sorry about that," Sarah says. "She knows not to do that on the weeknights."

Damon takes her hand and squeezes it.

We ride in silence all the way to my house, which is in complete darkness. Seeing the dark house gives me chills. I don't want to go inside.

"Sorry about tonight," Sarah says as she gets out of the car and pulls the seat forward.

I climb out. "Don't worry about it. I still had fun."

"It's freaking creepy out here. How do you handle it by yourself?"

I hate it. "It's not that bad."

"You want us to hang out for a while?"

"No, it's okay." Daddy doesn't want me to have anyone come over. He's afraid they'll mess up the house. "Thanks for the ride," I tell Damon.

"Anytime."

Sarah pulls me in for a hug. "See you tomorrow. Oh, and ask Zach about double dating." She gives a wide smile.

I watch them drive down the long dirt road from the screened in porch. My heart sinks further the farther they drive away. Once Damon's taillights are out of view, I walk inside the sweltering house.

Turning on the kitchen light, I search through the cabinets for Daddy's dinner. We really need to go to the store. Sighing, I reach for a can of Spam and a box of macaroni and cheese. I hate that we always get the powdered kind, but I'm grateful we can at least get that. Hopefully, this weekend, Daddy and I can work on my car together.

Sarah's suggestion about a double date with Zach crosses my mind. I know she wants me to ask him, but I don't want to get into trouble. Maybe Daddy won't find out. I'll come right home after the movies.

Taking a deep breath, I pick up the phone and dial his number. I try to ignore the heat that cloaks my body and the caterpillars gnawing at my insides.

"Hello?"

"Zach?"

ben

The mid-September morning is unusually cool, a welcome change from the brutally hot summer we'd been having. I don't mind the heat if I'm at a pool, but it takes a lot out of me when I'm running.

I'm finally free today to do what I want. Past two weekends, I had to take Hayden to the city for the mall. Twice. Like my life revolves around taking her and her friend to the damn mall because Mom is too busy screwing around to enjoy time with her kids.

Thinking about Mom makes me run harder, and I switch my brain to my date tonight with Courtney. Just a relaxing movie with my girl is exactly what I need.

When I spot Piggly Wiggly, I jog inside, needing some water. I'm completely drenched in sweat and gross, but I won't be long.

Then I see her. Her long brown hair is pulled back in a ponytail, and she's smiling as she talks to some blond woman with a fake tan. It's a genuine smile, like she's really comfortable. The sun beams through the front windows, casting Alisa in a warm glow. I've missed her. My heart hammers against my ribcage so hard I think it might break a bone or two.

Alisa turns around to her register. She works here. I had no idea. I hate that I don't know anything about her. When she finishes with her customer, she looks up. Our eyes meet and I swear my knees are about to buckle. Those beautiful, soulful brown eyes stare at me. Her cheeks flush, and I love it.

"I didn't know you worked here." I walk to her register.

"Yeah." She crosses her arms in front of her chest and looks away.

"Do you like it?"

Alisa shrugs.

I shiver, but it isn't from the air conditioning hitting my sweaty body. Alisa isn't a cold person. Her reaction is my fault. I hate this weird awkwardness between us.

"How long have you worked here?" I don't like small talk, but I want to hear her voice. I want to know more about her. This girl who was always there for me. The girl who made me soup when I was sick. Who made me laugh when I was frustrated over something. Who did anything in her power to cheer me up. But that was in the past. She's not the same, and neither am I.

"Since the summer. Are you going to buy anything?"

"What?"

She looks at me like I've lost my mind.

"You have to buy something. I can't stand around and talk. I'm on the clock."

"Oh. Right." I shake out of my reverie and snag a bottled water from the cooler next to the candy aisle. She rings it up, and I want to say something to keep the conversation going. Something to keep me here with her.

But I don't.

"A dollar seven."

I give her two dollars, and she gives me change. Our hands touch for the briefest second. It sets me on fire.

"Have a nice day."

Nodding, I put the change in my pocket and walk away.

"Ben," she calls, and my heart falters.

Turning around, I smile, hoping she'll change her mind and want to talk. "Yeah?"

Alisa holds up my water bottle.

Dammit. I take the bottle and leave.

What the hell was that? Why was I acting like some idiot? How could Alisa make me feel like that? No one has ever made me feel like that.

Maybe I can come back soon, visit her at work, and we can talk. If I decide to actually formulate words around her, that is. No one from school comes here. At least none of Courtney's friends. I don't even know what made me run through this part of town. I haven't been here since I was kid with Alisa and Sarah.

Shaking my head, I jog home trying to get my mind set for my date, but I'm so out of it from that bizarre encounter. I better get my head straight before Courtney sees me.

Courtney's dressed in a blue jean skirt and a sleeveless white shirt. Body glitter is all over her arms, and some is on her face. She's got her hair pulled back in a ponytail, but it looks like it took her hours to do.

When I hug Courtney, I inhale her peachy scent. I release her, and my hands are covered in glitter. I can't wait for this fad to go away.

We head to the movies with my radio on. Weezer's "In the Garage" plays. I start singing along, but Courtney changes the station to a Mariah Carey song. Doesn't matter who's driving. Always gotta listen to what she wants. If you ask her, though, she never gets to listen to her music.

We're quiet as I drive. I'm a million miles away thinking of another girl. Thinking about what it would be like with Alisa.

"Ben!" Courtney shouts.

"What?"

"That car is stopping."

"I see it."

"You weren't paying attention. I swear, you are the worst driver."

"Then maybe you should've driven."

"As if."

"Sorry. I've been struggling in practice lately," I say as an attempt to lighten the mood. She wants honesty. Here it is. "Zach kicked my ass the other day. Things at home are getting bad. I'm having a hard time concentrating."

Her pager goes off, and she reads it. She says nothing.

"Who is it?" I ask.

"Omigod. Why do you keep asking me that? It's Kim."

By the time we get to the theater, I'm on edge. I'm ready for the night to be over. Reaching in my wallet for money, I glance to the right and freeze.

Alisa is walking with Zach toward the ticket booth. Since when did he ask her out? And when did she say yes? I thought he told me they hadn't really spoken in a couple of weeks. Is he lying to me?

"Hello? Ben?"

I turn back to Courtney, but not in time for her to not notice who held my attention. I pay for the tickets and take Courtney's hand. I need water.

"Eww, why is your hand so sweaty?" She removes hers and wipes it on her skirt.

"Hey man, what's up?" Zach asks.

"Not much." I look at Alisa and almost melt. Under the lobby lights, I can see bits of copper in her light brown hair. She doesn't look at me, but her cheeks are flushed. She's wearing a gray and black flannel shirt with blue jeans. There's a hole at the knee and one on her upper leg. How did Zach get Alisa to go out on a date?

"Well, have fun." Zach puts his hand on the small of her back. I hate it.

"Are we going to just stand out here or what?" Courtney asks. "I don't like that girl. She stares at you."

"What are you talking about?"

"Please. Like you don't see it. She wants you."

I let out a groan and pinch the bridge of my nose. "Seriously?"

Courtney cocks an eyebrow. "I saw her the other day watching you play basketball. And just now, she kept glancing at you."

She did? I shouldn't be excited about that. "Did it ever occur to you that she was watching Zach? She's here with him."

"I'm not going in there if she's going to be here."

"I just bought the tickets."

"I don't care."

"Look, she's nothing to me. Besides, she's dating Zach, I'm pretty sure you're going to see a lot more of her." So will I.

"Ugh. I mean, who wears flannel on a date? It's like a thousand degrees outside."

I shrug. "You always get cold."

Her lips turn up into a smile. "But I always have you to keep me warm."

Rubbing her back, I coax her across the lobby. When I turn around, I catch Alisa averting her eyes as she pulls napkins from the dispenser, and my stomach sinks. I know she heard every word I just said.

It's for the best, I keep telling myself. The weight of not knowing how—if—Alisa can fit into my life is starting to pull me down. Though I'm pretty sure after the way I've treated her, she'll want nothing to do with me.

alisa

Clutching the napkins in my hand, my throat closes. I don't want to be here any longer. It's cold inside the lobby, but that isn't the only reason I'm shaking.

I lean against the counter, waiting for the room to stop spinning. As people pass, they whisper and laugh. Probably because I have holes in my jeans; my shoes are old; my hair is flat and boring.

Sarah was right. He won't even look at me, like he's embarrassed to be around me.

This pain hurts. He was nice to me earlier, at the grocery store. I don't know why I even care. I shouldn't. Why would he be nice to me? Why did I think anything differently? Just like he said, I'm nothing to him.

"Are you okay?" Zach asks, startling me.

No. "I'm fine."

"You look like you might be sick."

I shouldn't have come. "I'm fine."

He frowns and takes my hand. "Everything is okay. The movie's supposed to be really good."

During the movie, Zach is quiet, except when he's laughing at the funny parts. He's nice, but I get a weird feeling around him, and I don't know what it is. I don't know why he would even remotely be interested in me. It has to be one big joke.

"I'll be right back," I tell Zach and find a bathroom.

Inside the stall, I lift my shirt and trace the cuts across my stomach with one finger. I'm a terrible date. I'm sure Zach will tell everyone on Monday what an awful person I am. I'm no good at this.

I'm not sure how long I end up staying in the bathroom, but by the time I return to the movie, it only has twenty minutes until it ends.

Zach and I quietly leave. When we reach outside, I stop. "Thanks for the movie."

"You're welcome. Are you hungry?"

"Oh, it's okay. You don't have to."

"Is everything okay? You were gone for a while. Did I do something to upset you?"

"No, no. It's my stomach."

He nods and looks away as he plays with the keys. "I'll walk you to your car."

"Oh, it's not necessary." Zach doesn't know that I walked here. "Um, I'll see you Monday."

"Do you need a ride?"

I cross my arms in front of my chest. "It's fine. Really."

"Can I call, or would there be any point?"

No. You'll post my number all over the school like Austin Brown did to me. I like Zach, but I'm such a mess, and there's no way he actually likes me.

"That's what I thought." Defeated, he walks away, leaving me disappointed in myself.

ben

During the movie, Courtney's pager went off like five damn times. She's on the payphone talking to Kim or whoever while I'm waiting for her to finish. About twenty seconds later, a car pulls up in front of the theater and the door opens. One of Courtney's friends, Micah, gets out.

"Courtney, come on!" she urges.

Courtney hangs up the phone.

"Where are you going?"

"Sleepover at Micah's house." She gives me a quick kiss and runs out the door to her friends. She does this a lot. Especially when she's in a mood. Tonight, I don't mind. I'm exhausted, and I just want to go home.

As I drive, I see someone walking on the side of the road. The flannel shirt looks familiar. I pass by and realize it's Alisa.

What the hell? Did Zach just leave her? Why would he do that? I thought Zach was a better man than that.

I pull over on the side and get out.

"Alisa?"

She bites her lip as our eyes meet. The red taillights from my car shine on her face. My heart falters when I see her cheeks are wet. He made her cry?

"Are you okay? What happened to Zach?"

"Um."

"Come on. Get in. I'll take you home." I open the passenger door.

"Why? I thought I meant nothing to you."

Dammit. I let out a sigh. "That's not true."

"I have to go." She tries to walk around the car. When I reach for her, she flinches.

What the hell did Zach do to her? "Come on, Alisa," I say, my voice softer. "Just get in the car. I'm not leaving until you do."

We stare at each other on the side of the dark road, and I swear now we're trying to see who's more stubborn.

"I've got nowhere to be, so I can stay as long as I need."

Alisa bites her lips, drawing me to them. How soft are they? What would it feel like to kiss her? I squeeze my eyes shut for a moment.

She finally concedes and gets in the passenger seat.

The ride to her house is quiet. It's been six years since we've been in the same space this long, and I'm nervous for some reason. My insides twist in knots, but hopefully I can keep a cool exterior. I steal glances at Alisa as I drive, and she stares out the window the whole time. Her hands are clasped together tightly. I wish I knew what's on her mind. I can't believe she was walking on the side of the road. It's so dark someone could've swerved and hit her.

My stomach churns at the thought. "What happened to Zach?"

"Nothing. He went home."

"Why would he just leave?"

"Turn right up here."

It's weird that she's giving me directions to her house. I've always known where she lived, but it just occurred to me that she doesn't live in the same place.

"Did something happen?"

"Turn left."

She is so stubborn. But I haven't been fair to her. Guilt sinks in about the shitty way I've been treating her. She's just a friend. Or was.

"You can drop me off by the mailboxes over there."

I turn to look at her. "Where is your house?"

"I know my way home."

"That wasn't my question."

She doesn't answer. I slow to a stop, only to turn down the gravel road. It's so dark and creepy. I see chicken houses to my left and a cow pasture to my right. Nothing else around. The putrid smell makes my stomach flip, but I don't dare say a word.

She clears her throat. "My house is right here," she says, barely above a whisper.

I pull up in front of a one-story house, wondering why there aren't any lights on. My lights shine on her Escort. The poor thing has seen better days.

"Thanks for the ride." She opens the door, and I scramble to get out of the car.

"Are you going to be okay tonight?"

"I'll be fine." Alisa keeps walking onto her porch, and I watch her go inside the house.

I did this. I made her hate me. It's what I wanted, and I succeeded.

alisa

Leaning against the door, I release my breath, trying to stop myself from shaking. My skin tingles as I peek out the window to watch Ben drive away. I don't know why he wanted to take me home so bad. Why is he only nice to me when no one else is around? Even in the car, he seemed agitated that he had to give me a ride. Does he hate me that much? Am I that terrible?

The house is quiet, and Daddy won't be home for a couple of hours. Exhaustion wears on me, but I have to cook him something. Opening the kitchen cabinets, my heart swells when I see food. Daddy was true to his word. He bought groceries. I open the fridge, and there's more food. My stomach drops when I see two cases of beer. Closing the fridge, I lean against the counter. I want to drain the cans down the sink. I don't want him to drink. He's my dad when he doesn't. I take a deep breath. How can I get him to stop?

Shaking my head, I gather ingredients for spaghetti. I haven't cooked like this in so long, and it calms my nerves.

When I finish the spaghetti, I put a small amount in a bowl for myself and put the rest in a Tupperware container. I eat while watching TV, thinking about the weird night.

I was mean to Zach and Ben. I shouldn't worry about either one. I need to focus on saving money and getting good grades. It's the only thing that will save me. I don't want to leave Daddy, but I can't stay here forever. I love him, but I hate the drinking, and I'm not sure I can give him an ultimatum like Mom did in order to get him to quit.

I wait up for Daddy to get home, and when he does, he sits in front of the TV eating the spaghetti with a beer.

"This is good. Tastes like your mama's."

I smile a little, loving the compliment.

"I really miss her cooking," Daddy says. "Remember those pinto beans she'd let cook all day?"

"Those were good." She put bits of ham in the beans, and the savory smell would permeate throughout the house making my stomach growl.

"Did you get your homework done tonight?"

"Yes," I lie. "I talked to Sarah a little, too. Remember her?"

"From when you was little?"

"Yeah."

"How's her mama? I haven't seen her in years."

I clear my throat a little. "She's good. Works at the Busy Bee still."

"Maybe I'll drop in and see her."

He grabs his eighth beer from the fridge. I want so much to say something, but I don't. He's only been home for an hour, and already more than half a case of beer is gone. Anxiety begins to creep its way throughout me. I pick at my nails and ignore the cramps in my stomach. Maybe if I talk to him, he won't want to drink. Or maybe I can convince him to go to sleep.

He turns up the TV a little.

"How was work?"

No answer.

"Um, Daddy?" I need to ask him about my car. "Daddy?"

"What?" he snaps, his blue eyes glare at me.

"I-I was just asking to see if you could fix my car tomorrow."

He lets out a frustrated sigh. "What'd you do this time?"

"It won't start. My shift starts at nine."

Daddy doesn't say anything. He's engrossed in the sports highlights. I miss watching football games with him, but I'm usually working while the games are on.

"Daddy?"

"What? I'm trying to watch this."

I swallow hard. "W-will you look at my car tomorrow?"

"Goddammit. I'll fix it."

I nod, and pull my knees up to my chest, wanting to cry.

Daddy gets up for more beer. When he returns to his chair, he continues watching TV.

"I'm going to bed," I tell him.

"Fine."

Keeping the tears deep inside, I retreat to my room, missing the days he would tell me goodnight.

ben

I don't care how late it is. I need to know what Zach did to Alisa. Barreling into his driveway, I shut the engine off and slam the car door. The garage floodlights flash on, almost blinding me. Once I reach the door, I start pounding on it.

Lights on the inside come on, and his dad answers. "Ben? What's the matter?"

"I need to talk to Zach."

"What is it, honey?" Mrs. Miller ties her robe around her waist as she comes up behind his dad.

"Ben, do you know how late it is?" Mr. Miller asks.

"Yes, I'm really sorry. This won't take long."

Zach clambers down the stairs, and his parents retreat. As soon as Zach steps outside and closes the door, I grab his shirt and slam him into the brick side.

"What did you do to her?"

"What the hell are you talking about? Get off me!"

I slam him again. He tries to push me off, but I'm too angry. We've never fought before, but he hurt Alisa. "What did you do to Alisa, Zach?"

"Nothing. Jesus. What's your problem?"

"Why was she walking home by herself? She didn't drive because I saw her car at her house. Did you just leave her there?"

"What? No. We took separate cars. She wouldn't let me walk her to her car. Said her stomach was upset."

"You swear you didn't do anything?" I ease up on him, and he breaks free from me.

"You should know me better than that. No, I didn't do anything to her. Damn."

I believe him. But something is still not right. "Sorry, man. I just…she was walking on the side of the road. In the middle of the dark."

"What? Why? I thought she drove herself."

Did Sarah take her to the movies and bail on her? What about her dad? I didn't see his truck at her house.

"Look, man, I like Alisa, but you two obviously have some shit you need to work through."

"What are you talking about?"

He tilts his head, looking at me like I know exactly what he's talking about. "There's also something up with her."

"What do you mean?"

Zach shrugs. "I don't know, dude. Maybe it was her stomach. She spent a lot of time in the bathroom. She looked like she was about to cry at any given second. I tried putting my arm around her, and she recoiled." He shrugs again shoving his hands in his pockets. "Maybe it's me. She just acted like a wounded animal or something."

She did the same to me. "She lost her mom recently."

"Yeah, she told me."

She told him?

"That could be it." I hear the doubt in his voice, though. "I know you've been avoiding her for whatever reason, but I think you should talk to her. Stop being a dick to her. You can't treat her like crap then come try to beat my ass up. If you two were such good friends back in the day, I don't see what's stopping you now."

"That's not a good idea."

"Why? Because of Slutney?"

Clenching my teeth, I stare at him, challenging him.

He holds up his hands. "Alisa deserves better."

"Courtney already doesn't like her because she thinks Alisa likes me, which isn't true. Plus, you know my parents are all about appearances."

"Afraid of what people will say? Damn man. You really that shallow."

"No."

"Yeah, okay."

"What's that supposed to mean?"

Zach lets out a breath. "Look, man. Alisa obviously means something to you. She seems like she could use a friend. She won't let me be that person. She is so closed off."

"She has friends."

He rolls his eyes. "Just talk to her. No one's going to care."

Yeah, they will. And he doesn't know what she does to me.

Maybe he's right. But Alisa is closed off to me, too. She used to not be, and I wonder what happened to her in Kentucky.

"What makes you think she'll talk to me?"

"You really are an idiot. She'll talk to you. And if you care about her, you'll go find her and catch up with her."

Piggly Wiggly is sprawling with people today. It's Saturday, and the town practically shuts down for the college football games. The state of Alabama is so intense over football. As soon as you're born, you're baptized either an Alabama or Auburn fan. I'm an Auburn fan, thankfully.

Even though my team has a big game today, it's the last thing on my mind. That isn't what has my stomach in knots or why my throat feels like I drank sand. I need to talk to Alisa to see if she's really okay, then I can leave her alone, and there won't be anything weird between us.

But when I see her behind the register, an ache hits my chest, and I can't help myself.

Stay focused.

I scrounge around for something to buy, and I pick up whatever is near me. I get in her line and wait.

She smiles at every customer. Some of them know her by name and ask about her school. She answers them politely. Her smile is genuine and kind.

When she sees me, her smile fades, and her eyes dodge mine. Alisa scans the items I placed on the belt.

"Hi," I say.

"Hello."

"What are you up to?" I'm an idiot.

"Working."

"Yeah. What time do you get off?"

"Your total is $12.80."

What the hell did I buy? I hand her a twenty. "What time do you get off work?"

She counts out the change and puts it in my hand along with the receipt. I love the few seconds our hands touch.

"Have a nice day."

"Alisa, I just want to talk."

"Oh honey," the elderly lady behind me says to Alisa. "He's a handsome boy. I'd talk to him."

I smile awkwardly.

"Hi, Mrs. Aldredge." Alisa's lips turn into a friendly smile.

"Do you know he's the star basketball player?" Mrs. Aldredge tells her. Old ladies love me, and I like how she's trying to convince Alisa to talk to me. No way she can turn down the sweet lady.

"I get off at six."

"Sweet. I'll see you then."

I'm in such a good mood. It's like a high that I haven't felt since I was a kid. I forgot how good this feels. It's different than when I play basketball. I wait only a couple of hours before she gets off. I park next to her car, wanting to make sure she sees me.

Her car is ancient. I'm impressed it still works.

As I lean against my car, she rounds the corner, and my heart starts pounding like a dribbling basketball.

Alisa halts, gripping her keys. She stares at me with confusion or surprise. It's still hot outside, but she's wearing a long-sleeved shirt under her Piggly Wiggly shirt. I don't see how she's able to wear it. Fall doesn't start here until November. And it only lasts one week before the temperatures are in the twenties.

"Hey. How was work?"

"Fine."

"It's weird to think about you working."

"I know. It's different."

"Do you like it?" That was a dumb question.

"It's okay. Scanning groceries isn't exactly something I consider fun."

I chuckle. "Wanna come over and hang out?" What am I doing? It's okay, though. Dad's out somewhere. Mom is wherever and Hayden is at Janie's. Courtney's out with her friends again tonight.

"Um. I have to get home."

"Come on. My mom would love to see you again. And Hayden." I'll play dumb as to why they aren't there.

"I can't."

Damn.

She makes her way to her car like she's in a hurry.

"Can we at least talk?"

Alisa opens her door, and I hold it open for her. "Ben, I have to go." She turns the key, but nothing happens.

She tries again.

Nothing.

Her face turns red, and tears slightly well in her eyes. "He promised he'd fix it."

"What? Who promised?"

"Nothing."

"Is everything okay? Is this why you walked to the movies last night?"

Nothing.

"I can have your car towed somewhere to get it fixed."

She shakes her head as she gets out of the car. She slams the door, looking defeated.

"Are you sure?"

"My dad will fix it." Her voice is terse.

"Okay. Wanna come over. We can catch up."

"Why?"

"I've missed you," I blurt.

She blushes and meets my eyes. "What?"

"Come over. Then I'll take you home."

Alisa nibbles on her lip. "Okay."

Getting her to agree does wonders to my ego.

Just like last night, she clasps her hands together while peering out the window.

"I can't believe you're driving now," she says.

"Yeah, I know. Dad got me this car last year so I could practice." I hope I don't sound like I'm gloating.

"It's nice."

It's quiet again, and I turn on the radio to break the ice. One of my favorite songs is playing. It's "Today" by Smashing Pumpkins. The lyrics are dark and deep, yet the music is upbeat. Many people don't catch the true meaning of the song. It's amazing in that it describes suicidal thoughts in an ironic way. I wish I had writing talent like Billy Corgan. He writes straight from his life, and in a way, I can relate to some of the songs.

"I like this song," Alisa says. Her voice is soft and innocent. The sound sends shivers down my spine. I missed the sound of her voice. Her smile. The way her cheeks redden. The way she doesn't think she's beautiful but is.

"Yeah, it's one of my favorites. Are you a Pumpkins fan?"

"Um." She pulls some of her hair over her shoulder, hiding her face. I wish she wouldn't do that. I love seeing her face. "I don't really know them. Just what's on the radio."

"Ah. I should make you a mixed tape. Who do you listen to?"

She shrugs. "Nirvana. Pearl Jam. The Cure."

"I like Nirvana and Pearl Jam. Not a huge Cure fan, though."

"I like listening to the lyrics. I used to read along while the song played so I could memorize them."

"I've done that before. It's nice to sit back and relax while listening to the songs. It's nice to know I'm not alone." I glance at her, and she's looking at me with those beautiful brown eyes.

I pull up into my driveway. It's been so long since she's been at my house. When I meet her gaze, this peculiar, exhilarating feeling overcomes me. It's like she can see right through me or something. She breaks the staring match, and I get out of the car. I don't make it in time to open her door.

She smiles, and her cheeks flush. I wish she wasn't so shy around me, but I guess that is natural for her. She was always timid around people, except Sarah and me. It's been a while, so I guess it's returned. Alisa looks hesitant, almost paranoid. She keeps looking around her as if someone's watching or something.

We head inside the cool house.

"Ben," I hear Mom call out. I stiffen. I don't know why she's home, and it makes me nervous.

I hear rustling in the kitchen, and we make our way there. "Mom."

"I made pizza rolls for the game," she says, not looking up from whatever document she's reading. She hasn't wanted to watch football in forever. Or made pizza rolls in years. She used to cook them all the time for Alisa, Sarah, and me.

"Mom," I say again.

Finally, she looks up and through her glasses that sit low on her nose, her eyes widen, then narrow. "Ben, is that… Alisa?"

"Yeah."

Blood drains from Mom's face. She looks like she's seen a ghost. Mom recovers and gives a fake smile. Dread fills me. I know when she's not happy about something and refuses to make a scene. Why isn't she happy about seeing Alisa? When her eyes rove over Alisa's work shirt and dingy khakis, I cringe on the inside. I know immediately what's going on inside my mom's judgmental mind. She wasn't always like this, but ever since Dad became a city councilman, she has always worried about appearances.

Alisa just got off work. It's understandable she's not going to be dressed to the nines.

"Goodness, child. It's been so long." Mom steps around the island, but Alisa moves back a step. Mom takes offense by Alisa's lack of approach. "It's been so long since I've seen you. I take it you've moved back. How are your parents? Are you back for good?"

I briefly close my eyes. I want to end this awkwardness now.

"Mom," I tell her. I should've warned Alisa it would be like an interrogation, but I didn't know she'd be here.

Alisa blushes and bites her lip. "It's good to see you. Everyone's fine," she says, but I know she's lying. I can always tell when she lies. She never looks you in the eye, and she starts chewing on her lip.

"What brings you back?"

Oh crap. I should've told Mom weeks ago when Alisa first came back.

Her cheeks flush once more, and her eyes tear up. "Um, Dad and I moved back. Mom passed away."

My heart drops to my stomach as that tightness returns. I feel like a jerk hearing her having to explain. I should've said something for her.

"Oh, honey," Mom gasps. Finally, my real mom comes forth and before Alisa can react, she pulls Alisa close for a hug. Alisa winces for a second and doesn't hug back. Something eats at me. She doesn't like to be touched, which was never an issue before. Is this what Zach was talking about?

Mom holds Alisa at arm's length. "I'm so sorry to hear that. When?"

"March."

Mom shakes her head. "Well, I'm so glad you're here. I'm sure Ben is just as delighted to see you. Are you staying for the game?"

"No, I can't stay long."

Mom nods. "You kids hang out in the living room, and I'll bring in the snacks."

She never cares where my friends and I hang out. It's weird she said that. Does she think we're going to be doing stuff? I love my mom, but she's so odd sometimes. At least she's not forcing me to throw her out.

Placing my hand at the small of Alisa's back, I lead her into the living room. The simple touch makes me insane. I turn the TV on for the game, and we sit on the couch. I feel awkward though. I don't know what to say to her. And the couch is so big and makes conversations less intimate.

"I'm sorry about that."

"It's okay," she softly says.

"I'm also really sorry about your mom." I reach for her hand and squeeze it in mine. "I know we haven't talked in years, but I'm here for you." When she meets my eyes, I'm struck by her beauty once again. I want to hold her, comfort her. I want to be near her, like we used to. This distance is killing me, but I'm happy to have her back in my life again. "I've missed you," I utter. Again.

Alisa turns to me again, and I see that light in her eyes. She smiles a little and blushes but removes her hand. "You, too."

"What was Kentucky like?"

"A lot like here. Mom and Dad had good jobs. Things were good."

"How long have you been back?"

"We moved in June."

"You were here for the summer?"

She nods.

"Why didn't you call?" I don't know why it bothers me, but it does.

She gives me a pointed look.

I don't know what I would've done had I received a call one day from her. I'd like to think I wouldn't have been a jerk to her. "I wish I had known about your mom. I would've come to the service. How's your dad?"

"He's okay. He's sad. Mom had been sick for a while, so we knew it was coming." Her eyes well, and I make my move closer to her.

When I raise my arm to pull her closer, she flinches and cowers. There's a sinking feeling in my stomach, like something's not right with her. Did something happen in Kentucky? Did she date some guy who didn't treat her right? Instead, I take her hand, hoping she will allow it and that

I'm not being pushy. She does. Holding Alisa's hand takes that feeling away, and everything feels right.

"I'm sorry. It's in my nature to hold a girl who's crying." That is the dumbest thing I could've said. I swear, it's like I'm trying to get into her pants. But I'm not. She's different.

I can feel her relax into me, which boosts my ego. We stay like that for a little while, until Mom comes in with snacks. Alisa withdrawals from me as Mom gives me a warning look. I won't hear the end of it tonight, which I probably deserve.

Alisa feels so fragile right now. Scared. Almost like a timid animal. Just like Zach said. I remember as kids, she was fearless. Nothing scared her, except her parents fighting. She used to comfort me during storms, as much as I hate to admit it.

But I don't see that fearlessness in her now. It's gone.

alisa

I never thought I would be at Ben's house again let alone holding hands. I don't know how many times I imagined this. It makes me realize how much more I missed him. All those years away, I fantasized about us being together. Or him coming to Kentucky to visit and kissing me. It's a dumb dream. I don't know why he would think of me as more than a friend. I'm not worth it.

This whole time he's been so hot and cold unlike the Ben I've always known. But this is the real him. It's like he's been hiding or something. He seems more relaxed now, and not so on edge.

I need to quit fantasizing about something that will never happen. He is only comforting me as a friend. Nothing more. If that's what this is. He has a girlfriend. Come Monday the entire school will know what a sad, pathetic person I am.

My stomach growls loud enough that Ben hears it.

He chuckles and hands me the plate of pizza rolls. "I guess you're hungry."

I bite my lip. They look delicious, and I am starving. I take one, but he still holds the plate.

"They're all yours."

"Oh. Um. Thanks," I say and take the plate as he grabs his. "How come you and Sarah don't talk anymore?" I want to hear it from him.

He lets out a sigh, and I fear that I upset him. "We had a falling out I guess you could call it, right after you moved. I don't know. She just got weird. She met Damon and started dressing like him and listening to all this goth and heavy metal music. Not that there's anything wrong with that. The guy just changed her drastically. I didn't like him, but she wouldn't listen to me. It's like she resents me because I made the basketball team and started dating Courtney. I know things at home aren't great for her. I tried to help her through it, but it was like she didn't want to be near me. Damon seems to be good for her though. She needs him. Did you ever keep in touch with her?"

"No. We wrote a few letters, then I stopped receiving them after a while. Kinda figured neither one of you wanted to keep in touch. But life gets in the way."

"I always thought about you. I just…got busy with basketball and school." He clears his throat. "Started dating Courtney."

I'm not sure why but hearing that hurts, almost like he gave up on me. I'm not sure what makes me think he ever thought of me that way. I need to go. Daddy will be wondering where I am. I shouldn't have come over. "Um, thanks for the snacks. I should go."

"Are you sure? We could watch the game or a movie or something."

"I'm sorry. I have to go." I get up from the couch and take a step toward the kitchen with my plate, but Ben takes it.

"I got it."

When we walk out to his car, someone drops off a young girl, and I realize it's his sister, Hayden.

"Alisa?" she says and gives me a hug. "It's so awesome to see you. Are you two friends again? Has my brother straightened up?"

"Hayden." Ben warns. "I gotta take her home."

She rolls her eyes. "Good to see you. Hopefully, I'll see you again." She looks at Ben when she says that then walks inside the house.

As we drive down the road, he blasts the AC. I wish the AC at home worked half as good as this one. I find his story about Sarah interesting, because that was the first thing I noticed about her since coming back, but she really hasn't changed. It's like they both portray a different persona, but they're still the same people deep down inside. I don't know if I have changed, but we're all so different now.

Ben's car crunches over the gravel. I should've told him to let me out by the mailbox, but I don't see Daddy's truck. I wonder where he's gone. I try not to think about him being at a bar or something. I miss having both of my parents at home with me. I hate how so much has changed, and I don't know how to stop it.

For the second time in a row, Ben's expensive car has gravel dust all over it, and I'm sure some rocks have dinged the body. He pulls onto the grass next to the house, and we get out of the car.

I don't want people seeing the small house I live in with its chipped paint tucked away next to barns and cows. The smell alone is unbearable and embarrassing. My house is far from Ben's. His is two stories and brick with a u-shaped driveway and a basketball goal.

I reach the door to the porch and turn to face him. "Thanks for the ride."

"Can I call you sometime?"

I freeze. I'm not sure if I should give him my number since Daddy won't let boys call me. Maybe I can call him when Daddy isn't here. That is, if our phone is still in service. "Um, I can only talk certain hours. I can call you."

He frowns. "Oh. Well, here's my number and my pager number." He takes my hand and scribbles numbers on it, causing my heart to dance. "I'm really glad you're back, Alisa. I hope to keep in touch more."

He does? "Thanks."

"Do you need a ride to school on Monday?"

"No. My dad will fix my car. If not, I'll take the bus."

He frowns. "I can take you."

Why is he being so nice? What does he plan on doing once we show up at school together? He needs to leave. If Daddy sees Ben here, I will be in so much trouble. "You should go."

"Okay." He draws out the word.

I don't mean to be rude. "I'll call you."

"Yeah?" His face lights up. "Sweet. I'll talk to you later."

I turn the knob to the porch door and step up. "I'll see you Monday." There's a flicker of disappointment or something in his eyes, but he gives a warm smile.

"Have a good night."

"You too." Watching him leave causes a heaviness to tug in my chest. I don't want him to go. I didn't want our time to end. I shouldn't feel this way. He has a girlfriend. Am I going to see him Monday only so he can blow me off?

ben

The Cure's "Pictures of You," plays as I drive home. Ironically. I never cared much for The Cure. Now, though, I'm fascinated. I pay more attention to the song. It's a sad song, of course it is. It's The Cure. But it really speaks to me, because the lyrics talk about a lost love. At least, to me.

Shaking my head, I rub my face. What am I doing? I shouldn't be around her, but she makes me feel good. I feel like I can be myself around her.

I dread walking through the front door of my house, especially when I see Dad's car in the driveway. I'm sure Mom's already told him about Alisa. I wait until the song is over, then get out of the car. The nights are getting cooler.

When I enter the house, I head straight for the stairs.

"Benjamin," Mom calls, and I halt. I know I'm in deep shit. She only calls me that when I'm in trouble.

"She's in a mood," Hayden mumbles as she passes me going upstairs.

"I thought you were staying at Janie's for dinner."

"I *was*." She groans and stomps up the stairs. Apparently, I hit a nerve.

"Benjamin," Mom yells.

I sigh and make my way to the kitchen, annoyed. "What?" I snap. I don't mean to, but she is so impatient.

"Don't snap at me. Help me get this casserole out of the oven."

I roll my eyes. She can take it out herself, but she wants to talk to me and has to have an excuse. I open the oven with more gusto than I mean to, waiting for her to say whatever is on her mind.

"Did you and Courtney break up?" she asks, but it's more like an accusation.

"No, why?"

"You brought a girl home today, and you were holding hands."

"Mom, it's Alisa." I put the casserole on the counter and close the inferno. "She started crying because of her mom. I was comforting her. She's a friend. Am I not allowed to have friends?"

"Of course, you can have friends. You don't need any distractions between Courtney, basketball, and school."

"What? She was one of my best friends. Why do you think she'd be a distraction?"

"I don't want you to lose your focus. You and Courtney just got back together. She might not like it. Have you even told her?"

I should bite my tongue. "What does that matter? I did nothing wrong. Unlike her."

"Benjamin, having a girl come over like that is inappropriate."

Inappropriate? Is she joking? "You'd know," I mumble. Really, really should bite my tongue.

"What did you say?"

"You heard me. You're cheating on Dad, aren't you?" I can't help myself. Everything is starting to boil over.

Her mouth drops open, and tears pool her eyes.

Damn. I never meant to make her cry.

"He told you?"

That brings me up short. I have only been guessing this whole time. Assuming, which you should never do. Damn my intuition. And Dad knows? The knots in my stomach tighten and I feel like I'm going to pass out. How long has he known? How long has this been going on? It's been a little edgy for several months around here.

"Whoa," Hayden says as she walks into the room. "Uh… should I leave?"

"Set the table," Mom demands without breaking her glare on me. The tears vanish, and any emotion disappears from her face. She's always too good at that.

I can't catch my breath. I swear I'm going to throw up. This cannot be true. No matter how many times I close my eyes and open them, the kitchen still moves in waves. I need to sit down or something. It's hot as hell in here.

"Ben," Dad says as he grips my shoulder, startling me. "What's wrong?"

"He probably overexerted himself today." Mom presses a cool rag to my face, and while it feels great, I'm so pissed off at her. She's cheating on my father, yet he stays married to her. Though I guess I can't judge Dad too much. I stayed with Courtney. Has he forgiven Mom? Is that what we're supposed to do? Forgive and forget? Shove it under the rug like nothing is wrong?

"Nonsense," Dad says. "The boy can handle anything, can't you?"

"Alex, give him a break."

When the walls stop spinning, and my vision comes back to me, I see both my parents staring at me with confused looks. I know what Dad's thinking. That I'm weak. He would never react this way. He'd take it like a man.

"Sorry. Guess I need to eat something." I quickly regain my composure, and act like nothing is wrong. Guess that runs in the family.

The game is on in every room of the house. It's the only time Dad allows the TV to be on during dinner. Tonight, dinner is quiet and tense. I can't stomach my mom's casserole, even though I can usually put away food like I've got a bottomless pit. But the affirmation that Mom cheated…. I can't sit with them anymore. I need to get out of here.

"May I please be excused?" I ask. My parents always raised us to be incredibly polite, and they made sure Hayden and I upheld that. Whenever they have parties, we're always the children who can be seen, but not heard.

"Finish eating," Mom says.

Dad clears his throat. "If he's done eating, he's done. Although, running on an empty stomach in the morning won't be good."

"It's supposed to rain," I say, and I hope he doesn't catch on since he knows I run no matter what. I'm tempted to get up and walk away, but I can't move.

"Why do you always argue with me?" Mom asks, but when I look up, she's glaring at Dad.

Great. Now I started a fight.

"You're excused, Ben."

With that, I bolt from the table and practically sprint up to my room. I slam my door and immediately regret it because I know in a few seconds both of them are gonna come up and start yelling. I need to get out of here. Go for a run. Something.

Alisa flashes in my mind.

Then my door opens. "Ben, what the hell is your problem?" Dad demands.

"Nothing," I snap.

"I'll talk to him," Mom says from behind Dad. She's the last person I want to talk to, but she slips into my room anyway, giving Dad a knowing look. He shakes his head and leaves. Mom closes the door. "Ben—"

"I really don't want to hear your excuse."

"You don't even know what happened."

"Does Dad know?" He has to know something. Otherwise they wouldn't be at each other's throats all the time. "Who is he?"

"It's none of your business. I suggest you stick with your own issues and let me handle mine."

What the hell? "Yeah, you sure are handling them just fine. You're cheating on Dad, and you don't even feel the least bit sorry, do you?"

She slaps me across the face, hard. It's not the first time she's done that to me. I let it slide. "You have no idea what you're talking about. And don't point fingers at me when you bring home another girl while you're dating Courtney."

"Jesus, Mom, it's not a big deal."

"You will not see that girl again. She cannot be around here anymore. You were friends when you were kids, but times change. You have a reputation, Ben."

Her words are like another slap to the face. I can't believe what she's saying. I can't decide if the wine is making her spout all this craziness or what. Why is she so adamant that I not see Alisa? Does she think I'm going to break up with Courtney for Alisa?

This whole fucking night went downhill in a hurry.

"Are you actually forbidding me to see Alisa? She's a friend, Mom. You know some of us can actually have friendships with the opposite sex and not get involved."

She glares at me, and her face turns red. "If you don't listen to me, I will tell your father."

Is she crazy? Why do I care? Why does she say that like it's a bad thing? "He doesn't know?"

"Ben, you are the city councilman's son. You know he won't allow you to see someone from the trailer park hanging out with you."

I let out a laugh. "Wow. Really, Mom? I forgot. Looks are everything to you. Is that why you two are still married? Having your cake and eating it, too?" I'm so angry that I don't care what I'm saying.

"If you continue this with that girl, you can kiss basketball goodbye." She lowers her voice.

"Why are you acting so strange? You can't force me to stop playing basketball."

"You need a parent's permission."

"Okay. Dad will always let me play."

"No. He won't. If he finds out you're seeing that girl, he will take it away."

I clench my teeth. "I'm not seeing her, Mom! She's a friend."

"That's what they all say." Her lip quivers and tears pool in her eyes. Today is not my day with girls and crying.

"What does it matter that we're friends?"

"I know her family, Ben. She will do nothing but drag you down with her. You've come so far at such a young age. You don't want to blow it all away over some girl like her." She leaves the room without another word.

I start pacing my room, itching to leave. Quickly changing into jogging clothes, I grab my Walkman and bolt from the house in a sprint.

What the fuck just happened? Why can't she say Alisa's name? Why is she suddenly 'that girl?' What is so wrong with being Alisa's friend? I don't care how she dresses. She's not trailer trash. And she won't drag me down. We're not even dating. Why is she freaking out?

But I know if Dad finds out I'm hanging out with someone who they think is trailer trash, I have no doubt he'd do something to Alisa. Even though they have their issues, they have always controlled Hayden and me as a team.

I can't believe my mom and girlfriend both cheated. No wonder they're so close. Is that why Mom convinced me so hard to forgive Courtney? This is insane.

I can't believe she's making me choose. It's the craziest thing, it's laughable.

Then again, how would they ever know I hung out with her? Who am I kidding? Shit in that school spreads like wildfire so it will inevitably get back to them. I know I haven't seen Alisa in a long time, and I've missed her friendship, but is it worth all of this? Losing basketball? Or having Dad do something to her family? Should I keep ignoring her? *Fuck*. I don't know what to do.

alisa

Roosters wake me up early Sunday. I hate those roosters. I lay in bed reading until I hear Daddy shuffle about. Taking a deep breath, I get out of bed and change. I don't know what Daddy will say to me when he realizes he'll have to take me to work.

When I walk out of my room, he's rocking slightly in his recliner and watching some 70s TV show.

"Good morning," I say.

"Morning. Where's your car?"

I clear my throat. "It wouldn't start yesterday."

"Damn. Sounds like the starter. How did you get home?"

"A coworker."

"What time do you go in today?"

"Three."

"I'll work on your car. I'll get it fixed."

"Thank you."

We sit for a little while longer, and when he gets dressed, we go into town for a parts. People wave and smile when they see him. He talks to a few of them. We get the parts, and I'm impressed and ecstatic that he doesn't buy any beer. Maybe he's going to stop drinking. The thought makes me happy.

Daddy and I spend the afternoon working on my car. It reminds me of when I was a kid and I'd help him. Though, like when I was a kid, I don't do much, except hand him tools. Days like today make me guilty that I have a secret stash of money from Daddy.

But I still keep it to myself.

Work is busy for a couple of hours, but it's slow the rest of the night. Sunday nights are always dead. Daddy is out again when I get home. I end up making a mushroom soup beef casserole for dinner. It was something Mom concocted. Ground beef, powder macaroni and cheese, and cream of mushroom soup. I'm not sure if she got it from somewhere, but it's pretty tasty.

After I eat, I work on some homework. Knowing I have Ben's number weighs heavily on me. I want to talk to him. Spending the afternoon with him made me remember how much I enjoy being around him. I forgot how comfortable and easygoing he is. He calms me just by talking.

I stare at the phone. My pulse quickens each second. Will he care if I call? Is he busy? Maybe he's doing his homework. He did ask me to call him. Chewing on my lip, I reach for the phone. My hand shakes as I slowly dial a number. I don't know which one his pager is, which I'd prefer to call. My throat tightens. Heat fills my cheeks. I want to be brave, but I'm not.

"Hello?" Ben's mom answers.

I almost choke on my spit. "Hi, Mrs. Lamar. It's Alisa. Can I please talk to Ben?"

"Alisa, I'm sorry, but you can't talk to him. He has a girlfriend. And I don't think it's appropriate for young ladies to be calling young men."

"I-I'm sorry." Tears brim my eyes and I hang up. I can't breathe, and I can't stop the tears. Why did I think I was good enough to call Ben? Or good enough to be his friend? He has a girlfriend. Maybe this afternoon was all just a joke. I'm just a joke to Ben. Sarah warned me. She told me to be careful, and I didn't listen. I imagine his mom telling him I called and him laughing. All of them laughing at the loser that I am.

My eyes catch the glint of light on my scissors. I reach for them and open them. Lifting my sleeve, I close my eyes. I miss Mom so much. The woman who taught me to be brave, who taught me how to cook, who was always there for me smiling and congratulating me when I made good grades. The woman who could ease a tummy ache with a simple kiss. She's not here to ease this pain I feel every day, and I don't know what to do.

A few seconds later, the phone rings. I answer, and it's Sarah.

"Is it safe to talk?" she asks.

"Yeah. He's out."

"Good. Want me to pick you up? I need to get out of here."

"Okay."

I hang up wondering why she hasn't called Damon instead of me. It doesn't take long for Sarah to pick me up in her white Ford Probe. Soon, we're speeding through the night and end up at a park nearby.

She lights a cigarette, and I know something is wrong.

"Where's Damon?"

"Working."

"Are you okay?"

She lets out a cloud of smoke. "My fucking mom is using again. She told me she stopped." Sarah sits on a swing, and I take the one beside her. She shakes her head gives a small laugh. "I found pills. We got into a fight after I dropped them down the toilet."

"I'm sorry."

"She was passed out by the time I left. Pretty sure tomorrow will be interesting."

"I'm sorry. How long do you think it's been going on?"

"Who knows? She's good at hiding." She lets out a groan. "I really try to help her. I try to be a dutiful daughter, to support her, but it's like she can't survive without a man. Which is bullshit. She's a grown woman. And even though I've stuck by her side, it's like it's not good enough because Dad and Tonya left." She tosses out the butt of the cigarette and lights another one.

"Has she tried rehab? When my dad went, it changed him. But then he relapsed," I mumble.

"Rehab won't do shit for her." She pauses. "Let's run away. Leave all this shit behind. We're freaking kids, Alisa. We shouldn't be dealing with this."

"I have a plan. Before my mom died, she gave me money. She told me to use it for culinary school, but I have to finish school. That's what I'm going to do."

Sarah smiles. "I love it. You should do it. Where do you wanna go?"

"I don't know. I can't leave my dad yet. He needs me. And I know it's hard, but your mom needs you, too."

She lets out a breath and nods. "I know. Damon and I are already planning on leaving when I'm eighteen. We'll take Mom away from all this crap, too. You should come with us. I hear they have good culinary schools in Atlanta."

I glance at her. Is she serious? The idea sounds great.

"Anyway, how was your date with Zach?" She nudges me.

I smile. "I blew it. It was dumb. Ben and Courtney showed up and I overheard him say I was nothing to him. I couldn't relax. Zach is nice."

"But you're still hung up on Ben."

"I didn't say that."

"You don't have to."

"I did go to Ben's yesterday."

She gasps. "What? Really? Why?"

"He wanted to catch up, but I don't think his mom wants me around."

"She probably looked at you and judged you."

"She said I wasn't allowed to talk to him."

"She said that? Doesn't she remember who you are?"

"Doesn't matter."

"It surprises me that he's talking to you."

"Why? Because I'm so beneath him?"

"What? No! Don't ever think you are beneath him. He keeps to his clique, and that's it. Like he's hiding behind them. We aren't part of his clique and never will be. I wonder if he's got something up his sleeve. I mean, he knows you went out with Zach."

"We didn't talk about him, though. I don't know, Ben seemed like himself. Like the guy you and I remember."

Sarah cocks an eyebrow. "Good to know he's still in there. I'm glad y'all got to catch up. How are things with you?"

I shrug. "Good. I need to work more."

"Alisa, you work enough as it is. You're almost working full time for god sake. How do you even get your homework done?"

I don't, which is why I'm failing.

Sarah puts her arm around me and pulls me to her. She kisses the top of my head. "I'm so glad you're back."

"Me, too."

ben

Thunder crashes waking me. Rain angrily gushes out of the sky, pounding onto the house. So much is falling the sound blurs into one long whirring noise. My room is so dark. All I want to do is roll over and go back to sleep. I was hoping they'd close the school since there's a hurricane on its way, but no such luck. The storm outside matches the crazy, chaotic storm inside my head.

I never heard from Alisa. I don't know why Mom freaked out over the whole thing. All day yesterday, everyone practically stayed to themselves. When I was younger, I complained about having family time. We'd play board games, watch movies, whatever. It's funny when you don't have those things is when you want them the most.

I wonder if Alisa needs a ride to school and toy with the idea of driving out to her house to see. I wish I could call and ask her, but I don't have her number. How can I take Alisa to school without anyone seeing? I don't want to keep her a secret, but I can't let my parents find out. Or Courtney.

Fuck it. I don't care.

By the time I run out to my car, I'm soaked. Guess the shower I took was moot. I drive like a damn grandma toward Alisa's house during the torrential downpour, yet my tires still slip a couple of times. I don't think it can rain any harder.

When I pull up to her house, I see an old blue truck on the side of the house, probably her dad's. I brave the rain once more and race to her porch. I knock on the door, but no one answers. I call her name, but again nothing. Maybe she got her car working and left already. I hope she didn't take the bus. Is she sick? For a moment, I have this need to want to make her feel better. I am seriously messed up.

I wait a few more minutes, then my pager goes off. It's Courtney. I gotta go.

When I get to school, Courtney meets me at my locker with a strange look on her face. It's like she's pissed and amused. She looks completely hungover, too.

"I paged you."

"I was driving."

"Whatever." She crosses her arms in front of her chest.

"What's the matter?"

"Oh nothing. I just heard that you had some girl at your house Saturday."

I freeze. How the hell did she find out?

"What are you talking about?" Playing innocent will only get me so far.

"Don't play dumb with me. Who's the skank at your house? Kim said she saw some girl."

Shit. Kim must have been the one who dropped off Hayden from Janie's house Saturday.

"She's no one. She needed a tutor, so I offered to help."

"At your house?"

"She doesn't want anyone knowing she needs help."

"I can't believe you. You realize that's just an excuse to sleep with you."

"What?"

"Apparently, she's making quite a reputation for herself. She slept with Zach Friday night, so I'm guessing that's why she went to your house. Making her rounds."

What the hell? "Who told you she slept with Zach?"

"*Everyone's* talking about it."

Dammit. A sickening feeling churns in my stomach. "She didn't sleep with Zach."

"How do you know? Wait, did Zach deny it? Omigod she must have been that bad!" She covers her mouth.

I can't tell Courtney that I know for a fact the rumor is a lie. She can't know I took Alisa home Friday night. I know Zach didn't start the rumors. Some asshole thought it would be funny, but Alisa hasn't done anything to deserve that.

"What are you tutoring her in?"

"Math. Mom was there the whole time." Really wish I hadn't told her that.

Courtney presses her lips into a straight line, contemplating my story. I'm pretty good at hiding my feelings. I also know how to lie to her, which didn't start until after we started having issues. Guess I learned all that from Mom.

"Why couldn't she call Zach?"

"Zach was busy."

Courtney scoffs. "Yeah right. He's probably blowing her off after Friday. I hope he didn't catch anything from her. Someone said she hooked up with Adam Snyder in the bathroom a couple of weeks ago. *Ugh.* Why is Zach even into her? She's not even that pretty. She better not steal you away from me." She says this to be cute, but it annoys me.

"Trust me. There's nothing I want from her."

Courtney manages a smile. "Come on. Walk me to class." She hooks her arm with mine, and when we turn the corner, my stomach sinks. Alisa is braced against the wall; completely soaking wet, looking pale, and almost into panic mode. I want to comfort her. The rumors aren't true, and once I find out who started that bullshit, will wish they hadn't been born.

Alisa pushes off the wall, clumsily bumping into Courtney. I curse internally.

"Watch it, freak." Courtney pushes her, causing her books to fall.

I can't let this continue. "Courtney," I warn, and I know my next move is going to get me in heaps of trouble. Bending down, I pick up one of Alisa's books, and hand it to her without looking at her. I can't. I can't let Courtney see what I feel when I look into Alisa's eyes.

I take Courtney's hand and continue walking down the hall.

"What? She did that on purpose and got my shirt wet. Ugh."

Her name is Alisa. I wish people would stop saying 'that girl.' "I'm sure you'll live."

She playfully hits my shoulder, and as we continue to class, my stomach ties into knots. I'm not sure how much longer I can let Courtney, or my parents dictate who I am or who they want me to be. I'm not even sure why I let them. I can't keep doing this. I have to finally stand up for myself.

alisa

Gripping my books to my chest, my throat closes. I'm drenched from the rain, and it's cold inside. Everyone thinks I'm a slut. They all think I slept with Zach and some guy named Adam. Ben ignores me. Why does he keep doing this to me? I'm a joke to him. He wouldn't even look at me, like he was embarrassed to be around me. I can't take this anymore. I can't take the stares. The whispers.

No one wants me.

I need my scissors. Something. This pain hurts.

I want to get out of here, but I can't go home.

"Why don't you move along, hobags?" I hear Sarah behind me. When I look up, she's glaring at two girls who slowly pass by me. They walk away. "Are you all right?"

"I'm fine."

Sarah cocks an eyebrow. "Come on." She tugs me along outside, staying close to the covered ledges. We round a corner and meet up with Damon.

He inhales from his cigarette. "Hey. You okay?"

"They're just rumors. People like to come up with dumb shit. I'm sorry."

"I'll beat them up. Who started them? Was it Zach?"

I shake my head. Violence is the last thing I want. "It's okay."

"Some things haven't changed," Sarah says. "Those stupid bitches still laugh at us."

"They always will." Damon finishes his cigarette and tosses it on the ground. "If anyone fucks with you, I got your back. We'll find out who did this."

I'm not sure what to say or how to react. He doesn't know me. He shouldn't be so nice. I'm not worth it. I always mess up things.

"Thanks," I say. "I'm fine."

"I like your shirt," he says. I look down to see the Nirvana words sprawled across the top.

"Thanks." Mom gave it to me the week Kurt Cobain died. It was such a sad tragedy. She knew I liked them a lot.

The bell rings our five-minute warning. The three of us walk back to the building and my footsteps are heavy with fear. I know I'm weak. I don't belong. I'm undeserving. Maybe I can hide all day.

"I'll see you guys later," I say once we pass a bathroom.

"Okay." Sarah walks hand-in-hand with Damon.

I want to know what it's like to hold hands with a guy. Or to kiss one. Like that will ever happen though. I slip inside an empty stall and close the door.

My stomach cramps. It's cold in the bathroom, like everywhere else in this world. It's like the second Mom died, I've never been warm.

Clenching my teeth, I hold my stomach. I lift my sleeve to see my scars. They're starting to fade. I need to fix them. I need to go to my safe haven. The walls are closing in on me. I can't breathe. It's hot, and I can't slow my heart rate. I hate this feeling. I hate it when people laugh at me. Why couldn't Mom take me with her?

ben

I am the worst person on the planet. I just left Alisa in the middle of the hallway. All morning I've felt like the dick of the year. She looked so sad.

I should've stayed. Why do I care so much what people think? Probably because my father has ingrained that in me since I can remember. Make sure you're with the right people. Make sure you're always at your best. Someone could be watching at any given moment, and that moment could dictate your life.

Dad only cares about the scouts and what people around town think. Which is why on the outside, my parents are the perfect couple, but inside they're a volcano erupting.

The first two classes end, and I have no idea what we talked about. I don't care. I'm still thinking about Alisa and the shitty way I treated her. She always had this calm demeanor, even with all the crap she dealt with at home. Her parents always argued. I wonder what it's like now with just her and her dad. Quiet probably. I know she's struggling with the loss of her mom. I would be too.

Courtney waits outside the classroom as usual, and for once, I want to walk to the lunchroom alone. Or find Alisa and apologize. I can't believe Mom gave me an ultimatum. Doesn't she know I can air her dirty laundry? But I never will. I can't do that to Hayden. It would destroy her.

"What's wrong?" Courtney takes my hand.

"Nothing."

She stops in the middle of the hallway, making everyone move around us. "I know when something's wrong."

"It's just stuff at home."

She frowns. "Like what?"

I don't respond.

"Ben, what is it?" She knows I hate it when she presses. I don't like to talk about this stuff. Especially with her because she has an uncanny way of not paying attention to me. I tried talking to her the other night about it, and she ignored me. Why does she suddenly care now? Because she knows I helped Alisa?

"Nothing. Just let it go."

"Why don't you ever talk to me?"

"I do. I just don't feel like it right now."

"You never do."

I let out a sigh. "I don't feel like talking about this stuff in the middle of the hallway, okay? I'll tell you about it later." I won't, but it's enough to placate her.

She looks up at me with those piercing blue eyes. They used to bring me to my knees. But something lately has a hold over me, and I'm not falling for Courtney anymore.

She reaches up and caresses my cheek. "You know you can talk to me anytime. I'm always here for you."

Except, you're not. "I know." I kiss the top of her head. I look up and down the hall are Alisa, Sarah, and Damon talking. I need to apologize to Alisa, but now is not the time. Maybe I can catch her after lunch or after school. My heart picks up its pace, and I hope like hell Courtney doesn't notice.

I end the embrace so she can get away from my chest, and we make our way toward the cafeteria. For a moment, Alisa meets my eyes. I wish I could send some sort of message to her without saying anything. I want to take the sadness out of her eyes.

"Why don't you stop staring at my boyfriend like he's a piece of meat? Psycho." Courtney says to Alisa, and I want to die. "Not like he'd ever be interested in you." She laughs, tugging me into the lunchroom like I'm on a damn leash.

I can't do it. "Courtney." I jerk my hand away. "What the hell was that?"

She lifts an eyebrow and crosses her arms. "What?"

"You don't have to be so mean."

"Since when do you care?"

She's right. I haven't cared whenever she was mean to someone. Truth is, I never paid attention because I never wanted to get in the middle.

Damn. I've been such a selfish prick. "She's a new kid, Courtney. You don't have to pick on her."

"I knew there was something between you two."

"She's just a friend."

"Oh, she's a friend now?"

"I can't deal with this. I can't deal with you anymore."

"What's that supposed to mean? Why are you being a dick to me and not that trailer trash out there?"

I clench my teeth. "You don't know what you're talking about. She isn't trailer trash."

"You're kidding, right? You see the way she dresses. She's already slept with several people. Why are you acting like this?"

"Acting like what? Maybe I'm tired of you being a bitch to people."

Shit.

Her jaw unhinges. "You are such a jerk, Ben. I can't believe you are defending *her*. I'm your girlfriend. Whatever." She throws her hands up in the air and walks away. Several people are looking at me. It's not the first time they've seen Courtney and me publicly fight. I can't handle her anymore. I'm done. I have to find Alisa. I bolt out of the lunchroom and run smack into Damon, Sarah's tattooed boyfriend. He grabs my shirt and slams me against the wall. I don't wanna fight the guy, but I will if I have to.

"You need to get off me," I warn him. I stare at him, challenging him. The only reason I don't kick this guy's ass is because he's Sarah and Alisa's friend.

He scoffs and pushes me against the wall again. "Stop messing with Alisa. I know you and your friends started those rumors."

Clenching my teeth, I shove him hard. He finally releases his grip, but his dark eyes glare into mine.

"Damon," Sarah whispers and takes his hand. "Damon, let it go."

"I will when he leaves her alone."

"I didn't mean to hurt her and I didn't start the rumors."

"Whatever, Ben," Sarah says. It's the first time she's spoken to me in years. Her tone is just as bitter as I expected. "She's been through enough, and she doesn't need you or your girlfriend pushing her around. Why don't you do us all a favor and leave us alone."

"Where is she?"

Sarah gets right in my face and Damon keeps a watchful eye on her. "Leave. Her. Alone. You're a prick. Had I known you were only going to fuck with her, I would've told her to stay away from you."

"I didn't mean to hurt her."

"You keep saying that, but you do it anyway. Why do you treat her like shit when people can see? Yet, you're so nice to her when no one else is around. Just admit it. You don't want to be seen with her because of your status. If you don't leave her alone, Damon isn't the only person you need to be afraid of."

She takes Damon into the lunchroom. I release a breath.

I can't be getting into fights if I want to play basketball, but I won't hold back if that guy threatens me again. Sarah's right about everything. That's not who I want to be.

alisa

Sitting in the bathroom stall, I clutch the scissors that I stole from my teacher tightly in my hand. I hate this place. I hate that I can't talk to Mom anymore. I can't even visit her grave. I hate that everyone laughs at me. I hate how Ben's girlfriend called me a psycho, and he stood by like nothing happened. I hate that the first date I ever went on, the guy tells everyone we slept together.

Sarah wanted me to sit with her and Damon at lunch, but I told them I can't. It's the truth. I don't want more people laughing at me.

I need to feel something. I need to feel that high. My heart races with anticipation.

I raise my sleeve, and once I place the blade to my flesh, I'm far away again. The rush overcomes me, and I love it.

It only takes a few seconds for the bleeding to stop. Once I clean off the scissors, I shove them in my backpack and leave the bathroom.

The halls are empty, and I hope I don't get caught. The bell should be ringing soon. I meander down the hall and turn a corner. I come to a halt when I see Zach walking toward me. I cross my arms and keep my head down.

"Alisa," he says. "I'm so sorry about all this crap. I swear I never said a word. I don't even know who or what started it."

I swallow.

"Please believe me. I've told everyone they aren't true."

"It's okay."

"For what it's worth, I had a good time Friday. I like you, and I'd like to take you out again if you're up for it."

"You don't want to be with me."

"What?"

"Alisa!" I hear Ben call, and his voice draws me in. I hate that it does.

My pulse quickens, and nausea starts roiling inside my stomach. I pull my sleeves over my hands and dig my fingers into my sides. I can't look him in the eye. I don't want to talk to him.

"Are you okay?" He rushes up to Zach and me. "I'm so sorry. About how I treated you this morning. Courtney. The rumors."

I nod. "Okay." I can feel his eyes on me, judging me like everyone else does. I refuse to look up.

"She deserves better than this, man," Zach says. "I'll talk to you later, Alisa." He walks away.

Ben clears his throat and shifts his backpack. "Do you forgive me?"

I look up, meeting his apologetic eyes. I have always loved his hazel color. I remember thinking to myself that I could stare into them forever. But that was before. "I have to go."

"Can I walk you to class?"

"Why? So you and your She Devil can make fun of me?" I didn't mean to call her that aloud, but it's too late.

He frowns. Before he can say anything, the bell rings, echoing in the hallway. It makes me jump, and I walk away from Ben. Can't he leave me alone? Or does he have to continue to taunt me to make himself feel better?

alisa

It's a quiet evening. One that I need. I hung out with Sarah and Damon for a little bit after school instead of going to work. Daddy won't be happy when he sees my paycheck is short. I'll just take some from my savings.

I watch little bubbles spring to the surface as the water begins to boil. It calms me. I shouldn't be upset over Ben, but I am. I have to get over him. Once the water comes to a roiling boil, I put the powdered potatoes in and mix. Add a little mayonnaise, salt, pepper. I miss making things from scratch, and I'm tired of cooking from a box or a can. I don't even know if I have the skills to make it in culinary school. After eating a little, I go to my room.

I still have a picture of Ben and me when we were younger, both of us are smiling, a rare thing for me lately. Staring at it reminds me of The Cure's "Pictures of You."

I put the picture in one of my drawers. Pretty sure Ben will forget that I exist after today. And I'm okay with that.

I wake to the sound of a car door shutting. Then another. I hear murmured voices and one of them is a woman giggling. I pull the curtain back on my lone window and see Daddy and some woman with their hands all over each other. My heart pounds, and the potatoes I ate threaten to find a way out. I sit up in bed, waiting. Did Daddy bring a woman home? How can he do that? What about Mom? Cold sweat breaks out across my skin as I hear them come inside. The walls are so thin, and I hear every sound. I hear them kiss. Moan. Breathe. Something hits the wall hard, knocking a picture frame to the floor.

Unable to breathe, I grab my chest. The ache stabs me. Am I having a heart attack?

I hear Daddy and this woman go into his room, and he slams the door. I jump and cover my ears from the sounds. I can't believe he brought someone home. Does that mean he's over Mom? Does that mean he doesn't love her anymore? I can't help the tears that fall and try my best to keep silent.

Putting the pillow over my head, I curl up into a ball. I wish I had headphones. Or something. Something to end the pain of betrayal.

When the sun comes up, I remove the pillow. It's not even time for me to get up, but I want to get out of the house without anyone hearing me. I dress as quickly as I can and get my books. Walking out into the living room, my heart slams into my chest when I come face to face with a woman a little taller than me, leaning against the archway of the living room and kitchen, eating the potatoes I made, in nothing more than my father's t-shirt. The one he got when he, Mom, and I went to Panama City Beach. It was the only family vacation we ever had.

Something inside me rages. This stranger is eating our food and wearing my father's shirt. Who does she think she is?

"Are you just gonna stare? Who the hell are you?" She speaks with a thick Southern accent. Her dirty blond hair is short and misshapen. Heavy bags cling to her brown eyes. Her skin looks orange from all the fake tanning. Makeup smears at the corners of her eyes. I can't tell how old she is, but she doesn't appear to be as old as Daddy.

"That is not your food," I say through clenched teeth. I never get angry, but this woman eating what I made for my father angers me. The fact that she's still here angers me.

She furrows her eyebrows. "I was hungry."

Rage boils in my veins as she continues to eat. How can she make herself at home like she owns the place? "Stop eating!" I knock the bowl out of her hand, spilling the small remains of the potatoes on the floor.

Gasping, I stare at my hands. What have I done?

"What the fuck is all this noise?" Daddy screams as he comes out of the bedroom.

I freeze, my stomach clenching into a tight knot as the nausea returns. "I'm sorry. I didn't mean to wake you."

"She just came up to me and threw my bowl to the floor," the woman says.

My throat tightens. I didn't want her eating our food. But I did something wrong.

Daddy roughly grabs my shoulder. His blue eyes glare into mine. "What the fuck is wrong with you? She's a guest. You need to learn some manners." He slaps me across the face.

The woman gasps.

He pushes me, and I lose my footing, falling against the coffee table. The corner stabs me in my side and my finger jams. I stay down.

"Jack," she says.

"Shut up," he says. "I'm going back to bed, and I better not hear another goddamn peep outta either one of you."

The woman bursts into tears. I watch as Daddy lowers his shoulders and walks over to her, gathering her into his arms. "I'm sorry, baby." He kisses her forehead and her cheek. "I'm so sorry. I'm just grumpy when I wake up. It won't happen again. Come on, Diane. Come to bed with me."

She nods, and he kisses her. On their way to his room, Daddy looks down at me.

"Get your ass to school. And you'd better have dinner for Diane tonight as well."

When he shuts the door, I seize my backpack and hurry out the door. My hand trembles so much that I can't put the key in the ignition. Wiping my tears, I take a deep breath.

Who is that woman? I hated seeing Daddy comfort her. It should be Mom. Not this random lady.

I swallow hard, and turn the ignition, but nothing happens. The interior lights come on, but the engine doesn't turn. I try again. Nothing.

I throw the keys against the dash and punch the steering wheel.

"Fuck!" I look toward the house, fearing Daddy heard me. I clamber out of the car and run to the end of the driveway. My side and finger throb. Tears burn my eyes, but I refuse to cry. Nausea claws at my insides in the early morning heat. I can't hold it back. I throw up my dinner from last night.

ben

It's hot as hell outside and it's only six thirty in the morning. That's Alabama heat for you. I'm sweating like crazy, and I'm almost out of water. I know I shouldn't push it. Guys my age have died out in this heat. I slow my run to a jog and off in the distance, I see a girl wearing a backpack. Is she going to school this early? The buses don't start running until seven.

As I get closer, I realize it's Alisa. What the hell is she doing out walking this early? And how can she possibly be wearing long sleeves? It's like ninety degrees.

"Alisa?" I call out. When she turns around, she flinches and holds herself. "Hey," I say when I approach her. I'm panting. "Are you okay?"

She bites her lip. I can tell she's been crying by her red, puffy eyes and tear-stained cheeks. I itch to wrap her up in my arms and comfort her.

"What's wrong?"

She turns back around and starts walking again.

I grab her elbow, and she gasps, immediately jerking away from me. I hold up my hands. "Sorry. I just…. You can talk to me. I know I fucked up, but I'm here for you."

"Ben." She tucks her hair behind her ear, and I notice her cheek is bright red. "We can't be friends. You have your own life, and I have mine. Just stay away."

Her words cause an ache. "Alisa." This can't be it. "Please. I miss your friendship."

She looks up with a confused expression. "We haven't been friends in a long time, and I have no desire to be your secret friend. You have Courtney. I have to get to school."

"Alisa."

"What?" She turns back around to face me. "Why did you leave Sarah behind? Why are you so hot and cold with me? Why are you so cruel?"

I have no answers for her, and I hate it. "I don't know, Alisa. I never meant to hurt either of you. I just… it's been hard." I silently curse. Wrong answer.

"What do you want from me?"

"Alisa, I—"

"Ben, I get it. You're the popular guy. You have a girlfriend. You're a basketball star. You don't have to keep messing with me to drill it in my head that I'm no good for you and that you'd never be caught dead with me."

"That's not it at all."

"Why won't you and your little girlfriend leave me alone? We are two different people now. A lifetime ago we were friends. But that's over. I've moved on. You should try it, too."

Her bitter words sting. There's nothing I can say to make things right. "I am sorry, for what it's worth."

"Everyone's always sorry."

The bus arrives, and she gets on. It drives away, black exhaust shooting out of the back.

I run the rest of the way home when I should've been jogging. But I'm angry at myself, the situation. Basketball starts soon and that will help keep my mind off all this crap. When I reach the driveway, Dad greets me as he's about to hop in his BMW.

"Running late," he says, checking his watch. "Are you going to practice basketball twice as long this afternoon?"

"Yes," I snap.

"Hey! No need for the attitude, son." He gets in his car and drives off.

Hayden's inside the house still in her pajamas. Her eyes are red and puffy. Her hair is pulled back in a messy bun like she just woke up.

"You okay?"

"No."

"Need anything?"

Tears well in her eyes.

"What is it?" I hug her and she lets me for a little bit then pushes me away.

"Why isn't Mom here? Why can't she help me through this?"

"Through what?"

"Ugh. I'm *so* not telling you."

Oh. "Sorry."

"Are Mom and Dad getting a divorce?" Hayden looks at me with pleading eyes. Hoping I'll tell her that everything is going to be fine. That we'll be a family again one day. But I can't.

"I don't know."

alisa

After school, Sarah gives me a ride home so I can change into my work uniform. When I walk inside, the sound of the TV alarms me, and I stop once I see Diane sitting in Daddy's recliner. Daddy let her stay here?

Once she sees me, she scrambles out of the recliner. "Alisa, hi." She smiles, but it feels off.

"Hi." I should apologize for this morning, but the words don't come out.

"Your daddy told me about you, but I don't think he told you about me. I don't blame you at all for this morning. If I had seen some strange lady in my house, I would've reacted the same."

I nod, unsure of what to say to her.

"Listen, I really want us to be friends. I know it must be weird that your daddy is dating a woman much younger than him, but we really care about each other."

"Okay." I glance at the clock. I have twenty minutes to get to work.

"I know it's hard without a mama. I lost mine five years ago right after my twentieth birthday."

I don't know what to say or how to feel. Is this woman the reason for Daddy not buying beer the other day? Can she help Daddy recover? Can she really make things better?

"I know you have to get to work, and I'll be here when you get home. I'll have dinner ready, and we can talk more. Does that sound good?"

I hesitate. I'm supposed to be the one cooking. "Um."

"If you're worried about your daddy getting upset that you didn't cook, don't worry about that. Let me handle him." She smiles.

I don't know why she's being nice to me, especially after I treated her like I did this morning. "I'm sorry about this morning."

"No, it's okay. Really. Better get to work."

"Yeah."

I change, thinking about the weird exchange between us.

"Have a good night," she says as I walk out the door. I don't say anything, but maybe I should.

When I get back in Sarah's car, she lifts an eyebrow. "You're going to be so late. What were you doing?"

"Diane stayed. She-she's going to cook dinner tonight."

She puts the car in reverse, and once on the road, she speeds down the driveway.

"She's twenty-five."

Sarah's jaw drops. "What? Your dad is dating someone half his age?"

"She…seems nice though."

"Well. Maybe this is good for him."

Maybe. But I don't like the idea of anyone replacing Mom. Tears burn at the back of my eyes, but I push them away. Maybe it's time for me to move on, too. I'm not sure how healthy it is to still want my mom.

Sarah drives me to work and picks me up. I give her gas money, but she refuses to take it. Tells me to use it for my secret stash. When I get home, Diane was true to her word. She cooked dinner.

Though, I'm guessing it was her first time to ever cook, because the hamburger steaks are a little undercooked. The instant mashed potatoes aren't mixed well. I put the steaks back on the stove and she watches me. I notice she only cooked two steaks as well.

"I am so embarrassed. I need to learn how to cook if I'm going to be a good wife."

"It's easy."

"You make it look easy. Oh, Alisa, you're a lifesaver." Before I can react, she's got her arms around me, and I freeze. "Jack will be so proud of me."

"Yeah."

My stomach growls.

"Oh goodness, child. Are you hungry? Didn't you have dinner at work?"

I only get a fifteen-minute break, and I don't eat a meal. "No."

"I only cooked for Jack and me. I'm so sorry. Do you have a friend you can call? Maybe you two can go out to eat."

"Um. I have homework."

"Oh. Of course. I just…well, when Jack gets here, I didn't want you to feel awkward."

Oh god. "I'll be fine."

"You're such a good daughter. Better than me. My dad is so strict. I love that Jack is okay with me staying here."

How long is she staying? This whole situation keeps getting stranger.

"We're going to be a happy family. I promise. Go get your homework done. I'll clean up here."

"Okay. Um..."

"It's okay. I'll do it." She smiles.

I'm able to complete my homework, and I keep the pillow over my head. I still don't sleep. Maybe Sarah has headphones I can borrow.

Diane is true to her word. Each night I get home from work, she's got dinner prepared. I help her a little with things, and she even cooks something for me. I miss cooking, but it gives me a chance to focus on homework. Diane and I get along. I like her. Even Daddy isn't as angry every night. Can Diane fix us? Can she really make Daddy better? Things are finally looking up.

ben

It's a beautiful October day. The sky is a blue with zero clouds. There's a cool breeze in the air. The fall colors on the trees are probably the richest they've been in years. Yet, my world is dark and gloomy like a Cure song. I wanted to break up with Courtney, but I didn't. The thought of being alone scares me. Plus, we've been good. I stopped talking to Alisa for good. Nothing good will come of it. Basketball is the only thing I have going for me.

Zach's seventeenth birthday party is tonight, and I definitely need to let loose. Things at home aren't any better. Mom still travels a lot and works late. I just go along with everything, not caring about anything anymore. I'm like a robot. School. Basketball. Courtney. Do my best to ignore things at home. Do my best to ignore Alisa, but every time I see her at school, it takes everything I have not to talk to her. She's withdrawn more, and I hate the heavy sadness in her eyes. It kills me. I would do anything to see her smile, but she wants nothing to do with me, and I don't deserve her.

Music pounds throughout Zach's house, rattling the windows by the time Courtney and I show up. Thankfully, we haven't fought today, but it's still early in the evening. Zach's parents went away for the weekend, but we all know they did it on purpose. As soon as we walk in the door, Zach brings us solo cups with beer. I hope it makes me forget everything. If only for the night.

I get chatty when I drink, and I feel alive. It's been a while since I've felt this good. We hang out by Zach's pool, and some of the girls strip down to their underwear and jump in. They try to lure most of the guys in with them, except me. Because they know Courtney has tight reins on me.

By the time I finish my fourth beer, Courtney stumbles toward me and laughs. Her eyes gaze into mine and she wraps her arms around my neck. "I love you so much, Ben."

"I love you, too."

"Let's go upstairs," she whispers.

It's been so long since we've done anything, and the alcohol warms me and makes me feel good. Knowing I have zero chance with Alisa, I let Courtney lead me upstairs to an empty bedroom. I don't care anymore. I fucked up and I deserve what's coming to me.

Courtney kisses me, and it feels wrong, but I don't care. This is who I'm supposed to be with. I'm with the one who's supposed to make me happy. The one who loves me, who makes me feel good.

But it's all a lie.

The world doesn't let you have what you want. It holds you back in the cruelest way.

The next morning greets me with a throbbing headache, a sickening feeling in my stomach, and a bad taste in my mouth. Rolling over, anxiety washes over me when I see Courtney sound asleep next to me, naked. We had sex, and my dumb ass didn't use protection.

Fuck.

I rub my face trying to wake up more and get dressed.

I wake her up and she sits up, moaning.

"We didn't use a condom."

Courtney groans. "Good morning to you, too. I have my pills." She slurs through her words, half-asleep.

We're quiet on the way to her house, and I feel sick. She doesn't even kiss me before she stumbles out of the car. I should help her, but I know if I move, I'll throw up.

When I get home, I go straight to bed, hoping like hell Courtney isn't pregnant and that I didn't just ruin my life more than I already have.

"Courtney, I'm just asking if you feel any different," I say to her over the phone days later.

She laughs. "Jesus, Ben. Why are you freaking out? You can't get me pregnant. I'm on the pill."

I breathe a sigh of relief. It's been bothering me ever since the party. I can't have a kid right now, and deep down, I don't want one with Courtney.

"Is this why you won't have sex with me? It's been several days. You're my boyfriend. You're supposed to show me how much you love me."

I let out a groan. "I told you I haven't felt like it. I'm stressed out."

"Oh, is basketball stressing you out? Really? Throwing a ball into a basket stresses you out? Gah, what a baby."

I'm used to her belittling, but it's gotten worse lately. She never understands the pressure I'm under. Which is strange because I know she deals with the same from her parents. She doesn't get how much Dad hounds me about it. She doesn't see the intensity that lives in this house either. Yet we all carry on like nothing is wrong. We act like everything is perfect. I'm tired of acting. I want to be me for once.

alisa

Sarah, Damon, and I skip school. No one stops us. It feels dangerous, and even though we're breaking the rules, I can't help but feel high from it. I love it. Once we're strapped in Damon's car, he peels out of the lot.

We arrive at Sarah's house, and without missing a beat, Sarah takes my hand and leads me into the bathroom. She dyed her hair black and wants to do the same to me. "You'll wanna take off your shirt and drape this towel around you.

I can't let her see my arms. "No. I'll just drape the towel."

"But it'll mess up your shirt. Come on." She attempts to raise my shirt and gasps. I know she sees the cuts, and I push her hand away. "What happened, Alisa?"

"Nothing."

"Alisa! That's not nothing. What happened?"

"Nothing." I turn for the door, but she stops me.

"Did you do that to yourself?"

"It's nothing, okay?" I stare at her, completely horrified and ashamed. I don't want anyone to know my secret. "Just leave it alone."

She raises her hands in surrender. "Okay. You can talk to me about anything. I won't tell anyone, not even Damon, and I won't judge you. God knows I have my own issues."

Nodding, I place the towel around my shoulders, and she opens the box of dye. When she puts it in my hair, the stench is overpowering.

"Yeah, sorry. It stinks."

"That's an understatement."

She laughs and continues squeezing the dye into my hair. When she's done, she sits on the edge of the tub while we wait.

"Where's your mom?" I lean against the sink.

She frowns. "Probably sleeping last night off. She's gotten worse since Ray dumped her. I keep telling her he's not worth it. He made her cry all the time."

"I'm sorry. Is she still using?"

Sarah lets out a long sigh. "Unfortunately. I can't get her to stop. He's the jackass that got her the pills."

"How'd you get him to leave?"

She shrugs. "He left on his own. Said he didn't want to be here anymore. She stays in her room a lot, really depressed, thinking no man will ever love her again, but I keep telling her it's not about that. She has me and Damon, who sees her as a mom."

I remember Sarah's mom always had a boyfriend. Some were good, some weren't. She was never alone because she hated it. "I'm sorry."

"I'll go check on her in a minute."

A few minutes later, Sarah directs me to lower my head under the faucet. The warm water rushes over me and I relax a little as she massages my scalp.

"I wish I could stop," I say, and for a second, she pauses. "But I can't."

After she finishes washing my hair, she wraps the towel around my head after and holds me at arm's length. "I'm your friend, and no matter what, we'll get through this."

I nod, biting back the tears.

"Can I ask why?"

I have no answer. It's a way to cope, it makes me feel better, but I don't want to say that to her.

"It's okay. I understand if you don't want to talk about it. I'm here for you."

It takes about an hour, but when she's done, my hair is black as night. It definitely pales my skin more, but it looks cool.

"I love it!" Sarah says. "It makes you look badass!"

I smile, liking it, too. It's better than my boring brown.

We hang out the rest of the afternoon playing Mario Brothers 3 on her Nintendo. Sarah and Damon drop me off at my car and follow me to my house to make sure my car makes it. Turning onto the gravel road, Damon speeds past.

The air has gotten colder, which means it's cold inside the house. I hate walking inside the cold dark place. It always feels unwelcoming.

I decide to make fried cubed steak, mashed potatoes and gravy, and green beans. Mom taught me how make the gravy from scratch, and now I've learned to perfect it.

There's nothing on TV except some 80s movie, but I watch it anyway while I eat. The movie reminds me of hanging out with Ben and Sarah when we were kids. We laughed and acted goofy. I miss those days. We built a fort in Sarah's backyard and came up with obstacle courses like we were on American Gladiators.

A car door slamming jolts me awake. I blink as I realize I fell asleep on the couch. Glancing at the clock, I see that it's after midnight. The front door bangs closed, and Diane's got her tongue down my father's throat. Gagging, I turn off the TV and head to my room.

"Alisa," Daddy says, and I stop in my tracks.

"Yes, Daddy?"

"What'd you do to your hair?" he asks, the smell of alcohol lingering.

Clearing my throat, I clench my fists. "Um…I dyed it."

"With what money?"

I swallow hard, not meeting his eyes. "Sarah bought it."

"Why would she buy that for you? Did you make her?"

"No. It was a surprise."

"Makes you look like a whore."

"Oh, Jack no. It just looks…I don't think it suits you dear."

I nod and bite my lip to keep from crying.

"Diane needs her clothes washed." He tosses a bag of clothes at my feet. "Tonight."

I don't know why, but I wait for Diane to say something to help me out of this situation. But all she says is, "It shouldn't take long. I'm sorry. My dad kicked me out, and—"

"She don't need to know that. Just get it done."

"I have a test to study for," I tell him, regretting it as soon as it slips past my lips.

Daddy stops touching Diane and as he walks toward me, he backhands me. I fall to the floor. He kicks me in the back with his boot. "How many times do I have to tell you not to backtalk?"

I nod. "I'm sorry."

"Stupid bitch, you should be. You need to learn your damn manners and stop being so goddamn unruly. I wouldn't have to hit you if you behaved. You understand?"

"Yes, sir."

"And make sure her laundry is done by the morning."

They go to the kitchen as I sit up, grabbing her bag of clothes. The laundry room is past the kitchen, and once I enter, I shiver. No heat comes into the room. I stay most of the night washing her clothes that reek of cigarette smoke. I don't want to touch them.

There's a small tap on the door sometime later, and Diane sneaks in, wearing just a t-shirt. "Alisa, that wasn't a very nice thing. I know that if you mind your daddy, he won't reprimand you."

I nod.

"What's your test on?"

"Chemistry."

"Oh dear. I know nothing about that. I feel awful. Why don't you leave the clothes as they are? I'll finish them in the morning. I would've said something earlier, but I don't want to come between you two."

"It's okay. I'll finish them."

"No. Let me do them tomorrow. Go study, okay?"

"A-are you sure?"

"Yes, of course. Just don't tell your daddy."

I nod. "Thank you."

"Absolutely."

Diane shouldn't be so nice to me, though I appreciate her help. I shouldn't have fallen asleep on the couch. When I get to my room and start reviewing my notes that I copied from Zach yesterday, I still don't understand them. I should've taken him up on his tutor offer, but that ship sailed long ago.

I wish I could be good for Daddy. I wish I was smart enough to make a passing grade on any of these chemistry tests. I shouldn't have skipped today. We may have reviewed the test, and it could've helped me.

Doesn't matter. I'm not going to pass.

Grabbing my scissors, I go into the bathroom and let the bleeding bring me solace.

alisa

Diane holds up a gold chain necklace. "Oh, I love this one."

"Daddy gave that to my mom."

"Oh, it's so pretty. Do you think I'd look good with it?"

No. "I can't let you wear it. It was my mom's."

"Honey." She places a hand on my arm. "I'm really sorry that she's not here. But you can't let this jewelry sit here unworn. It'll start changing colors and collecting dust. I promise I'll keep it safe."

I bite my lip.

"I won't tell your Daddy about you hanging out with your friends. I keep all your secrets from him. It'll be okay."

I don't want her wearing my mother's jewelry, but she has been so nice to me. "Okay."

She smiles and hugs me. "And these earrings, too."

She holds up my mother's small diamond studs. Daddy gave them to Mom right after we got the news of her lymphoma. I swallow the lump forming in my throat and nod. I don't know what I'm doing. She lets me leave the house, and Daddy doesn't have to know. I feel wrong and selfish.

Sarah, Damon, and I meander outside the shopping center on a cold Friday night. The temperatures are supposed to go down this weekend, and I dread it. I lost my jacket in Kentucky, and I've not had a chance to replace it. Sarah let me have an old hoodie of hers. I didn't want to take it, but she forced me.

Diane told me she'd cook for her and Daddy before I left. As long as I'm home by eleven, Daddy will never know I'm gone.

"Diane seems cool," Sarah says.

"Yeah."

"What's wrong?"

"She wanted to borrow some of my mom's jewelry. Said she'd keep my secrets from my dad if I let her."

Sarah furrows her eyebrows. "What?"

"She's really helping out. I was supposed to do her laundry the other night, but she offered to do it so I could study for my test. She cooks so I don't have to when I get off work."

"Don't let her use you."

"Use me? She's helping me, Sarah."

"Okay."

Damon intertwines his fingers with Sarah's. I look away because I know they're about to kiss. I love Sarah and Damon, but I feel like the third wheel all the time. Shivering in my hoodie, I stare at the ground wondering if I'll ever find someone like Damon. Someone who loves me no matter how many mistakes I make, or despite my unintelligence. I know it's all wishful thinking. Even Daddy found someone else to love.

We make our way to the ticket counter for the movie theatre. Sarah and Damon insisted we all see a movie. I hate that they have to pay my way. We find seats near the top in the center. No one else is in the theatre.

"Seriously though," Sarah says. "It's weird that she's taken up residence there."

"She makes Daddy happy."

Sarah rolls her eyes. "Yeah, but does he still take a lot of shit out on you?"

"I deserve it. I can't do anything right."

"Bullshit, Alisa," Damon spits. "Don't believe anything he says to you." He leans forward and looks at me, then Sarah and back at me. Sarah's eyes widen, and her lips press into a thin line like she's warning him. "Alisa." He hesitates. Damon never hesitates. "Has he ever hit you?"

His question brings me up short. "What? Why would you think that?"

"You just…have a lot of bruises."

"I'm clumsy, and I bruise easily. I've told you this before." My fingers clench into tight fists in the pockets of my hoodie. Why are they accusing me? Nothing happens that I don't deserve.

Damon looks at me like he doesn't believe me. It's not bad. Daddy does it to teach me a lesson, but I can't tell him that. He'll think it's not right.

"Alisa, you can trust us," Sarah says.

They're both ganging up on me. My throat tightens. "He gets upset and raises his voice. He's just very strict. That's all, okay?"

Sarah bites her lip. "Alisa, if he ever does anything to you, we've got to turn him in."

"Why would you do that?" I raise my voice. "He hasn't done anything to me. You two are being ridiculous."

We stop talking when we hear a group of people laughing as they enter the theatre. As I turn to the front, I see Ben, Zach, Courtney, and another couple. Ben looks exhausted and worn down. He sees me, then sits down with Courtney. Zach makes his way to where we are.

"Hey, Alisa," he says. "How are you?"

"I'm okay. You?"

"On an awkward double date." He laughs.

"Why don't you sit with us?" Sarah asks.

"Sure. If that's okay?" he asks me.

"Yeah."

He sits down next to me. "Thank you. I can only take so much of Courtney's bickering."

"Why were you with them on a double date?"

"I think they feel sorry for me. I don't know. I had nothing else going on. Oh, I finished reading *Fight Club*. That was insane."

Zach and I easily fall into a conversation before the movie starts. I like that we can always talk, even in class.

Trying to pay attention to the movie is difficult when Sarah and Damon decide to leave for a period of time. Ben and Courtney keep whispering to each other several rows in front. I feel the distance as if I were all the way in China.

Damon returns with a sullen and shocked look on his face. "Alisa, we gotta go," he whispers.

"What's wrong?"

He shakes his head.

"Um, I'll see you later Zach." I follow Damon out of the theatre. Once we near the glass doors, he turns to me, hesitating. He refuses to meet my eyes. "Sarah's mom… overdosed."

I gasp and close my eyes, willing the tears away. The weight in my heart pulls me down. I'm brought back to the night that my mom succumbed to her death. How the nurses had to pull me out of the room.

Ben and Zach run out, and when Ben takes my arm, I don't wince. It takes me a minute to notice the tears rolling down my cheeks. I can't bring myself to say anything.

"I gotta take Sarah home, can you take Alisa?" Damon looks to Ben and Zach.

"Of course," Zach says.

Damon bolts out of the theatre. I need to be there for Sarah. Pushing my legs to walk, I run after Damon.

"Alisa! Wait," I hear Ben say.

I turn around. "I have to be there for her."

"What happened?" he asks, catching up to me with Zach in tow.

Damon's much faster, and as I see him peeling out of the parking lot, I stop, panting in the middle of the parking lot.

"Is Sarah okay? What's going on?"

Tears well in my eyes. "Sarah's mom. She died."

Ben's eyes widen, and blood drains from his face. "Okay, let's go."

"Wait," Zach holds Ben back. "I can take Alisa. You go be with your girlfriend."

I don't want Zach with me. I want Ben. He knows Sarah and her mom.

"I have to take her," he tells him, and Zach nods, understanding.

"What's going on?" Courtney demands as Jared and Rebecca follow.

"Ride with Rebecca and Jared. I have an emergency," Ben calls as we race to his car.

"Are you serious?" she screams after him, but he ignores her as we climb inside.

He shucks off his jacket and hands it to me as we buckle up. "Here. Why don't you ever wear a jacket?"

Because I don't have one. "I'm wearing one. I'm okay."

He looks at me in disbelief. "Put it on. For my sake at least. A hoodie isn't enough."

I take the jacket and put it on. It's warm and smells like him.

"Courtney won't be happy with you."

He frowns. "You're right. But this is important. She'll deal."

My pulse races as we head to Sarah's house. Fear courses through my veins. I'm not sure I want to be there. I remember the night my mom died. The confusion. The chaos. The silence.

And now Sarah's mom died.

We're quiet on the way, and when we get there, Ben parks far enough away so he's not intruding. Staring at the blue and white lights, I freeze in the seat. I want to be there for Sarah, but I can't bring myself to move. My stomach churns with a sickening feeling as I grip the door handle. I don't want to be here.

ben

I take Alisa's hand. It feels like she soaked it in a bucket of ice. My stomach aches at the scene before us. There's a police car, an ambulance, and several more parked in the cul-de-sac in front of Sarah's house. I haven't been here since we were kids. A few people stand around watching the depressing scene.

Mrs. Downs is dead. It's something that rolls around my head like a ball inside a dryer. It doesn't sink in. She was always so sweet to us. She always let us hang out at their house, and she never once raised her voice to any of us.

Tears roll down Alisa's pale cheek, and the blue lights illuminate her now black hair. I wish I knew what to say to her. There's nothing that can be said, but I want to comfort her.

Slowly, she moves her hand to open the door. I turn off the engine and get out, hurrying around to open her door, but she's too quick. I slip my hand in hers, hoping she won't pull away, and she doesn't.

Alisa starts walking toward the lights, completely dazed. I can only imagine she's thinking about her mom. I don't know how she died or how Alisa feels. She stops, and Sarah looks up. Tears have filled her eyes and smeared her mascara. A stabbing pain hits me deep in the stomach. Alisa releases my hand and wraps Sarah in a hug. I keep my distance, and Damon nods at me.

An officer tells him something, then Damon takes Sarah's arm. "Let's go sit in the car."

"Why?" Sarah asks.

"Come on."

"I'm not leaving!" she cries.

"You don't want to see this." Alisa calmly takes her hand, and without a word pulls her toward Damon's car. I realize, they don't want her to see the coroner wheel out her mom's body. The Mexican food I had earlier threatens to escape, and I turn away, not wanting to see it either. A chaplain follows us, speaking to all of us. I feel awkward since we've not been friends in so long.

It feels like hours that we stand out in the cold. Where is the rest of Sarah's family? I know her dad bailed years ago, but where's her sister? I remember when we were kids, her house was full of people for the holidays. I don't know what will happen to her now, and regret overpowers me as I realize what a jerk I've been over the years. I should've been Sarah's friend, no matter what, and I hate myself for how easy it was to be pulled into the popular crowd. Feeling like I lost myself, I watch Sarah weep into Damon's chest. I'm a selfish person. Even as she cries for her mom, I'm thinking about myself.

Knowing I don't deserve her friendship or Alisa's, I vow to make it up to them. I just hope it's not too late.

I squeeze Sarah's arm, and she turns to me, giving me a small appreciative smile.

"Thank you for being here."

I nod and glance at Alisa who looks as though she's seen a ghost. When I follow her eyesight, I see the coroner wheeling the stretcher out. Sorrow punches me in the gut, and I move in front of Alisa's view.

Peering at Damon for a second, I see his eyes are glued to the scene as he clutches Sarah tightly to his chest.

Alisa starts crying, and I gather her in my arms. It's only a matter of time before she pulls away and hugs herself.

alisa

Ben gives Damon and Sarah money for a hotel, after offering them to stay with him. They refuse both, but Ben insists on the money. I wish I could help them like that. We get inside his car, and he blasts the heat. He sighs, leaving the car in park.

"What?"

"I have missed you so much, Alisa. It's been so long since we've seen each other, and you come back into my life, and I treat you like crap. The last two months have been hell for me. I regret leaving Sarah, and I hate what I did to you. I miss you."

My heart lurches forward at his confession. I don't know what to think or say. Is he messing with me again? "We can't be friends."

"Why?"

"I'm not…I can't…I don't belong, Ben. Your friends hate me, and if they knew we were friends, they would cast you out, too."

"That's not true. And besides, I don't care what they think."

"But you do. You would always be nice to me when others weren't around. You said the meanest things about me. You told Courtney that I was nothing to you."

"I did that on purpose. She's very difficult to be with and I…I don't want to be with her anymore."

"That's no excuse. Why are you with her if she's so bad?"

"It's complicated."

I nod, not completely understanding the meaning, but I understand how it can be difficult to explain things. Sarah and Damon never understand when I tell them I'm fine at home.

"I cheated on a test once. Not proud of it. Courtney took the fall for me. I realized then that she'd do anything for me. I confessed later to it. She didn't want me to get in trouble or lose any of my basketball privileges. But it's different now."

He puts the car in drive, and we leave the neighborhood. I'm not sure if I'll ever see it again, and the thought brings tears again. Taking a deep breath, I keep them at bay. Glancing at the clock in Ben's car, I curse to myself, knowing Daddy's home from work. Briefly, I wonder if I should even go home. Anxiety weighs heavily inside my stomach and shoots through my veins, twisting around my heart and lungs, making it difficult to breathe. I start to shake and close my eyes tight, willing it to go away.

"I'm really sorry, Alisa." Ben's voice brings me back, calming me.

"For what?"

"Everything. I've taken so many people and things for granted. I've always gone with the flow and did what my parents wanted me to do. They control every aspect of my life. Everything I do is for them."

"That's not true."

"What?"

"You like basketball. I know you do."

"I don't know," Ben says. "I've been playing like shit in practice. Thinking about giving it up."

"You definitely don't want to do that."

"Why?"

"Because you're at your happiest when you play," I tell him as he slows to a red light. Its glow fills the car.

"I wouldn't say that."

"What do you mean?" When I look over, his heavy gaze clues me in, and heat rises to my cheeks. It feels like there's an animal stampede going on inside my chest. I love the way he looks at me, but I don't know if I can trust him.

The light turns green, and I peer out the window. We're quiet again, but his words about taking people for granted rotate inside my head. He sounds genuine.

"When I lost my mom, I thought I lost everything. My dad's family is gone, and my mom is the only child. I barely knew her parents. When Dad and I moved here, I was nervous, but excited to see you and Sarah. You've both changed, but Sarah accepted me, even though she shouldn't have. And you... You say your parents control you, but I think others are to blame and maybe other influences." As soon as I say the words, I want to take them back. He's going to hate me.

He lets out a long sigh as he pulls up next to the mailboxes and cuts the engine. It's so dark I can't see my hand in front of my face, but I welcome the darkness. It's comforting in a way.

"You're right. I let everyone decide for me. Including Courtney."

Ben reaches over for my hand. The simple touch makes my heart beat wildly. I love the gentleness of his hand, the warmth. I wish I could be with him. He's the first boy I ever fell in love with. But it's stupid.

"Are you going to be okay tonight? Stupid question, I know."

No. "I'll be fine."

"Will you call me if you want to talk?"

I want to so much, but I can't. "Maybe."

He squeezes my hand, and I relax. I don't feel on edge or afraid. Being with him calms me and it's peaceful, but I slowly withdraw my hand. Daddy always tells me I don't deserve nice things and that I'm not allowed to have a boyfriend. No matter what, I still want more time with Ben. More time to sit in the darkness with him. Just…more time.

Losing Mom, and now Sarah's mom passing, makes me feel like there isn't much time left to live and that we all should live in the moment.

But I have rules to follow, and I've broken so many tonight that I'm not sure when or if I'll get to see Ben again. I don't even know if I'll be able to attend Mrs. Downs' funeral.

Glancing at the time, a jolt of panic shoots through me. I have to face him. "I'll talk to you later," I tell Ben as I open the door. The rush of cold air hits me.

I softly close the door and Ben gets out, meeting me in front of his car. Above, the stars overwhelm the sky. There is no moon to light my way home, but tonight I prefer the dark.

Ben removes his jacket and as he moves closer to me, I flinch. He pauses and wraps it around me. The closeness makes blood rush to my cheeks, and I inhale the clean scent. "I don't need this." I move to take it off, but he stops me.

"Keep it," he says. "I'll get it Monday."

"It's okay. I—"

"Keep it."

We're inches from each other, and I can feel his eyes on me. Slowly, he pulls me into him and warmth curls around my heart. The urge to break down and cry overcomes me, but I hold back. I want this moment to last forever. He kisses the top of my head and tenses. "Sorry. I…I'll see you Monday. Um…call me. If you want to talk."

Nodding, I pull away from him reluctantly, wondering if he feels as empty as I do now. Walking down the long gravel road toward the house feels like it takes forever.

Inhaling a deep breath, I bite my lip as my shaky hand touches the front doorknob. I breathe a short sigh of relief to find it unlocked. My entire body turns to ice as I walk through. Daddy is sitting in his recliner, sound asleep. Careful not to wake him, I softly close the door and turn the lock. Diane is nowhere to be found, and I wonder where she is. Inching my way toward my room, I hold my breath, listening to my pounding heart. When I reach inside my room, I exhale, closing the door.

I'm still not out of the woods as Daddy will ask me questions tomorrow when he comes home from work, but for now, I relish in the silence, remembering how Ben's hand felt on mine. I can still feel his warmth around me, and as I curl under the heavy blankets with his jacket, I cuddle with Mr. Zebra, wishing it were Ben. I imagine feeling his arms holding me as I drift off to sleep.

ben

To hold Alisa all night would be a dream. The few seconds she allowed me to hug her felt amazing. Even without my jacket, I was warm. I know I'm crossing lines I shouldn't, but I want to comfort her. I want to be the person she comes to, but I know I've made that difficult, and she's afraid of me. Or being with someone altogether. I hated hearing her say we couldn't be friends. I want to be more than friends, but that's not possible.

I would give up basketball for her. I would do anything for her. But she's right. I let everyone else make my decisions, and if I do anything, it has to be for me. I don't even know if she feels the same way as I do. She deserves so much more than me.

Being around Alisa, I feel so calm, like I used to when I was younger. I haven't felt that since she left, and I forgot what it was like. I miss it. I realize being on edge all the time is what I'm used to, and I hate it. I need to change it.

When I get home, it's late, and the house is quiet. Fatigue and sadness weigh heavily over me. Once I enter my room, I see a Post-It note on my monitor. *Courtney called.* She already filled my pager. I'm not looking forward to that conversation since I practically bailed on our date. No matter what I tell her, she's not going to be happy. Why do I stay with her? Am I really that afraid of being alone?

It's hard to believe Sarah's mom died tonight. One second, she was there, and the next, gone. I can't begin to imagine how Sarah or Alisa feels. I know I don't get along with my parents a lot, but it would devastate me if one of them died. Don't they appreciate each other? Or do they just tolerate each other for the sake of me and Hayden? I don't know what will happen with Sarah, but guilt overwhelms me even more. Everyone abandoned her, including me. And I abandoned Alisa.

Unable to sleep, I grab my portable CD player, press the headphones to my ears, and hit play. Smashing Pumpkins drowns out my thoughts as I slip into sleep knowing what I have to do.

alisa

The smell of coffee invites my eyes to open. As I hesitantly remove the blankets, the weight of last night's event clings to me. Sleep was off and on as I dreamed of Mom dying all over again. Daddy is never up this early making coffee. Diane. She must be here.

I quickly dress in layers. The house is cold again because we can't afford kerosene for the heaters. Daddy bought little heaters to place throughout, but there isn't much insulation in the house at all. It makes me feel guilty having a secret stash of money.

Gradually opening the door, I listen for whatever noises, and the only thing I hear is low voices on the TV. I take a deep breath and come into the living room to find Daddy sipping coffee in his chair.

"G-good morning," I mumble as I sit on the edge of the sofa.

"Morning."

We sit quietly for a few seconds.

"Where were you last night?" he asks in a calm voice. He's not drunk. He looks tired, and a little sad.

"Sarah invited me out." I clear my throat. "Um, but, her mom…died." Tears rush to the forefront of my eyes.

Daddy stops rocking and looks at me. "What? What happened?"

"She…overdosed."

He closes his eyes and rests his head against the chair. "Damn."

"I'm sorry I was out so late."

Daddy waves his hand. "Don't let it happen again."

"Yes, sir. Um…can I go to the funeral?"

He takes a sip of his coffee. "Yes."

"Thank you."

He nods. "It's a real shame. I think about your mom every day."

"Me, too."

"We're doin' okay though, aren't we?"

"Yeah. Is Diane coming over today?"

"No. We broke up."

The news hits me hard. I'm not sure how to feel. She made things better. "I'm sorry."

"She was too needy. I need to change the oil in your car. There's some laundry that needs to be done."

"Yes, sir."

"Also, your birthday is coming up soon, but I don't have much money."

"It's okay."

"You're a good kid." He pauses. "We need to go to the store."

I nod with a small smile. "Okay."

"Things will get better." Once he finishes his coffee, he stands and drops his cup off in the kitchen. "Maybe we'll rent a movie tonight." He walks by me on his way to his room.

I nod. "Okay."

I wonder if we'll do anything for my birthday. But watching a movie tonight sounds good. It will keep my mind off things. I just hope he doesn't drink.

ben

"Did you call Courtney back?" Mom asks as I sleepily make my way into the kitchen. Dad's already in his office with the door closed, as usual. What does he do in there that is so important? Why can't he be a normal dad and play basketball with his son or do something with his daughter? Or mow his own lawn?

"Not yet," I mumble. I didn't get much sleep, and I'm tired as hell.

"What happened last night? She said you left in a hurry with some girl." She stirs the eggs in the pan as the oven dings for the biscuits. One thing I appreciate about Mom is that she still cooks instead of hiring a maid. There are only four of us, and it would seem so excessive. Dad, on the other hand, hires a professional lawn and landscaping company.

Rubbing my eyes, I let out a sigh. "Sarah's mom died."

"Oh dear." Mom turns off the stove and turns to me. Her blond hair is pulled back in a perfect bun. She looks like she's dressed for work, but it's Saturday. "Who is Sarah?"

Another sigh. "Remember Alisa, Sarah, and I used to hang out when we were kids?"

"Oh right, I remember. I was glad when you stopped hanging out with them."

"Why?"

"Some things are better left unsaid. That poor girl though. Her mom was always dabbling into drugs and alcohol, so it doesn't surprise me."

"Could you be anymore insensitive?"

She narrows her eyes. "This doesn't explain why you drove off with some girl."

Mom has never questioned me like this before, and I can only imagine it's from Courtney freaking out telling her god knows what. "We went to the movies and saw Alisa and Sarah. Sarah's neighbor paged her, and Sarah's boyfriend took her home. I gave Alisa a ride there."

"Alisa. Didn't I tell you not to see her?"

I roll my eyes. "Are we seriously getting into this? What was I supposed to do, Mom? Leave her there?"

Slamming down the pan in the sink, she turns to me with her hands on her hips. "Benjamin, her father is an alcoholic, and chances are she is too. Sarah's family is into drugs. You don't need to be around that. They will do nothing but bring you down and distract you from what's important."

"Alisa isn't an alcoholic, okay? There's something else going on." None of this is adding up. She's hiding something from me. Something about Alisa. "Why are you so set on me being with Courtney? Why do you care? Don't you want me to be happy?"

"Of course, I want you to be happy. Courtney is a wonderful person for you. Alisa is not."

Where is she coming up with this? Is she just making it all up? "So it's okay for me to date Courtney, who cheated on me and broke my heart, but I can't be friends with someone whose father's an alcoholic? When my own dad can't even acknowledge the fact that we exist half the time?"

"Benjamin! That is enough!"

"What did you just say?" Dad enters the kitchen.

"Nothing." I shake my head as I walk out.

"I didn't say you could leave," Dad says.

"So you think you can be a dad now? When it's time to punish or yell? I was helping a friend last night whose mom died. I was being good. Isn't that what you want? As long as whatever we do is good for our image—"

"I never said that."

"You never had to!"

"Okay, maybe we all need to calm down." Mom places a hand on Dad's shoulder.

He doesn't react much to her touch, just continues to glare at me. "What is going on with you? Why are you being so argumentative lately?" Mom still hasn't mentioned Alisa to him. What is up with this?

It's pressure from you. Courtney. Mom. Coach. I feel like I'm about to break. "Nothing."

"Then stop acting like an immature boy. You are sixteen years old, and you need to respect your parents."

A small laugh escapes my lips, which angers him more.

"Where are the keys to your car?" he demands.

I laugh again. "You're going to take my car away? Are you going to take me to school now?"

"You can take the bus."

"Whatever."

"Until you can prove to us that you're mature enough to drive the damn car, it belongs to me."

Tossing my keys to him, I turn around and walk out the door. I don't care. I don't need the car. I need to get the hell out of here and do something I should've done a long time ago.

alisa

Daddy and I went to the store, and unfortunately, he bought more beer. I don't know what to do to get him to stop. Maybe I can find Diane and find out what happened. Maybe I can bring her back and they can patch things up. I don't want her replacing Mom, but Daddy was happy. Things were good.

When we get home, I put away the groceries while Daddy changes the oil in my car. He's quiet today, and I wonder if he's thinking about Mom or Diane. I wish I could visit Sarah or talk to her. I hope she's okay. I can't believe her mom died. I still have a hard time believing mine is gone. But it's my fault she died. She was in so much pain, and I thought…I thought I was helping her. I made things worse. Like everything else in my life. Pain and anger build inside me, and I need my solace. Taking my scissors into the bathroom, I close the door, anxious to put the blade to my skin. I need to let it out. All of it.

After I make dinner, Daddy and I eat in the living room and watch the action flick he rented. We are quiet for the remainder of the night, and when the movie ends, I go to bed. Hours later, I wake to Daddy yelling and slamming doors. With my heart lodged in my throat, I hide in the small bathroom.

Daddy's drunk and angry. With Ms. Downs' death, we're both thinking of Mom.

While I hold the door closed, I pray that he doesn't find me. I pace my breathing and hope my thumping heartbeat can't be heard. Each time he raises his voice, cursing at nothing in particular, I jump. I hate this anger…this volatile, anger. I remember hiding in the bathroom every time Mom and Dad fought. Why can't it be like it was earlier tonight? Why can't I go back to when it wasn't so loud? When Mom and Sarah's mom were still alive. When Daddy gave me stuffed animals and told me everything would be okay. When Sarah, Ben, and I were friends.

The minutes pass. No sounds for a moment. I grab my scissors and place the cold, silver blade to the flesh of my arm. Daddy yells again, then I hear the shattering of a glass against a wall. Baring down, I move the scissors across my skin. The dark, red blood seeps from the opening.

"Please stop," I whisper softly, cutting once more. Blood drips onto the carpet and I inhale a deep breath, ignoring the tears. Why did Mom have to die? Why are Daddy and me hurting so much? Why is this happening?

The house becomes quiet and when I look down at my arm, I'm still bleeding. I cut deeper this time without realizing it. In a panic, I tear off some toilet paper and wrap it around my arm. I don't want to do this anymore, but I can't stop.

I don't want Daddy to be angry and hurt anymore. I just want all of this to end.

When my arm stops bleeding, I make my way out into the living room and find Daddy passed out. I breathe a sigh of relief, knowing he'll be out for a while. I return to my room and sit on the edge of the bed, wanting to call Sarah, but I don't want to bother her.

Pillow-like clouds sail across the grey sky. The wind cuts through, blowing debris across the parking lot. Usually on my breaks, I hang out in the breakroom, but today I wanted to be alone.

Concentration is lost on me, and I've been making mistakes all day. Scanning items twice. Typing in the wrong produce codes. Counting change wrong. I can't do anything right and it's a wonder I still have a job since I've been calling out a lot.

I see Damon's maroon car pull into a spot. He walks toward the building, and when he sees me, he heads my way with a sullen look etched onto his face. Something is wrong, not just about Sarah's mom. His arms are crossed, and his look scares me to walk any closer. I stop mid-stride, not wanting to hear what he has to tell me. I don't have the willpower to move.

An anchor pulls my heart into my stomach. This isn't good at all. His eyes are bloodshot, and I know it's not from pot. There's a heavy sadness in them. Worse than Friday night.

"Sarah—"

"I don't wanna know." I shake my head.

He frowns. "Sarah's uncle has custody of her now."

I finally look up, ignoring the tears urging to escape. "What?"

Damon nods. "He came down yesterday along with her sister, Tonya."

I don't like the heaviness in my stomach when he says that. Her uncle hasn't been around in so long. Why care now? Both of them left Sarah to care for her mom by herself.

"Is he going to care for her? Is he going to provide for her, or will she have to fight for herself?" I'm getting angry. If Sarah's uncle is a good guy, why hasn't he ever taken Sarah before?

"She never wanted to leave her mom, Alisa. Both her uncle and Tonya tried."

I can understand that. "Oh," is all I muster up to say.

"The guy seems okay. There's something else."

What else can there be?

"She'll be ten hours away. In Tampa."

My heart crumbles inside me. The world spins so fast that I can't keep a hold on anything. My mom left. Diane's gone. Ben…And now Sarah.

Damon hugs me. I don't mind though. He's the only one here for me. And I'm the only here for him. I'm sure he won't stay now that Sarah's gone. His whole purpose for being here is because of her. He will leave after today. But for now, I welcome the embrace and wrap my arms around him as tight as I can because he's the only thing holding me together.

Damon draws back a bit and lets out a long sigh. Running his hands through his thick hair, he takes a step back and lights up a cigarette.

"How are you?" I ask.

"I'm okay. Just worried about everything. I'm being selfish because I don't want to lose Sarah."

"Go with her. What's really keeping you here?"

"She is, but I'm not eighteen yet, and I can't just leave my brother's home."

"Why? It's only a month away. She needs you, and you need her."

"She needs you, too. She wants you to come with us."

I shake my head. "No, I can't."

"She's serious. She wants you to accomplish your goal of culinary school. Todd can help with that."

I meet his dark eyes. They've talked about me to her uncle? Live in Tampa with Sarah and her uncle? Leave Ben for good? Daddy? The thoughts create a new ache. I'm already going to have to repeat my junior year with my failing grades. Culinary school is looking less and less likely. "I have to stay here."

"He's not your responsibility, you know."

But he is. I swore to Mom that I would take care of him. There isn't anyone else who can now that Diane is gone. It will always be my responsibility. I can't let Mom down. I won't.

"You have every right to live your life. You deserve that and you can get out."

I'm stuck here.

"Will you at least think about it?"

"Yeah. Sure."

But my mind is made up.

ben

I have to do this. My feelings for Alisa are too much to ignore. Being around Alisa and Sarah reminds me of who I used to be. Someone who wasn't so moody and angry. Someone who could be themselves without any judgement. No pressure.

Taking a deep breath, I knock on Courtney's door.

When it swings open, her blue eyes immediately glare at me with hatred. "You're a piece of shit," she yells.

"Will you please listen to me?"

"Why should I? You've changed, Ben."

"Sarah's mom died, Courtney."

She crosses her arms in front of her chest. "So? Since when do you care about those low life trashy people? You just bolted from our date. For *her*."

"I had to be there for a friend."

She raises an eyebrow. "Friend? Since when have you ever hung out with them? Why are they suddenly so much more important than me?"

Bees swarm my stomach. I have to do this. "This isn't working out for me."

"What isn't?"

"Us. We aren't right for each other. We should never have gotten back together."

"Are you kidding me? Are you breaking up with me? What is with you?"

"I'm finally realizing who I am. And I'm not someone you can push around anymore."

"What are you talking about? Have you been taking drugs?"

I roll my eyes, ignoring the anger thumping in my head. "No, Courtney."

"Are you seeing someone?" Her face turns red as she pins me with her glare. "It's because of that girl, isn't it?"

"I'm not seeing anyone. It's you. You make me feel like shit, and I'm tired of it."

"Are you kidding me? For months, *you've* been the one treating me like shit. You don't care about me. You never have. Why do you think I cheated on you?"

Ouch. "Don't blame that on me," I say, hearing the icy tone in my voice. "I'm tired of you blaming everything on me."

"*I* blame *you*? You really are messed up."

We take a beat. I'm pissed, she's pissed.

She sighs, and her eyes soften. "Ben, I don't want to lose you. You're everything to me. I don't know what I'd do without you."

"Courtney…it's over."

"You don't mean that."

"Yes. I do."

"You'll change your mind. This is what we do. We break up, but we always make up." She smiles and runs a finger down my arm.

I back away. "Not this time."

A tear slides down her cheek. I can't comfort her. I can't be sucked back in. I turn around and jog away.

alisa

The heavy scent of refrigerated flowers engulfs me. The scent screams death. There are flowers everywhere. And black. Everyone's dressed in black, including me. The same dress I wore to Mom's funeral. Everyone's quietly whispering like they're afraid to talk. And tears. So many tears.

Seeing Mrs. Downs' still body…I close my eyes and see my own mom inside her silver casket lined with pristine taffeta.

Watching from behind the chairs at the graveside, I hold myself, needing my scissors. I need to get rid of this pain. It starts closing in on me. I need an escape. My fingers dig into my arms as I clench my teeth so tight to hold back the tears.

When I feel a warm body close to mine, I tense. It's Ben, and I relax a little. I wasn't expecting him to show up, but I'm glad he did.

The wind blows, and I shiver. Ben shrugs off his suit jacket and wraps it around me. I love the clean wintery scent.

When the preacher finishes the sermon, Ben turns to me. "How are you?"

"I'm okay. You?"

He shrugs. "I'm all right." But I can tell he's lying because there's a weight in his eyes. "Why don't you ever have a coat?"

"I forgot it."

He rolls his eyes.

"We're going to Sarah's house," I say. "Do you want to go?"

He hesitates. "Are you sure that's a good idea?"

"It'll be fine. Sarah appreciates you being here."

When we get to his car, he opens the door for me, and it makes me feel awkward. No one's ever done that. I don't know why he's being so nice to me.

"I've been worried about Sarah." He starts the car and puts it in drive. "And you."

"Me?"

"I know this is hard for you, Alisa. I can't even imagine how difficult today has been. I've never lost anyone close to me. I don't even know what to do or say."

"There's nothing that can be said or done. Knowing someone is there to lean on helps."

"You didn't have anyone but your dad. I wish I could have been there for you."

I nod, not knowing how to respond. He reaches for my hand, and I let him take it, but I release it after a few seconds, even though it felt amazing.

We're quiet on the way to Sarah's, but it's not an uncomfortable silence. It's relaxing for a change. No crying. No yelling. Just peaceful quiet. It's nice. We arrive and inside, we walk through a crowd of people and make our way to the kitchen.

Sarah comes into the room, and her eyes are bloodshot and puffy. "So here's where the cool cats are."

I give a small smile and hand her a glass of water.

"Thanks. Thanks for coming, Ben."

He nods. "I'm sorry, Sarah."

"I know. Thanks." She leans against the counter and sighs. "This sucks. I barely know half these people. This house gives me the creeps."

I know what she means. It wasn't until after Mom's funeral, after everyone had left that it really hit. The house held an emptiness. A void or something.

"I leave this weekend for good."

Tears threaten to escape, but I hold them back. "What am I gonna do?"

"Wait, what?" Ben asks.

Sarah clears her throat. "Yeah. Uncle Todd is bringing me to his house in Tampa."

Ben curses under his breath. "I'm sorry."

She wraps an arm around me. "I know we won't see each other, but I'm always a phone call away."

I nod, not meeting her eyes. An ache stabs my chest knowing I'll probably never see my best friend again. We parted ways once before, but for some reason, this feels different. It feels final. I hate it.

"Wanna get out of here?" Damon asks Sarah.

She nods and looks to me and then Ben. "Come on."

We don't go far. Just to the abandoned tree house in Sarah's backyard. It used to be one of our favorite places to play. It was a place where we could pretend that life had no problems. Where we could be ourselves and not worry about anything.

Damon pulls out a joint and lights it. Sarah sits in between his legs, leaning against his chest, while Ben and I sit next to each other. Damon passes the joint to Sarah, and after they each take a hit, they offer it to Ben and me. We both turn it down. Although, looking at Sarah and Damon, they look so relaxed. I want to know what that feeling is like, but I refuse any drugs and alcohol.

"Remember that day we were hanging out here and one of the neighbor's wild turkeys appeared. Ben took off and the turkey chased him, and Ben ripped his pants wide open?" Sarah laughs, and we follow.

Ben rolls his eyes. "My mom got so pissed at me for that."

"Why?"

"Because I was always destroying clothes. But a *turkey* chased me."

We laugh again.

"Remember when that thunderstorm came?" Ben whispers in my ear. "We hid in here until it passed."

I nod, thinking back to that day. It was the day I knew I liked Ben. We were so young, and he hated storms. He held onto my hand so tightly while we waited out the storm together. He kissed my cheek that day as a thank you. Things were simpler then.

For the rest of the afternoon, we hang out in the treehouse, reminiscing about our childhood, and when it's time to go, I don't want to leave. I don't want to say goodbye to Sarah again. It feels like I'm losing part of myself, and I hate that.

She pulls me into a tight hug, and I try my best to hold back the tears. "Take care, Alisa," she whispers in my ear. "Things will get better, I promise. I hope you change your mind and come to Tampa."

She hugs Ben as I hastily make my way to the door. I hate crying, especially in front of people. When I'm outside, a rush of cold hits me, and I hold myself, not looking forward to the drive home. I don't want to go yet.

"Alisa," Ben calls from behind.

I turn around.

"Need a ride?"

"Sure."

Leaving Sarah's house amplifies the ache.

"I shouldn't have stayed," Ben says.

"Why?"

He tugs on the back of his neck. "I gotta get home before my dad sees I took the car."

"What? Isn't it yours?"

"He took the keys."

"Why?"

"We got into a fight."

"I'm sorry. Want to talk about it?"

He's silent, and when I look at him, it looks like he's struggling with his words. "He wants me to be who I'm not."

"Who do you want to be, Ben?"

He thinks about it for a moment. "Someone who's good enough. Sometimes they make it hard. Everything I do is for them."

"What do you do that's for you? What is it that you want?"

"I don't know," he says, but I know it's a lie.

"You shouldn't let people dictate your life."

"What about you? What do you do that's for you? Do you ever go after what you want?"

I look away. "It isn't that simple for me."

"Why?"

"Same reason it's not easy for you."

He nods. "Fair enough. I broke up with Courtney."

My heart skips a beat. He broke up with her? "Are you okay?"

"Honestly, I feel like a huge weight has been lifted. It was a mistake to try and fix things."

"Why did you stay with her?"

"I don't know. I fell in love and thought that what we had was good. She was sweet and cool. She was fun to hang out with, and she was caring. But over time she got worse. Super jealous and controlling. I can't stand how she treated you."

"Then why did you stand by and do nothing? I'm sure she does it to other girls. Did you never notice it before?"

"No." He frowns. "I'm sorry. I never paid attention because I didn't want to get involved in her drama. I ignored a lot, hoping it would all go away. I made several mistakes. I didn't care."

"Maybe you should've said something to her."

"I know. I guess I used all that as a distraction from all the crap I deal with at home."

"Like what?"

He shakes his head, but I know something is wrong. I want to be there for him, but I don't know how. "I don't wanna bring you down. Look, what I said the other night, I meant it. I miss you. But did you really mean that we can't be friends?"

I release a long sigh unsure of what to say. Of course, I want to be his friend. And more.

"My parents can't tell me who to be friends with."

I look over, meeting his hazel eyes. "What?"

"It's nothing."

"Your parents won't let you be friends with me either?" I shouldn't feel hurt by it because I already knew.

"They can't make me."

"Was that why you fought? Was that why they took your car?" Guilt settles in my stomach.

"Alisa, it's okay. It was an empty threat. I'll have my car back soon."

I nod, but I can't get rid of the guilt. I feel sick. Ben got into a fight with his parents over me. I'm not worth it.

When we approach the edge of the long road leading to my house, I see Diane's yellow Pinto next to the house. Did Daddy forgive her? Is she back to patch things up?

"Are you okay?" Ben asks, slowing to a stop beside the mailboxes.

"I'm fine." Diane doesn't know about Ben, and I'm not sure I want her to. Yet.

When he does, I get out of the car. "I'll see you at school." Closing the door, I take a step toward the house. Ben gets out of the car and takes my hand, turning me to face him. His skin is soft, and it sends warmth all over me. He's so close that my entire body is humming. I wonder what it's like kissing him. Not that he'd ever want to kiss me. I'm a freak, and I'm messing up his life.

"I'm sorry," he whispers. Tears burn at the back of my eyes as I turn away from him. He tips my chin up, forcing me to look at him. "I'm here for you. I promise you that. I don't care what anyone one thinks. I will make this right."

"Being around me will hurt you."

He crinkles his forehead. "What?"

I reluctantly slip from his hands and take a step back. "You shouldn't be seen with me. It will ruin your reputation. You have your future laid out for you, and you don't want to destroy it. I don't want you to get into trouble, Ben. We can't be friends."

"Alisa—"

"I gotta go."

As I head down the long driveway away from Ben, my heart sinks further. When I look back, he's still standing there, watching me, but a second time, he gets back into his car and heads toward his house. What I would give to go with him to where it's safe.

ben

Exhaustion latches on to me like a wet cloak by the time I get home. I'm drained, and all I want to do is sleep. Recharge my batteries. As miserable of a day as it was, it was nice spending time with old friends and remembering what it was like being with them. It's sad that I'm realizing that too late. But maybe there's still time with Alisa, even though she keeps pushing me away. I can't stand the look on her face when she told me we couldn't be friends. Again. Why does she think she'll ruin my reputation? Why does everyone say that? It's like she repeated the same exact words Mom said. Has Mom talked to her?

Someone knocks on my door, and I can guess it's Mom.

"Come in," I say.

She slowly enters and sits on the edge of my bed. "How did it go? How is Sarah doing?" she asks like she cares.

"She just lost her mom. How do you think she's doing?" I'm not being fair, but I'm still upset with her.

"Ben, please. You haven't said two words to me all week."

I let out a sigh. "What is so bad about Alisa, Mom? We used to be friends when we were kids, and you were fine with it."

"No, I wasn't. But you were young. I knew you'd find your way eventually."

"That's just it. I haven't found my way. I've lost it. And when I'm with Alisa, I feel like myself. She doesn't get pissed if I don't put up enough points on the board. Or if I would rather go to a concert than some lame ass party. She doesn't get mad when I don't call back. She doesn't expect anything from me."

"Ben, I am your mother. Of course, I'm going to expect things of you."

"You and everyone else. Tell me. What's so bad? Why does everyone have it out for her? She's the sweetest person, and has done nothing to me but be nice, even when I've not been the best person to her."

"You have a future. Don't ruin it by wasting your time with her. You have a good thing with Courtney."

I guess Courtney hasn't called Mom with the news, but I don't feel like getting yelled at by Mom, so I say nothing.

"I don't want to see you make the same mistakes as me."

"What do you mean?"

"Stay away from Alisa. She will only bring you down. I'm not discussing it any longer. I came in here to tell you that we are giving your car back."

"So long as I stay away from her?"

She doesn't say anything as she hands me my keys. The whole thing is dumb since I already drove my car today.

"Mom, what mistakes? Will you tell me what the hell is going on? I'm so sick of this."

She turns around. "Yes, I had an affair," she screams. "I did everything I could to make this work, but he never wanted to. I stopped trying. I slept with someone because I needed to feel something. Your father didn't care."

Was that how Courtney felt about me? "Are you kidding? He's been miserable."

"Only because he doesn't want a divorce. It looks bad."

Divorce? The word stabs me in so many places, making me dizzy. I lower myself down on the edge of my bed. Mom's been thinking about divorce? My throat is so dry, and I keep trying to swallow the bulge.

Her lip trembles, and I immediately regret saying anything. I don't want Mom to cry. I don't like that she's hurting. I don't like that my parents have been like this for so long.

"I don't know what else to do, Ben. I'm not happy. I haven't been for a very long time. None of this is healthy for any of us."

"Have you tried therapy?"

"Your father refuses to go."

"Make him. He has to care. I mean, when's the last time you talked to him? Actually talked."

"I've tried multiple times."

We sit in heavy silence for what seems like an eternity.

"Why won't you let me see Alisa?"

She lets out a long sigh. "That's what's on your mind right now?"

"This is the first time you've been honest, and we're talking."

She sighs again as she sits next to me on the bed. "Ben. I-I'm not proud of this."

Mom never stutters. What could be worse than what she's already told me? I wait until she's ready.

"When you all were kids, we didn't really run in the same circle as Alisa's parents. But one night, I…" She takes a deep breath and looks to the ceiling. "I went to a bar."

Oh no.

"Jack Hopewell was there."

Alisa's dad? I don't like where this is headed.

"I always had sort of a crush on him."

"Okay. What does this have to do with Alisa and me?"

"We drank more than we should have—I was upset with your father about something I can't even remember now—and we fooled around."

"Fooled around?"

She gives me a knowing look.

I'm going to be sick. "W-when was this?"

"Several months before they left town."

"That's why they left?"

Mom wipes a tear. "April found out. She threatened to leave Jack if he didn't stop drinking and said that they needed to be closer to her family."

How has Alisa gotten through all of this? I feel even worse now because I didn't keep in touch.

"Does…Dad know?"

"Yes. It was a mistake, and I regret it."

"But…you cheated on him again."

She takes a deep breath. "I'm not perfect."

Jumping up from my bed, I cross the room to my desk, squeezing the back of the chair. "You don't have to be perfect, Mom. This was all in the past. This has nothing to do with me and Alisa."

"Ben, that family is bad news. You don't need to involve yourself with her. You have such a bright future, and I don't want to see it wasted."

"Stop saying that. Just because something happened with you and her father, you can't stop me from being friends with her. She's not a bad person."

"You need to focus on basketball, school, and Courtney. You two went through a lot. Give yourselves a chance."

"Mom, do you even hear yourself? Stop trying to force yourself in my relationships. It's not like you're exactly an expert."

"Benjamin!"

"He forgave you, Mom. And you did it again!"

"I've said my piece."

I shake my head. "This isn't about me at all. This is about you and Dad."

Mom bites her lip. "Ben, I have spoken to a lawyer."

The way she says it sounds final.

I swallow hard and try not to let the nausea take over. "What will happen to Hayden and me?"

"Well, you're sixteen, so you can decide. Hayden will come stay with me."

The queasiness threatens to reach my throat again. Saliva collects in my mouth, and I take a deep breath. Hayden and I might not live in the same place?

What will that do to Hayden? How is she supposed to cope with all of this? It's too much to handle.

"I can't believe you did this. You ruined our family."

She bursts into tears, but I can't feel sorry for her right now. I'm so angry. I have to leave, or I'll say something I'll regret.

"I gotta go."

"Where?"

"I don't know. I'll be back later."

I'm shaking. Curling my hands into fists, I want to hit something. I don't know where I'm going, but I need to run. I know I can't run away, but it feels good. As soon as the cold air hits me, it soothes me for a second.

alisa

Taking a deep breath, I hesitate outside my house. I'm not sure why. Maybe I just want to be alone. When I walk inside, Diane's sitting in Daddy's recliner, eyes glued to the TV.

Is she supposed to be here? Did Daddy forget to get the key from her? Did they make up?

"Alisa!" She jumps out of the chair and gathers me in her arms. "I thought I'd never see you again." She holds me at arm's length. "Jack and I made up. It's so wonderful. What did I miss? Why are you in a nice dress?"

Lowering my head, I tell her. "I went to a funeral."

"Oh, that's terrible. Is it okay that you missed school? Does Jack know?"

"Yeah."

"Well, you go work on your homework or rest, and I'll get dinner started."

I retreat to my room to change. Closing the door, I inhale a deep breath. I change into a long-sleeved flannel shirt and jeans. I'm close to tears, but something on my dresser catches my eye, and when I examine closer, I see that my mom's jewelry box is broken, and several pieces are missing.

Pain lurches to my throat and stays there. I can't breathe. Did Diane do this? Did she steal Mom's jewelry? Was it Daddy? Why would he take it? Are we that low on money? Daddy would never do that. Anger fills every nerve in my being as I march out to confront her.

"Give them back," I demand. My hands shake and I'm breathing hard.

She looks up. "Excuse me?"

"You heard me. Give them back."

"I don't know what you're talking about."

"My mom's jewelry. You stole it!"

Diane gasps. "No, no I wouldn't do that."

"So many pieces are gone."

She approaches me with caution. "Alisa, I promise I would never do such a thing. Do you think your daddy could've taken them? Maybe pawned them off?"

"He wouldn't do that."

"Your mom is gone. Maybe he needed the money to pay for something. It's okay. It's just stuff. Having them won't bring her back."

I know that. I release a breath. She's right, though. Mom's gone. I never wore any of it. I could never bring myself to. If Daddy had to pawn the jewelry off to pay for kerosene or one of the bills, I feel worse. I have the money, and I need to stop hoarding it. He needs help. It's my fault we're struggling.

Clenching my teeth, I make my way into the kitchen and pull out some boxed dinner. The whole time I cook, I try keeping the tears down. Most of my mother's jewelry is gone. Pieces she had growing up. Pieces Daddy gave her. I feel like my insides are going to explode. I can't control what's going on. It's too much to process, and I'm seconds from shutting down. I need my scissors.

When dinner's done, I scoop some out for Diane and me. Maybe eating will help ease things, but I don't feel like eating. I bring her a bowl and sit on the couch.

"What is this?"

"Cheeseburger mac. It's Daddy's favorite."

"Oh." She plays with the food, looking at it like it's a pile of dirt.

"I'm sorry about earlier."

Diane puts her fork down and takes a breath. "Alisa." She hesitates. "I think you have anger issues. It would be best for all of us if you fixed it. It scares me."

"What?"

"Don't you think you get worked up over nothing a lot of the time? I'm only being helpful. Every time something doesn't go your way, you explode. Then apologize. You hurt my feelings a lot."

Guilt harbors inside me. I never meant to hurt her, and I shouldn't have assumed it was Diane who took the jewelry.

"I'm really disappointed in you. I thought you liked me, and I hate that you accused me of stealing. I don't think you should have TV privileges. You should probably put your food in the kitchen and go to bed."

Biting the tears back, I return my bowl to the kitchen and retreat to my room.

I can't believe how awful I've been. I don't deserve anything. Locking myself in my tiny bathroom, I pull out my scissors and return to my solace.

My best friend is moving. My mother's jewelry has been pawned. And I've been a terrible person. I'm nothing but trouble. Wasted space. No one will love me, and there is no point to any of this.

ben

Two weeks have passed since the funeral and since Sarah left. And since I found out the truth from Mom. I haven't said a word to anyone about it, but things at home are even more tense if that's possible. The news swims in my head. I hate that when I think about Alisa, I think about her dad and my mom. I'm worried about Alisa. I haven't seen her much. Funny that when I break up with Courtney, I see Alisa less now.

I'm sitting in my room checking my email, and I see one from Sarah. I can't remember the last time she emailed me.

Hi Ben

How are you? Tampa is hot, but it's actually kinda nice. Damon worked something out and is able to come down here. The reason I'm emailing you, as awkward as this is, I've tried to call Alisa, but I get no answer. Diane tells me she's busy studying or working, and that she's grounded. Normally, I wouldn't ask this, because Alisa is private, but if you really meant what you said about wanting to be her friend again, now is the time. She needs a friend. She needs you more than she thinks. I'm worried about her and I need you to check on her. She always says she's fine, but you have to learn to read between the lines. Just like you. You both haven't really changed. I can still tell when you're lying or holding back. Also, you are so much better than Courtney and you deserve better. Life is short, Ben. Do what makes YOU happy. Not anyone else. Promise me you will take care of Alisa.

Write back.

Sarah

That's probably the weirdest email I've ever read, especially from Sarah. She's really worried about Alisa, and it's almost like she's trying to tell me something but won't. Or can't. She knows something. Does Sarah know about my mom? I lean back in my chair, staring at the email.

As I open an email to reply, an instant message pops up on my screen from ravengirl97. It's Sarah.

ravengirl97: hey

basketball_guy24: hey

ravengirl97: have you read my email yet?

basketball_guy24: yeah. what was all that about?

ravengirl97: just worried bout Alisa. i haven't talked to her since i left

basketball_guy24: neither hav i. i haven't seen her much at school eithr

ravengirl97: i thought u were gonna be her friend

Damn. She acts like Alisa can't take care of herself.

basketball_guy24: i am. she's been avoiding me.

Or maybe I've been avoiding her.

ravengirl97: :/

basketball_guy24: i'll call her tonight.

ravengirl97: sorry. i just worry about her and i miss her

basketball_guy24: is there something going on with her that i should know?

There's a long pause, and it worries me even more.

ravengirl97: i know you both like each other. just remember who u really are, ben. she needs u and u need her.

As I read her words over and over, my pulse quickens. It's almost like it's okay to give in to my feelings. But is it, really? She types Alisa's number, and I'm nervous.

basketball_guy24: i'll call her. I broke up with Courtney.

ravengirl97: what!! For good?

basketball_guy24: yes

ravengirl97: good for you!

We chat a little bit longer. She tells me more about Tampa and all the alligators she's seen. How the weather is good to her, and that there are no reminders of her mom or dad. She misses her mom a lot. It's hard to believe that both my best friends have lost their moms, and at such early ages. It's weird Alisa hasn't reached out to Sarah or taken her call. Or that even if she's grounded, her dad or Diane could let her talk to Sarah given the circumstances.

I miss Alisa. I constantly crave to talk to her. To touch her. To be near her. My eyes shift to the phone. I want to call. It's an itch that I need to scratch. I want to know if she's okay. I would stop by, but I'm not sure how that would go. Especially if her dad is there. I pick up the receiver and dial her number.

"Hello?" she answers, tiredly.

"Hey, it's me, Ben."

"Hi."

There's complete silence between us. I hate this awkwardness. "Is it okay that I called?"

She clears her throat. "Yeah. My dad's at work."

"How have you been?"

"Okay, I guess. I miss Sarah."

"I know. Me too. She sent me an IM and wants you to call her."

"She talked to you?" Her voice sounds hurt.

"She said she's been trying to call." I give her Sarah's number. "Look, what you said the day of the funeral, you're wrong. I want to hang out with you. You aren't going to ruin my reputation. Either way, I don't care." I want to tell her so much that I want to be with her, but I'm scared.

She's silent. I hate the phone. I need to see her face. "Do you want to hang out tonight?" I blurt.

"I-I can't. I-I have to stay here. I have a lot of homework to do."

"Maybe we could study together." Not that there would be any studying going on.

"I can't. I'm so sorry," she whispers.

Something's not right. I hear the sadness in her voice. Sarah's email comes to mind. What is going on? Is it because Sarah left? "Are you okay?"

"I'm fine."

No, you're not. "Are you sure?"

She clears her throat again. "Yeah. Homework is frustrating."

"Do you need help?"

"It's okay."

"Can I take you to lunch tomorrow?"

"Oh. Um…I don't have any money." She always has an excuse.

"It's okay, it's my treat."

"I can't go. I'm grounded."

"Grounded? Why?"

"I…talked back and didn't listen to my dad."

"Ah. Yeah, I tend to do that as well. How long are you grounded?"

"Um…I don't know."

"I'm sorry. That sucks. Are you allowed to be on the phone? I don't want to get you into trouble."

"No, but it's okay. I like talking to you."

Her words create a warmth around me. "I like talking to you. I've missed it a lot. Do you have plans for your birthday yet?"

"No."

"Well, we'll celebrate. I'll see if Sarah can come back for the weekend."

"Really?" Her voice edges up a notch, and it makes me happy knowing I made her happy.

"Yeah. Of course."

"Why are you so nice to me?" I don't miss the shakiness in her voice.

She asks this a lot, and I know because of how I treated her before, she's wary around me. The internal storm that's been brewing inside me isn't an excuse for the way I treated her, and I will never forgive myself for hurting her. "Because I like you. I was wrong in how I treated you."

"Aren't you afraid to be seen with me in public?"

"No, I'm not," I say firmly. "I'd be a proud man to have you by my side. If people say shit, let them. But don't you dare believe for a second anything they say about you. You are beautiful, smart, and brave."

"No, I'm not. No one understands me, and they all want to believe rumors. I wish I could be more like you and not let it bother me."

"You are so much more than those people at school. You have to believe that."

"I-I don't know what to believe."

"I wish I could see you. I miss you."

"What? You miss me?"

"Yes. Why do you sound so surprised?"

"Ben, don't do this," she says, and I can hear the quiver in her voice. "You're not making this easy."

"Oh god, I-I didn't want to make you cry. It's so easy to tell you these things. I guess it's easy to be myself around you. Please talk to me. What's wrong?"

"I like you, too, Ben. A lot. But we-we can't…we just can't…" Her breath hitches on the other line. "I gotta go," she quickly says. "Don't call back."

And with that, the line goes dead.

alisa

Diane stands in my doorway, arms crossed, staring at me. I thought she was passed out on the couch. I hide the cordless phone behind my back, hoping she didn't see me on the phone, but I know she did.

"Alisa, you know you're grounded."

"I had to ask someone a question about a math problem."

Diane looks at me with pity. "I don't see no homework. I've been so patient with you, but you never listen to me. I don't know what else I can do to make you mind me."

"I'm sorry."

"You say that so many times that it's lost all meaning," she says, and leaves my room when Daddy's truck tires crunch over the gravel. I'm so disappointed in myself. I don't know what my problem is. I really try to do the right thing.

My heart pounds as I wait for Daddy to make his way inside the house. The way he slams his truck door and the porch door, I know he's upset.

Daddy walks inside the house, and I brace myself. I can barely make out what he and Diane are saying, but my heartbeat pounds in my ears.

He bursts through my door, flipping on the light. He pulls his belt off and whips me with it.

"Daddy!" I cry. The belt hits my arm, my legs, my back. Nothing is safe. White hot pain shoots throughout me, leaving my skin to burn and throb. I know welts are starting to form. It hurts so much; all I can do is cry.

"What the fuck is wrong with you? Making Diane do all of the chores? Pawning off your mother's jewelry? Where's the money?"

I freeze. She knew about my secret stash? Did she take it? I slowly sit up. "What money?" I have to play innocent.

My father glares at me and breathes hard. "Don't fucking play dumb. Where is the money?"

"I don't have any money. Diane pawned off the jewelry."

She gasps, covering her mouth with her hands. She stares at me in horror. "Alisa?"

Seeing the rage in his eyes, I expect the lashing across my arm. "Lying bitch! Give me the money or get the jewelry back."

"Did you hide the money?" Diane asks.

I want to hurl myself across the room and strangle her. How could she do this?

Daddy moves to the chest.

"No." I grab his arm, but he pushes me away.

He tears open the drawers, tossing everything out, not caring where it lands or what it is.

"Daddy, stop!" He can't see it.

He reaches the last drawer.

I can feel my heart ripping apart. It's all over, and I crumble into a thousand pieces when he pulls out my bag of money. Every single penny I've saved. All of the money Mom gave me.

"Where did you get all of this? Ain't no way you pawned jewelry and got this much."

Diane's jaw opens. "There must be thousands. How could you blame this on me?" Her chin quivers.

"Where did this come from, Alisa?"

"I saved it."

"Saved it? You mean to tell me you've been giving me less than your paychecks? What do you plan to do? Run away?"

"No."

He flips through the cash and shakes his head. "What were you thinking? Hiding all of this from me? Don't you know how hard I work to keep food on the table?"

"I do."

Daddy clenches his fists. "You selfish bitch. I've had it with you. You better apologize to her."

"I'm sorry. I never meant to hurt you."

"Don't you ever lie to me or blame her."

He and Diane leave me crying in the corner. Clothes, pictures, drawers are scattered all over the floor. I can't move. I lie there feeling the throbbing pain all over my body. Why would she blame me? Why does she hate me?

Because I'm trash. I'm a terrible person who only causes problems. I don't deserve to be here. Maybe I should run away. No one wants me.

There's a soft knock at my door, and seconds later, Diane enters. "Alisa?" she asks, timidly. "Are you okay?"

"I didn't pawn the jewelry."

"I think it's best that you stop lying. I don't understand why you do." A tear falls down her cheek. "I really like you, and I really want to be your mom, but it's obvious you hate me. I hope this lesson will teach you to mind me. My heart is so broken."

I never meant to hurt either of them. I shouldn't have hidden the money. Daddy took it. I have nothing left.

"Put this ointment on your skin." She hands it to me. "It'll help. Maybe from now on you'll help me with the chores around here, too."

I meet her eyes. "I do."

"I've let a lot of things go. You've been out with your friends a lot, even though you're grounded. This was the only thing left I could do. Will you mind me from now on?"

I hate you. I nod.

"Good. Now, get some rest." She leaves.

Why can't I be good? Why did I think I could go to culinary school? I should've been helping Daddy instead.

Every time I move, I wince. Staring at my body in the mirror, I see every single raised welt on my skin, red with anger.

Sleep doesn't come since it hurts too much to lie down. I don't want to go to school, but I can't stay here.

Changing clothes hurts. The welts and cuts from the belt still sting. Luckily, Daddy missed my face, and my flannel shirt and jeans cover everything. My black hair is starting to fade like my memories with Sarah. It looks awful, and I wish I could wear my hood over my head all day.

At school, one of my worst nightmares come true in chemistry. Zach isn't here today so I have to sit by myself.

Mrs. Greene asks me a question, but I don't know the answer.

"Alisa, we went over this the other day."

I feel stupid and embarrassed as heat scorches my cheeks. I want the class to be over. I can hear kids around me laughing, and I do my best to ignore them.

"See me after class," Mrs. Greene says, and a few students oooh.

Biting my lip, I walk up to Mrs. Greene's desk when class is over.

She removes her black-rimmed glasses and lets them hang around her neck. "Alisa, are you okay?"

No. "I'm fine."

She raises an eyebrow. "You don't appear to be okay. Things at home all right? School?"

I stare at the way her neck jiggles when she speaks. "Things are fine. I-I didn't get any sleep last night."

"You know we have counselors if you need to talk to any of them."

I let out a sigh. Why do people say that? Am I crazy? Diane said I have anger issues. Is that true? Do I need to talk to someone? "I'm just tired, okay?"

"Your grades haven't improved, and I know Zach helps you with notes and even tests. I recently talked to him about it. He can't help you with the tests anymore. Other teachers have mentioned your grades as well. Do you need a tutor?"

There's no point. "I'm okay. I'll get my act together. I promise."

She presses her lips together. "I hope you do. The semester is almost over, and I don't want you repeating these classes."

I nod.

Instead of going to lunch, I hide in the bathroom with my scissors. They're my only comfort. Watching the blade slide across my skin, thinking of a time that was good. Anger is the only thing on my mind. It spreads to the blade of the scissors and leaks out my arm. Some of it drips onto the bathroom floor.

When the bell rings, I jump, not knowing how long I've been in there. I clean up and walk in a daze to my next class. I hate all of it. I want it to end for good.

ben

Alisa is seventeen today. It's hard to believe. It seems like yesterday we were kids running around riding bikes and skinning our knees. I got a card for her and a little red bear. I hope it's not stupid.

When I get to school, I'm surprised the entire place isn't buzzing with the news of mine and Courtney's break up. I don't even see her at school, and a small part of me feels bad, but I have to ignore it.

As I walk down a hallway, I see Alisa on the ground, books all around her, kids laughing, but what really catches my eye is the huge welt on her stomach.

Dammit. I rush over to her. "Why don't y'all leave her alone?" I snap, and they leave. I'm so sick of this. Why do kids push her around all the time? "Are you okay?" I hand her a book.

She snatches it from me. "I'm fine."

I try helping her to her feet, but she waves my hands away. Clutching her books to her chest, she moves past me.

I follow her. "What happened?"

"Leave me alone."

I seize her arm, and she cries out. I let go. "What? What is it?"

"Nothing." She won't look at me, but the pain on her face hurts me.

Stop being so stubborn. "Alisa. What can I do?"

She shakes her head, and I can only think of one thing.

"Do you wanna get out of here?"

Finally, she looks up with tears in her eyes, and nods.

"Okay. Come on."

We reach outside and she shivers. I don't know why she only wears a hoodie when it's freezing. Maybe I should have bought her an actual coat for her birthday.

Something happened, and it wasn't just today or last night. She hasn't been the same since Sarah left, and the cryptic email I received from Sarah scares me even more.

Alisa eases into the car like a wounded dog. She winces every time she moves. I have to find out what's going on.

When I get in on the driver side, I stare at my keys, trying to find the words to say to her. "Alisa, what's going on?"

"What do you mean?"

"You aren't yourself. Sarah…told me to look out for you."

"She said that? When did you talk to her?"

"Last night. She said she's tried calling you multiple times, but Diane tells her you're grounded. Who is Diane?"

"She's my dad's girlfriend."

We're quiet for a moment.

"Why would Sarah tell you that you needed to look out for me?"

"I don't know. You tell me."

"Does she think I can't take care of myself? Is that why she and Damon hung out with me? And you?"

"No, Alisa. We're your friends. We care about you."

"You care so much that you abandon people. You care more about your image and reputation than anything else."

"Not anymore. I'm sorry for that. I really am. I know it was a dick thing to do, but I'm here now."

"Is that why you're suddenly talking to me again? Because you feel guilty?"

"No, it isn't. I wanted to wish you a happy birthday, and I saw you in the hallway. I've been wanting to talk to you since the funeral."

"But you haven't."

Damn, she's tough. "I haven't seen you much."

"It doesn't matter."

"What doesn't?"

She doesn't answer.

Damn that wall. Reaching into my backpack, I pull out her card and the bear. "Happy birthday."

"You remembered?"

"Of course." I hate that she asked that. "Do you remember my seventh birthday? We went to the park and rode the merry-go-round until we literally puked."

She lets out a soft laugh. "I'm still dizzy thinking about it."

I chuckle, loving how easy it is to fall into a conversation with Alisa, even when she's pissed at me. "Happy birthday."

She bites her lip as she stares at the bear. "Thanks," she mumbles, and just like that I've lost her. She put up her wall.

I put the key in the ignition and start the car. We drive in silence as I head nowhere in particular. I just want to be with her, even if it is in a car as she ignores me.

"The first game is Saturday night. You wanna come watch? We could hang out afterward."

"It's okay. I'm sure you'd rather be with your friends."

Only friend I want to be with is you. "Alisa…."

"Just…can you just drop me off at my mailbox?"

I don't want to. It bothers me that the last two times, she's asked me to drop her off at the damn mailbox.

We're quiet again the rest of the way and I'm trying to figure out what to say to her. I pull up to the mailbox, but I decide to drop her off at her door.

"Ben! Stop!" she cries. The stark fear in her eyes forces me to hit the brakes. "Just drop me off here."

"Are you that repulsed by me that you won't even let me drop you off at your house?"

"No." She looks nervous and refuses to look at me. "I gotta go." She opens the door and my heart races. I have to say something.

"I like you, Alisa. A lot. I've been too scared to say anything, but that's the biggest reason why I left Courtney. Because I want to be with you. I've always wanted to be with you."

Alisa halts, and slowly turns around. Her big, brown eyes meet mine. "What?"

"It's true."

She settles back in her seat, shock written all over her face, then she shakes her head. "You don't like me. You can't."

"Why?"

"This is some twisted bet, isn't it?"

"No, it's not." Why won't she believe me? I know my previous stunts don't earn me a lot of trust, but she's so quick to disbelieve everything I say. "Please come Saturday. We can talk afterward. I promise this isn't a joke at all."

"I'll think about it."

That's all I can hope for at this point. I know I won't play my best if I don't see her in the stands. She gets out of the car and closes the door. I wait until she reaches her house, then I drive off. I don't know why she won't let me drop her off closer to the door, but maybe this weekend we can talk.

Alisa is such a mystery, but I will do anything I can to win her heart, or her friendship.

alisa

Saturday morning, I wake, butterflies flying around in my stomach. It's so bad I have to take deep breaths to calm down. I haven't decided if I'm going to the game tonight to watch Ben. I know I shouldn't because I'm grounded. But I want to. Just for once, I want to know what it feels like to be a normal high school kid. To go to a game and cheer on my school. To laugh and cut up with friends. I know if I go, I'll be by myself. It makes me miss Sarah and Damon even more.

Work is crazy busy since the news mentioned an ice storm. I must have scanned a thousand milk jugs and loaves of bread. All day I contemplate going to the game. Daddy will probably be out late with Diane. Maybe I can leave a note at home letting them know I'm working. I just have to pray that they don't show up here. I feel awful facing Diane now. I hate how I've treated her, and I hate how Daddy found out about the money.

Since my car died, I've been walking to and from work. I take the bus to school though. Once my shift ends, I leave the store and take my time walking. When I don't see Daddy's truck, I relax.

It's cold and overcast. Colder than it's been in a long time. My fingers and toes are numb by the time I reach the inside of the house. My skin is dry and cracked and I long to find gloves. After changing clothes, I brave the cold once more and head to school. I wish I had a car, but I can make it.

Once I reach the school, I envelope myself in the warmth. There's an excitement in the air and I can't help but feel caught up in it. Students shout, talk loudly, as they head toward the gym. Once I reach the gym, I freeze. The bleachers are packed with people wearing blue and gold. I never realized how many people came to these games. I don't know where to sit and as I search the seats, I pray I can find one. I swallow hard. I can do this. Ben wants me here. Taking a deep breath, I climb the stairs hoping to find an empty space somewhere in the crowd.

I see a girl in one of my classes who's nice to me, at least the two times we've spoken. I slide in next to her and she smiles.

"Hi," she says.

"Hi."

"You're Alisa, right?"

"Yeah."

"I'm Brianna. Did you come alone?"

It must be that obvious. "Yes."

"Oh. Well you can sit with us."

"Thanks."

The lights in the gym go down and everyone gets to their feet in applause. Music blares through the speakers as they start announcing the players. My heart dances, and I'm eager to watch Ben play. I've never done anything like this, and I want to forget all of the bad, just for one night. One night to leave it all behind.

ben

I'm pumped. There's an electrical current buzzing through my veins, and it's the best high. When they call my name, the cheers are loud. I can't wait to get this season underway. Should be an easy win, but I don't ever underestimate our opponents. Anything can happen. Best of all, Courtney isn't here, and we broke up.

When the lights are turned up, I scan the crowd, and I zero in on *her*. She came. Alisa came to the game. When she meets my eyes, her lips curl into a simple, but sexy, smile. Seeing her adds a huge boost in my confidence, and I play one of the best games of my life. My layups are spot on. I put up several points on the board, and we win 54 to 14.

After the game, I shower and change quickly, hoping to catch Alisa. I don't see her in the gym, but as I walk to my car, I see her on the sidewalk, moving in the opposite direction from me.

"Alisa," I call out. Is she seriously walking home in this freezing cold night? The weather people have been talking all week about how it's going to snow and ice starting tonight. Of course, the entire town has gone into a frenzy. Part of me is surprised anyone came to the game, but the other part of me knows nothing will stop them. It won't snow and if it does it won't stick. It never does. It was like fifty degrees yesterday.

She stops and turns. "Hey."

Catching up to her, I feel a rush of exhilaration, but the awkwardness in the air is thick and for once, I have no idea what to say. Her brown roots are showing, and I gotta admit that the black hair turned me on.

"You played a good game," she says.

It was because of you. "Thanks." I should say something, but seeing her so close to me, and knowing she watched my game, has me tongue-tied. Does this mean she likes me, too?

"Look, I just wanted to…what you said earlier…I-I miss you." Her cheeks flush, and she looks away.

Heat rises inside me. I want to kiss her, but I have to refrain. "I miss you, too."

"I know I don't fit in your world, and I shouldn't even be talking to you. I don't get what you want."

"I want to be your friend." More than that. "I shouldn't have treated you so poorly before. I was a dick and only cared about what people thought."

Something flickers in her eyes, but I can't tell what it is. Hope?

"Do you wanna get out of here?" I ask. "It's freezing. And why the hell aren't you wearing a coat?"

She looks around hesitantly and shifts, withdrawing from me. "Um. I don't party."

"We don't have to. Are you hungry? We could grab a bite."

"Okay."

Shucking off my coat, I wrap it around her. She tries to remove it, but I stop her. "Take it."

I lead the way to my car and open the passenger door for her. She slides in causing my pulse to race. I know my parents will never approve of us dating. But I don't care what happened in the past. That's on them.

Getting in the car, I toss my bag in the backseat. She shivers, and I start the car, cranking up the heat.

"What do you have a taste for?"

"It doesn't matter."

"Let's celebrate the win. What's your favorite type of food?"

"Greek," she says. I half expected her to shrug and tell me she didn't know. "I had it once with my mom. I had this grilled chicken in a pita. It had lettuce and tomatoes. Sounds simple, but the way they seasoned the chicken was delicious."

I chuckle a little. "You know food."

A beautiful pink color reaches her cheeks, but I can see a slither of a smile on her lips. "I like to cook. I've never been able to make that chicken though."

"Why?"

She's quiet for a minute. "I just haven't. What's your favorite food?"

I shrug. "I like Mexican. Italian. Never had Greek before. The only thing that's open this late is fast food. Or we could cook some Greek?"

"Um." She pulls her sleeves over her hands.

"I bet you're a great cook. I'll even help. My parents are out of town, and Hayden's at a friend's house." I don't want to sound desperate but seeing that smile makes me think that maybe if she's in her comfort zone, she'll smile more. And I want to be the one who makes Alisa smile.

"Okay."

Finally. A win.

alisa

When we get to Ben's house, it's quiet. Warm. The giant brick house is empty, and like the first time I came back to the place, its beauty and size take my breath away. I forgot how big it was. Hardwood floors throughout. The doorways are all arched. The ceilings are vaulted. I'm certain my entire house will fit in their living room and kitchen. The enormous kitchen has black granite countertops and wooden cabinets. There's an island big enough for four stools.

When I was here last, we sat in the living room on the white sectional sofa that took over two walls.

"I'll take your coat."

I shuck off his jacket and hand it to him. I hate how he gives up his coat every time he sees me, but I'm grateful because the cold is almost paralyzing. One day I'll be able to get a coat.

Being around Ben makes me comfortable, like being with Sarah, but more. I'm not afraid of him, and he's warm. I know I'm not good enough for him. I'm definitely not beautiful like Courtney, and there's nothing special about me.

Ben unloads the ingredients he bought at the store and shows me where everything is around the kitchen. I gasp when I see a cupboard full of herbs and spices. To be able to afford so many. I shake my head as if trying to remove the surge of jealousy. Taking a breath, I reach for oregano, garlic, rosemary, thyme, and lemon juice and pull them out of the cabinet. My veins pulse as excitement runs throughout me. This is what I want to do. Cook for people.

An ache slices through me because I know it will never happen now. Taking Sarah up on her offer to come to Tampa flashes through my mind, but I haven't spoken to her since she left. And there's no way I can leave. I need to call her.

Grabbing the chicken, I take it out of the Styrofoam and rinse it. I look up and see a cutting board. It's like everything I need is here. There is no improvising in this kitchen, and while it feels weird, it feels great.

"What can I do?" Ben asks, and I almost forgot he's standing next to me.

"Oh. Um. Does Hayden or your mom have any hair ties?"

"Yeah."

When he leaves, I place the chicken on the cutting board and start cutting it into strips. The knife easily glides across the chicken as if I'm cutting soft butter. I could cook forever in this kitchen.

Ben returns, and as I go to wash my hands, he stops me. "I got it."

He gently gathers my hair, and my body stills as his fingers graze the nape of my neck sending an unusual chill down my spine. His fingers through my hair make my heart somersault, and I can't breathe. I grip the knife to contain myself. He's so tender as he gathers my hair into a ponytail, and each time his fingers touch my skin, it feels like fire. No one's ever touched me like this, and I don't know what to think. When he's finished, I clear my throat and resume cutting, although my hands are shaky.

"I'll put on some music," he says. "What do you wanna hear?"

I shrug. "It doesn't matter."

"You're not into the Spice Girls or anything like that, are you?" He raises an eyebrow.

"No. I like Tori Amos, Bjork, Better Than Ezra. Stuff like that."

"Ah. Tori's cool. I may have her CD around here somewhere."

"It's okay. Radio is fine."

He nods and turns on the radio that's attached to the underside of the cabinets. A slow tempo song plays through the speaker. A deep voice sings about one headlight. I like the sound a lot. It feels rather nostalgic and sad.

"Want me to cut the vegetables? I'm no expert, like you appear to be, but I can try."

When I look up, our eyes meet. I can't tell what he's thinking, but his heavy gaze forces me to look away. My cheeks fill with blood. "Um. Okay."

After a few seconds of us cutting, he sighs. "This is awful."

"What?" I look over and see his cutting job. The vegetables aren't perfect, but they'll still taste the same. I can't help but crack a smile.

"It's that bad, huh?"

"No. It…it's fine."

"You are such a liar!" He laughs.

I can feel the smile on my face, and it feels good. It's been a long time since I've felt like this: happy and content. It feels nice, but I know it won't last long. I'll mess it up inevitably, like I do everything else.

I mix the ingredients as the radio continues to play songs. I love music, but I never get to listen to it since we don't have a radio at home. My mom always sang along when we were in the car. The Eagles were her favorite band, and in seventh grade I became obsessed with them. I remember one night I caught my mom and Daddy dancing in the kitchen to "Peaceful Easy Feeling," and I thought I want a love like that. That seems so long ago.

Ben sets the island with plates, forks, napkins, and drink glasses. I can't remember the last time I ate at a table or something with a surface. He pulls out a stool for me, and I climb into it as he sits next to me.

I'm so hungry, and it smells good. Hopefully, Ben likes it.

I'm nervous as he bites into the chicken. "Wow. This is really good. Where'd you learn how to cook?"

I shrug. "I watched my mom. I kinda just play around with ingredients, but I haven't in so long."

"How come?"

"No time," I lie as I take a bite of the chicken and rice. The warm and savory flavors swim in my mouth, and I want more.

"That's a shame. It makes you happy."

"How do you know?"

"Because the first time you stepped foot in the kitchen, your face lit. When you started cutting vegetables and throwing in all the spices, you were like a kid opening birthday presents. It was cute."

Heat rushes to my cheeks. I don't know why he's being so nice to me, but it's probably a prank. I can't let myself fall in the trap, but it feels good to be treated so nicely for once. Whatever happens, I'll deal with the repercussions later.

"You could work in a restaurant. Work your way up. All the way to chef."

But all the restaurants I applied to before didn't want me.

He squeezes my hand, jolting my heart into overdrive, and he smiles at me. Biting my lip, I slide my hand into my lap.

"Let's watch a movie."

"Oh. Um, I should go."

"Please don't. Not yet."

"Why? Why are you being so nice to me? What's in it for you?"

"You're my friend, and I want to spend time with you."

"Is that what Sarah told you? That I need to be babysat 24/7?"

"No! I just…I want to spend time with you. Why is that so hard for you to believe?"

"Because no one wants to hang out with me except Sarah and Damon. What else did she say to you?"

"She didn't. She was very cryptic. Is there something I need to know?"

"No," I say, my tone harder than I mean, and my cheeks turn red.

"Don't shut yourself off. I won't force it, but I am here for you."

"Until Courtney returns."

Ben sighs. "No. She and I are done. I want to be with you, Alisa."

"Why now?" I ask, ignoring the hammering in my chest. He's saying everything I've wished he would say, but I have a hard time believing it.

"Because I'm finally doing something that I want. Not what my parents want or anyone else. And because seeing you every day and not being able to talk to you or touch you has been driving me insane for months. I've always liked you more than a friend. When you left, it crushed me. Yeah, I got busy with basketball and other things, but really it was a way to keep my mind off you. They were all distractions. Now that you're here, I don't want to let a second chance pass by. I missed you."

"Maybe you miss the idea of who you think I used to be, but I'm not the same person, Ben."

"I know you're not. Neither am I, but that's the point. I like who you are now. I liked who you were then."

"You don't know who I am," I whisper. I don't understand him. How can he possibly like a shell of a person? I'm nothing.

He moves closer, sending his winter scent my way. "You're not far from the girl six years ago. She's in there somewhere. You've been through a lot, which would change anyone. But you're brave. Smart. Caring. You still love music and cooking, and I'm learning new things about you. I want to learn more."

We sit in silence for a little longer, and I'm unsure of what to say or do. Glancing at the clock on the stove, I see that I have two hours before I have to be at home. I don't want to go home though. Being here with Ben is safe, warm, and comfortable. But it's supposed to snow, and I should get home before it starts.

"Let's watch a movie," he says.

I nod, not wanting to think or talk anymore, but I need to piece together my thoughts. My mind is boggled with all these feelings. I've always liked Ben, but once he sees what a horrible person I am, he'll leave. I push the thoughts away, hoping that he won't. But these thoughts overwhelm my mind, threatening to pull me deeper into an abyss.

As we watch the movie, sweat gathers in my palms by being this close to him on a couch. In the dark. Thankfully, he can't see my blushing face, or hear my thoughts.

Ben slides his hand in mine, and I freeze. I know he wants more, but I can't give him what he wants. I'm not good enough for him.

But I also know Daddy will never allow this to happen.

ben

Alisa sits next to me, our hands are touching, but her body is rigid. The last thing I want to do is make her uncomfortable or move too fast. I want to know what happened to her. She says she's never been with anyone, but something happened when she was gone during those years. Did she find out about our parents?

Whatever it is, I can wait until she's ready. Sitting here with her is good enough. As we continue watching the movie and holding hands, she loosens her guard a bit, and soon she rests her head on my shoulder. I swear it makes my insides burn. All I've wanted is this girl. I was never drawn to anyone like I am to Alisa. Even after she left, I imagined what it'd be like to be with her. Every fight with Courtney led to those thoughts and how Alisa would handle certain situations.

This girl next to me is broken, and maybe I can help put her back together. I will do anything for her. She was always there for me, and I never forgot that.

Throughout the movie, Alisa ends up lying on a pillow in my lap and I stroke her hair. When the movie ends, she's sound asleep. I don't want to wake her, but it's late, nearing her curfew.

"Alisa." I gently shake her, and she moans. "It's time to go home." I can't help but notice she becomes rigid again at the mention of home.

"I wish I could stay," she whispers so softly. She sits up and rubs her eyes. It's a simple, innocent movement, but it's sexy as hell. "I'm sorry I fell asleep."

I smile. "It's okay." I cringe at my next words. "Come on. Let's get you home."

Alisa nods and bites her lip. I get up and walk to the coat closet, pulling out one of Hayden's bazillion coats. She's twelve and oddly about the same size as Alisa.

When I come back into the dark living room, Alisa is standing in front of one of the windows, watching snow coming down. I see that it's covered the street.

"Wow," I say, completely shocked. It doesn't snow often in Alabama, but when it does it's like some beautiful magical occurrence. A rare beauty. And no one really thinks it's going to be as bad as it ends up being, so the entire state freaks out.

"It snowed a lot in Kentucky," she says, completely somewhere else. "Mom and I would watch it all day."

I come up behind her and take her hand. I love the softness of her skin and the way she grips my hand like she never wants to let go.

I need to know how she feels, yet I don't want to ruin this moment.

It looks like already two feet of snow has piled up on the ground. I can't remember the last time it snowed in Alabama.

"Remember when we were five and it snowed on Christmas? Your mom wouldn't let you come out and play so Sarah and I went to your house to play in your backyard."

Damn. I can't believe I forgot about that. Mom was scared I'd get sick, which is exactly what happened. The next day Alisa brought some chicken noodle soup her mom made. How did I forget about that?

"Yeah," I say.

"Your mom's not here."

"What?"

Before I catch on, Alisa is out the door, without a freaking coat on. When I catch up to her, she plows a snowball in my chest. Then I hear the sweetest sound. Alisa's laughter. Grabbing as much snow as I can in my hand, not caring how damn cold it is, I launch it at her, but she runs away. We play like that for I don't know how long. Until our hair is wet, and we're out of breath. I can't remember the last time I was this happy and carefree. I want it to last forever.

alisa

Snow falls constantly as Ben and I run around his massive front yard. We're both covered in snow, having too much fun to care about how cold it is. Ben throws snow at me. As I dart to avoid it, I slip and fall. It hurt, but I laugh so hard it hurts my stomach. He comes up to me, holding out his hand as he laughs.

I love his laugh. It's heartwarming and real. One that makes my stomach tickle. I take his hand, and he pulls me up to my feet. As I look at him, his eyes change. There's something deep and majestic about them. The way he looks at me makes heat rise to my cheeks. When he reaches up, I flinch. He carefully touches my cheek. His fingers are cold, but they leave a trail of fire down to my neck.

He leans down, slowly. I close my eyes, holding my breath. When our lips touch, it's magical and romantic and more than I ever hoped it would be. Sparks ignite inside me as he cradles my head in his hands. Ben Lamar is kissing me. My entire body is zooming with pleasure. Pleasure I've never felt in my entire life. Warmth envelopes me in places I never expected. He holds me so close to him. Even in the cold, his body warms me. I'm so in love with Ben. I never thought this would happen.

His lips are warm and gentle. I feel a rush all through me. It is incredible. I never thought there could be another high, but I am hooked.

Ben draws back for a moment; the rush still tingling inside me. My heart thumps so loud that I'm sure he can hear it. Pressing his lips to mine once again, that high hits me like a jolt to the heart, awakening me. I feel like I'm floating as he holds me tightly against his body, like he never wants to release me. I never imagined someone could be so tender with me. He cradles my face with his hands, and I slowly reach around him, touching his back. I feel faint for a moment, and I need air. It's too much.

"I've wanted to do that for so long." He rests his forehead against mine, breathless.

"Ben." I don't know what to say. I feel the butterflies multiplying, and my head is spinning.

He tips my chin up and gazes into my eyes. "Let's go inside." The fire in his eyes forces me to look away, then reality sets in. I'm still at Ben's, past curfew. The roads are too dangerous to drive on. We kissed, but we can't do this. The cold rushes over me, and I hug myself to keep from shaking.

Ben takes me inside the warm house and wraps a blanket around me. His hands rub my arms. "Want me to start a fire?"

"I have to get home."

"Maybe we can call your dad and let him know you're safe and—"

"No, I have to go. I'll just walk." I start for the door, but he pulls me back.

"You can't walk out there in this. I'm sure your dad didn't drive home in this. Just…hold on." He leaves the room for a minute and when he returns, he has a worried look on his face.

"What? What is it?"

"The phone lines are down."

The roads are too treacherous to travel. I have to get home…somehow. It's too far to walk without getting sick or something more severe happening.

Why did I think I could have fun?

Daddy will kill me. I don't know what to do. I can't breathe. I try taking breaths, but nothing fills my lungs. It's hot and I can feel sweat gathering at my hairline and the base of my neck. I'm going to pass out.

"Alisa!" Ben yells, causing me to face him. "It's okay."

Placing his hands on my shoulders, he instructs me to breathe. After a few minutes, he helps me to the couch. I feel so drained and sleepy.

Ben leaves and returns quickly with a cold rag, pressing it to my forehead. "Are you okay?"

I nod, feeling embarrassed. I don't know why it happens to me, but I hate it. I hate feeling like I'm going to die.

"I promise we'll get you home tomorrow morning. I'll explain to your dad—"

"No, it's okay. I'll tell him what happened."

"Are you sure? You said earlier you wanted to stay."

"I do. But…I can't."

"It's okay. I'm positive your dad cares more about your safety than a curfew. We'll try the phones first thing in the morning. If it doesn't work, I'll walk you."

There isn't much to do at this point. Maybe I can sneak out when Ben falls asleep. Maybe Diane will be there to cushion the blow. "Okay." I want nothing more than to be asleep on Ben's shoulder again, and I shouldn't want that because he's better than me. And I'm not allowed to have a boyfriend.

"Let's watch another movie."

"Okay."

It isn't until a few minutes into the movie that I begin to relax. I love being here with Ben. It feels real. Panic captures me as I think of tomorrow for ways to explain to Daddy why I wasn't home. Why I didn't cook dinner. Or wash clothes. I don't know what I'm going to tell him. For now, I just want to enjoy this night with Ben. Even if it's the last night we'll have together.

ben

Alisa had a panic attack. Does she know what's happening? And why is her dad so strict to cause such panic? Does he know she's been talking to me? Does Alisa know about Mom and her dad?

She's curled into a ball on the couch, her head is on a pillow in my lap, and even though my legs are asleep, the last thing I want to do is wake her. As I grab the blanket from the back of the couch, she shifts, and her flannel shirt exposes part of her stomach. I would give anything to touch her, but in the faint early morning light, I begin to see red lines across her flesh. At first, I think it's just pen lines, but as I focus more and adjust to the dim dawn light, I realize they're cuts. Deep, angry, red cuts.

My pulse quickens. I don't know what happened, but it looks awful. My hands itch to explore her skin because she's beautiful, but also to see what the marks are. What happened? Did a cat maul her? It looks painful. I can't look further.

Instead, I bring the blanket over her. I lean my head back and close my eyes, wanting this to last forever.

But I can't sleep because I'm too wired having this beautiful girl sleep in my lap. And the cuts on her stomach now consume my head. What are they?

In the morning after bundling Alisa up in a coat, scarf, and gloves, I take her hand and we head to her house. She was very insistent on going home, but the roads are still icy, so I agreed to walk her. The sky is dark, like it's about to storm again. Even though I'm glad to be holding her hand, I wish the gloves weren't in the way. I want so much to ask her about the marks on her stomach, but I don't know how to broach the subject. It's probably nothing, but it didn't look like nothing.

"It's beautiful out here," I say in an attempt to comfort her or distract her from whatever she's about to face. I always knew her dad was strict, but it seems to be worse now. She looks like at any second, she'll faint. Something doesn't sit well with me. Is this what Sarah was talking about?

"Yeah, it is." She grips my hand the closer we reach her house.

I can't take it any longer. "Alisa, are you okay?"

"I'm fine. When we get to my mailbox, you can head back."

She's so quick to get rid of me. My first instinct is to be offended, but I push it away. "Why don't we spend the day with each other?"

"I can't."

Of course, she can't. Once her house comes into view from the road, Alisa immediately relaxes. I'm not sure why.

"I hope my dad's okay."

She allows me to walk with her to the house. When we reach her door, she turns to me. "I had a good time. Thank you."

"You're welcome." I know she's trying to get rid of me, but I can't just leave her here by herself in the middle of a snowstorm. There doesn't seem to be anyone else here. What kind of person would I be to just leave? "You know I can't leave you alone, right?"

She starts removing the gloves, but I stop her. "Alisa, you can take them off inside where it's warm."

Biting her lip, she nods. It's like she's ashamed of her house or something.

"I hope my dad called," she says as we enter the house. It's a small farmhouse, a little cozy, except it's freezing.

"Is the power out?"

"I don't think so." She moves toward the answering machine and presses play.

"Alisa. I got stuck, and I'm staying with Diane. Make sure the house is spotless. I don't know when I'll be home."

That was his message. He didn't even ask that she call or say I love you. A little weird, but maybe that's their relationship. God knows my relationship with my parents is messed up.

Alisa continues staring at the answering machine, her fists clenched. She takes a deep breath. I touch her shoulders and she jumps.

"Sorry. What's wrong?"

"Nothing." Her eyes say something else. Anger? Fear?

"What is it?"

"It's nothing."

I wish she wouldn't shut me out. "Why don't you pack an overnight bag and stay at my house?"

"I can't. I have to be here. I have to clean."

Clean what? I scan the room. "Alisa, this house is spotless. Come on. You don't need to be alone in this. It's cold and snowy."

"I'll be fine."

"Then I'll stay here. I can help you clean."

Her eyes widen. "No. If Daddy sees you, I'll get in trouble."

"He won't. I can hide or sneak out. It'll be okay." I don't want to push the issue, but I don't want to leave her alone in such a cold house.

"Ben, you can't. Okay? I don't want anything to happen to you."

"Why would something happen to me?"

Alisa bites her lip and fidgets. I move closer, but she recoils. I hate it when she does that. She acts like a wounded animal. "You should go. I'll be fine."

No, you're not. "Why isn't the heat on?"

"Because we turn the heaters off when we're not here. Fire hazard."

Lie. "Do you have enough food? I can go to the store. I don't know how long this storm is going to last. We could—"

"I'll be fine, okay?" she snaps. "I don't need a babysitter."

Fuck. I crossed a line. "That's not what I meant. I just meant…we could cook again. Like last night."

"It was fun, but you can't keep paying for things." In a haste, she starts removing the gloves, scarf, and coat, throwing them at me. "I don't need your charity."

"Alisa, stop!" I shout, dropping the clothes. I take a step closer to her, scared I'm going to do or say something wrong. No matter what though…"I love you. I want to take care of you. That's all. I'm not babysitting you or anything." I take her head in my hands, gazing into her eyes. When they soften, I lean down, pressing my lips to hers. I will never tire of how soft her lips are or the way my body shudders when our mouths meet. Tangling my hand in her hair, I pull her closer, and she moans. Heat pours over me as she ends up against the wall. She makes me crazy when her hands roam around my back. My hands slip to her stomach, my thumb barely grazing her skin. Her breath hitches, but as my thumb moves higher, she pushes me away.

I accidentally let out a sigh, and I know it hurts her. But that isn't why I sighed. I'm not frustrated she won't sleep with me, just hate it when she shuts down so quickly.

"You should go, Ben."

I'm striking out left and right. "I'm sorry. I wish you wouldn't push me away all the time."

Alisa sighs and crosses her arms in front of her. She has such a tough wall. "I have so many demons, Ben. I'm not… good enough for you. I'm not the right person for you."

"What?" I tip her chin up, coaxing her to look at me. "You are more than good enough. If anything, I'm the one who doesn't deserve you. I haven't been good to you."

"I don't know how to do this."

"What? Kiss?"

"All of it."

"It's okay. We can take our time. You are definitely worth waiting for, Alisa. If you'd rather we not kiss, I can refrain."

She bites her lip again. "I've never felt this way before. I don't know how to handle it.

"Do you like me?"

A blush creeps up her cheeks. For a moment, it looks as if she may cry, but she meets my eyes with an intense gaze. "Yes, I do. I've always liked you."

"Do you want to be with me? I mean, I don't want to put myself out there for no reason. I'll understand. You're all I've thought of for several years."

"Ben…" She hesitates. Suddenly my heart slams into my stomach, and I don't feel on top of the world anymore.

"It's a simple question," I say, trying to ignore the twisting agony inside my stomach.

"I'm not allowed to have a boyfriend."

That brings me up short. A boyfriend? Or not allowed to be with me? "What? Why?"

"Ben, it's something my dad told me. It's complicated."

Fuck. Complicated. He knows. I don't know too many girls who aren't allowed to date, so I can guess he knows she's been talking to me. Maybe I can talk to her dad. Tell him that what happened with him and Mom has nothing to do with us. Will he even listen? Usually, I would talk to my dad for advice, but given the situation, and the fact that they're preoccupied with themselves, that won't help.

The weight of everything forces me to sit on the couch with my head in my hands. I feel the seat dip next to me.

"I'm sorry," she says, her voice a whisper.

I shake my head and face her. "Alisa, you have nothing to be sorry for. I'm sorry." Why are our parents so against us being together? Why do they let their mistakes dictate our lives? I love this girl, but love isn't enough to convince adults that it's real, especially at our ages.

alisa

Ben and I sit on the couch in my cold home, miserable, and in love. Maybe we can make this work. We'd have to tread lightly. I want it to, and I hate making him sad.

"My parents won't let me see you either."

"What?" I ask. It's because of what I am. Poor. Not good enough for Ben.

He clears his throat. "Alisa…my mom told me something."

She knows about Daddy's drinking. I'm a girl from the wrong side.

Ben shakes his leg and clenches and unclenches his hands. "I don't even know how to say this."

I'm scared. "Just…say it."

He takes a deep breath and exhales. "She told me that she and your dad had an affair months before y'all left."

My stomach drops. *What?*

"She said that was the reason y'all left."

I shake my head. "No." Daddy would never do that. He loved Mom. She's always been his world. Is that really why we left? No. It was because of his drinking. He went to rehab as soon as we got to Kentucky.

"Alisa, please say something."

I can't. I don't know what to say. My mouth refuses to work. Why would Mom stay with him? Why would she ask me to promise that I would take care of him? Because this never happened. Ben's mom made up the whole thing.

"She's lying."

"What?"

"She has to be lying. That's not why we left. Daddy had a drinking problem. We left so we could be closer to Mom's family. He went to rehab. My dad would never cheat on my mom."

"I know it isn't easy. I found out a few days ago."

He believes it? How can it be so easy for him to believe his mom would do something like that?

"Alisa, I don't care what happened between our parents. I don't care if it's true or not. I'm not saying you should follow suit, but I'm just…I'm tired of doing everything they say and them telling me how I should live my life. Why can't I be with the one I want? I don't deserve you, but I will do whatever it takes to be someone who deserves you. You make me happy. You don't stress me out. You make me feel worthy, and I love spending time with you."

His confessions are unexpected, and I don't know how to react. I take his hand, loving how warm it is. I wish I could turn on the heat. I know we should go back to his house, but I'm scared. "I…I want to be with you, too."

His mouth is on mine, slow, and yet yearning. I love how gentle he is. He keeps holding my hand as he kisses me. I've never felt this way, and I feel *good*. It's a high like I've never known. It's different, and my body warms as his hand skims down my arm to my stomach. I'm on fire, and I don't want to stop kissing him.

When he pulls away, I feel the heat rising to my cheeks.

Ben gives a small laugh. "I love that."

I bite my lip and avoid his gaze. I can't believe I'm in Ben's arms and he kissed me. Again. I know it's just a fantasy though. It won't last. He'll soon realize I'm not worth his time and that I'm nothing.

"What is it?"

Our eyes lock. "What?"

"You look sad. I hate seeing you that way."

"Oh." I pull my hands away.

"What is it? Please don't hide from me."

Heavy tapping on the roof starts. A loud thunder erupts causing me to almost jump out of my skin. I hate storms, and all I remember from every storm I've been through was that my mom held me each time. She always told me that no matter what she would always be there for me and that she wouldn't leave me alone. She always said I never had to be afraid because Daddy only does it to teach her a lesson, and that he would never hurt me. But he does. And it's her fault she left me. She didn't have to leave. She could've stayed and helped me with Daddy. But now he's with someone else who doesn't like me anymore. I'm not worth being loved. Everyone has abandoned me because I'm a mess. I make mistakes, and I'm not good enough. I'm worthless and a waste of space. I am a mistake.

"Alisa," Ben says, touching my cheek. "Why are you crying?"

I touch my cheek, unaware of the wetness. I don't cry. Only babies cry. I wipe the tears away and look away.

"Talk to me, please."

I shake my head.

He squeezes my hand. "When you're ready, you know I'm here for you."

I nod.

He intertwines his fingers with mine and kisses my forehead. I can't tell him. Daddy would hurt me, and I don't want him to leave me. I don't want Ben to leave either, but I know that's what he'll do. Maybe I can keep the fantasy going long enough so I'll have something to remember when he leaves.

"I always hated storms," he says. "You'd always comfort me, though. Do you remember coming to my house a few times?"

I can't believe I forgot that, but he doesn't realize that I was running away from home because my parents were fighting. I hated being around it. "Yes."

"You have always been a comfort to me. Whenever I fight with my parents, or Courtney, I always think of you, and it makes me feel better. Because I know you'd never treat me like that. I really want this to work."

I let his words sink in. "How?"

"I don't know, but we'll make it work."

"Ben, do you really believe what your mom said?"

He squeezes my hand and frowns. "I don't know. She's been cheating on my dad for several months now. I don't even know if she's ended it yet."

My heart falls. "Ben. I-I'm so sorry. I had no idea."

"No one does. I've not said a word to anyone about it. She wants a divorce."

I pull him into my arms, hoping I can bring comfort or something. After a few moments, I hear him sniffling, and my heart breaks for him. Sarah was right. Everyone's families are messed up. I want to make it all better for him, but I don't know how.

ben

Alisa holds me as I let out all the building emotion and stress. I can't remember the last time I cried, and it's embarrassing. But she's comforting. No matter how many miles I ran, or basketballs I've bounced, or songs I've listened to, none of it came close to making me feel better like she has.

I finally kissed Alisa. There's this crazy invigorating sensation charging through my veins. This has never happened before. Kissing her was amazing, and I want to kiss her again.

But she started tearing up and I don't know why. She was so open to me, and then she shut down. Or maybe she's still thinking about her parents. Then I broke down.

I don't know what to say to her, but I hate seeing the sadness in her eyes. I know it hasn't been a good year losing her mom and starting back at her old school. And I didn't make it any better when I acted like an ass. I just didn't see what was important at the time. Now I do. This girl sitting next to me has always had my heart. She always helped me when I had a bad day. She was always my rock.

Now that she's back in my life, I can't help but think she's going to say goodbye again. I know I can't handle it if she leaves me.

I squeeze her small hand in mine as we sit on a dingy, sunken couch in her living room. The house is freezing, and we can't go anywhere because the storm has worsened.

"Where's the restroom?" I ask her.

"Oh. You should use the one in my room. I can't let my dad know anyone was here."

I nod. "I've never seen your bedroom before." As I head down the hall, I open the door and look around. It's a plain room. Nothing is on the walls. No picture frames. There's a broken jewelry box on her dresser and there's barely anything in it. Maybe she hasn't had time to decorate since moving. I head into the bathroom and see scissors on the counter with spots of dried blood.

When I get out, I see her sitting on the edge of her bed. "It's getting worse out there."

"I'm not going anywhere, if that's what you're worried about. Let's go cook something."

She takes my hand, and we head to the kitchen. "Um, we've not gone grocery shopping yet. I need to work more."

"More? You work all the time." Are they struggling so much they can't afford heat? Food? It's all starting to come together because I'm slow. She works all the time, as does her dad, and they still barely manage to get by. It's a long shot, but maybe Dad can help them. Or something.

We settle for some ramen noodles and find the *Goonies* on TV. It's not fancy, it's not at the movies, it's just me and her hanging out, and I love it. It's easy being with her. I don't feel pressured to entertain. I'm relaxed, and after all the shit we've been through, we definitely deserve a quiet evening.

The phone rings causing both of us to jump. Guess the phones are working again. Alisa leaps up so fast, she answers it before it starts a second ring. She talks so low I can only make out certain words.

"…cleaned the house. No…homework. Yes, sir."

Then she hangs up.

"I'll be right back," she says without looking at me.

"Are you okay?"

"Yeah."

Lie.

She disappears into her room, leaving me to watch Chunk feed Sloth a Baby Ruth candy bar. This whole scene used to make me laugh so hard, but I can't pay attention to it. Next thing I know, thirty minutes have passed, and Alisa still hasn't come out of her bedroom. I get up and softly tap on the door, but she doesn't answer.

"Alisa?" I open the door, but I don't see her. I hear faint sounds coming from the bathroom. I tap on the door. "Are you okay?"

She clears her throat. "Yeah. I'll be out in a minute."

I don't like the uneasy feeling settling in my stomach. I wait for her on her bed.

When she emerges, I can tell she's been crying by the redness in her eyes. "Sorry. I missed the rest of the movie, huh?"

"What's wrong?"

She shakes her head. "Do you wanna watch another movie?"

Not really. I wanna find out what's on your mind. I want you to open up to me, but I highly doubt that will happen. "You can talk to me."

"I know. Everything's fine." She forces a smile, and I hate it.

I can't drag it out of her.

"Sure. Let's watch a movie." I take her hand, and we leave the room, settling onto the couch. We start watching *The Breakfast Club.* I guess it's an 80s night on this channel. It's a classic movie though.

Inviting Alisa to lean against me, she slowly wraps her arm around my stomach, and I kiss her forehead. We stay like that through the entire movie. When it's over, she lifts her arm, and I see spots of blood on my shirt.

"What happened?"

Her eyes widen, and she immediately stands up. "I'm so sorry. I accidentally cut myself the other day. I guess I still need a band aid."

"Let me see. Do you need stitches?"

"No." She pulls away from me, holding the ends of her sleeves in her hands.

"Alisa, if it's still bleeding, let me see." Something is going on, and I have to protect her.

She tries to go around me, but I catch her hand. She tries to escape my grip, but the amount of red through her shirt concerns me. I pull up the sleeve and gasp.

"Alisa, what—"

"Let go of me!" she screams.

I release her. "What happened?" Deep, red scars clutter her arm in a chaotic pattern, just like the ones I saw on her stomach. I remove my shirt and wrap it around her arm. Pulling her into my arms, I hold her so tightly. Was she trying to kill herself? What is this? I feel sick. "We need to get you to the hospital."

"No. No hospital. I'm fine."

Is she crazy? "Alisa, I…I don't understand. What happened? Did you…did you do this?"

She doesn't answer, which says a lot.

"Why? What for?"

"It's nothing."

"Nothing?" I clench my teeth. How can she seriously say that?

"You should go."

"No," I say sternly. She's not getting off that easy.

She pulls out of my grasp and leans against the arched frame of the kitchen. "It's-it's you wouldn't…understand if I told you."

"Why wouldn't I? Why do you shut me out? You always assume I can't or won't understand."

"You shut me out, too, Ben."

I deserve that. "You're right. I'm not used to being with someone who I can actually talk to."

"Neither am I. I told you, I don't know how this works."

"Neither do I." But I can try. I let out a long breath as I sink onto the couch. "I keep all this stuff inside because no one wants to hear it. I have no right to complain."

She sits next to me and slides her hand into mine. "You can tell me."

"My parents aren't exactly the right ones to get advice on communication. Courtney wasn't someone I could ever talk to about stuff that's been going on. She would never listen. And my dad pressures me into being this perfect basketball player. Mom wants me to be the perfect boyfriend to Courtney. I guess. I don't know."

"I'm sorry. Does your mom know she cheated on you and hurt you?"

I nod, letting her change the subject. For now. "It doesn't matter. I think she pushed me to get back with Courtney because of what was going on with her and Dad. But I don't know."

"Have you talked to her?"

"She doesn't care."

"Maybe something's trying to tell us something."

"What do you mean?"

"Ben, there are so many factors against us."

I squeeze her hand, meeting her eyes. "Something is always going to test us. But we're strong enough to get through it."

She nods, and we're quiet for several minutes, listening to the tapping on the roof. Holding her in my arms calms me, but I need to know why she cuts herself. She needs help.

alisa

"Why do you do it?" Ben asks quietly.

I don't really know. I can't believe he found out. I don't even know what to say or do. "It's not an easy or simple answer."

"It's okay," he says. "Whatever it is, we can get through it together. I promise. I'm not going anywhere."

I can't sit still. I move away from him and pace. I'm shaking, unable to settle down.

Ben puts his hands on my arms. "Hey, it's okay. We don't have to talk about it right now."

"You can't be here. If my dad sees you, I'll be grounded."

"I'll leave tomorrow. I'm definitely not leaving you tonight. Your dad isn't coming home tonight. Please stop trying to get rid of me."

"I don't feel like talking."

"Okay. I don't want to leave you."

"I'm not going to hurt myself."

"It's not about that. I want to be here."

I clench my fists, feeling sick to my stomach. Something in the carpet catches my eye. A piece of fuzz. Or dirt. I need to get rid of it. "I have to vacuum."

"Alisa, take a deep breath. The house is fine."

I do what he says, but I'm embarrassed. I don't want him knowing, and I don't like that he can see me. I want to cry, but not in front of him.

"D-do you want to die?"

"No! It's not like that."

He nods.

"I'm tired."

"Okay. I'll sleep here on the couch."

I cross my arms, trying to calm down. He moves closer and wraps his arms around me. I let him comfort me, and I begin to relax into him.

"Come on. I'll tuck you in."

Ben takes me into my room. I slip under the covers while he sits on the edge of the bed, holding my hand. I shift to the other side of the bed inviting him to lie down. When he does, he pulls me close and kisses my forehead. We lay like this for a while. His fingers lightly brush my hair away from my face. His touch is insanely gentle.

The moonlight barely lights his face, but I look up into his eyes.

I lean in, kissing him. His lips are soft, and I want more. Ben grips my stomach and deepens the kiss. My insides are boiling, reaching that high that I need. That I crave. It's so cold, but the heat between us is enough to set the house on fire.

Ben slides his hand under my shirt, and I moan. I'm feeling higher than high as I slowly move my hand beneath his shirt. When I touch his bare skin, he makes a sound, and I jerk my hand away.

"It's okay," he whispers. "Are you okay?"

For once, yes. "Yes."

Bringing my hands back to his back, he rolls on top, and there's a throbbing in my ears and other places. I don't want to go far tonight, but I love this incredible high. I need it. It isn't painful at all. It's an amazing feeling. I need it.

ben

My brain is mush as I kiss Alisa, touching her bare skin. I want to go further, but I know she isn't ready, and I want to take my time. Feeling her hands on my back drives me crazy. She lifts the shirt over my head, and when her hands touch my chest, I about lose it. I kiss her with more pressure than before. When I kiss her neck, the low moan that escapes her lips excites me. I want her, but we're moving too fast. I slow my kissing and move beside her. Both of us are breathing hard. Gathering her in my arms, she lays her head on my chest and I hold her hand.

"I love you," I say.

She raises her head and meets my eyes. The look on her face pains me. She's struggling with something, and I dread what she's thinking. I don't think I can handle her breaking my heart. I love her. The first time I've ever truly fallen in love, but it's with a girl who doesn't love me back.

"I-I don't know what to say. I—"

"It's okay. I was just telling you how I feel."

She rests her head on my chest and squeezes my hand. I hate the silence and the uncertainty of it all, but I will be patient for her. I don't expect a lot. She's dealing with a lot, too. I hope I'm not complicating things further.

"I've…never said it."

"It's okay. I promise."

We lie in a comfortable silence.

"I don't know why I do it. It helps…with everything."

"What do you mean?" She's talking about the cutting, and I hope I don't say the wrong thing to scare her. This is the closest I've been with her.

"It's hard to put into words. I want to stop, but it's hard."

"Are you seeking help?"

"No."

"I don't know how, but I will help you quit."

She nods.

I rub her upper arms and tighten my grip around her. I kiss the top of her head, loving the way she relaxes into me, and soon she's fast asleep.

I don't sleep well. The cold in the house is ridiculous. I stay under the blankets with her, hoping I'm keeping her warm. I can't believe she sleeps like this every night. My mind keeps me awake all night with worry, and I don't release her. I've never known anyone who cuts themselves. I don't even know how to help or if I can do anything. She wants to stop. That's a good sign. Maybe I can convince her to see a therapist.

alisa

When I wake up, I feel something soft against my cheek. I gasp when I realize it's Ben. In my bed.

I bolt upright, breathing hard. I shiver once the blankets fall off me. Did Daddy come home? My heart beats unsteadily, and I shake as I peer out the window.

"Hey, are you okay?"

His voice startles me, but I relax once I don't see Daddy's truck. Instead, a thick blanket of snow covers the ground and the drive. I remember now. It snowed, and Daddy stayed at Diane's. But given the shining sun, the snow will probably melt soon.

"Yes." When I glance at the clock, I gasp. It's after twelve. I never sleep this late.

"What is it?" he asks, taking my hand.

I jump out of bed, ready to start cleaning and doing laundry. It has to be clean for Daddy.

"Alisa, slow down." Ben stops me in my tracks, taking my hands between us. I can't help but stare at his bare chest. I love it, but it makes me nervous. "What's going on?"

"I just…I never sleep in." But I haven't slept that well since before Mom died. I feel…*good* for a change.

"It's okay. I'm not used to it either."

"Thanks for staying."

"You don't have to thank me. Did you sleep well?"

I nod. "You?"

"Yeah. Like a rock." But he looks exhausted, which makes me feel bad. "What's wrong?"

I shake my head. "Nothing."

He puts on his shirt and shoes. "I have an extra heater at my house that I'm going to get for you and your dad."

"No. It's okay. He'll pay the bill soon."

"Okay, but you need something in the meantime. And I know you won't come home with me for the night."

"I can't."

"I know. It's okay. Do you want to come with me to get the heater?"

"I can't leave."

"Your dad won't be here. The roads still look frozen."

I shake my head. "I shouldn't."

He nods. "I won't be long."

"If you come back, and my dad's truck is in the driveway, turn around and go back home."

"I'm just a friend delivering a heater."

"No, Ben."

"It's okay. I promise." He kisses me, and I don't want it to end. The way his warm lips press against mine makes my pulse quicken.

When I draw back a little, he rests his head against mine. "I love you, Alisa. I'm so glad you're back. You've made me the happiest I've been in so long."

"I haven't done anything."

"You do more than you think. I'll be right back."

He leaves, taking the warmth, the comfort, the peace with him. He makes me feel things I've never felt before. Excitement. Happiness. Love. I'm addicted. The second he leaves, I miss him. I hate being away from him. I feel too antsy and on edge. It's hard to believe he feels that way for me, especially finding out my secret.

ben

I'm freezing by the time I get home. The warmth feels amazing, but I feel awful knowing I've been warm and cozy while Alisa's been freezing this whole time. I get why her dad's strict. He doesn't want her to have a boyfriend and lose focus on school which could hurt her college chances. But we can make this work. I can't lose her again.

Does her dad know about her cutting? Does Sarah? Is that what Sarah wanted me to know?

The phones are working so I call Dad and check on them. They're stuck for the night and will try to come home tomorrow. Hopefully this weekend away together will help them patch things up. Or at least begin.

I call Hayden at Janie's, and she's going to stay again. Maybe I can bring Alisa back here for the night.

I shake my head. I can't get too greedy. But last night was one of the most amazing nights of my life. Despite finding out some truths.

Once I find the heater, I grab some snacks and head back to her house. The sun is out, and the snow is melting. I decide to take my car, driving like my grandma, since no one here knows how to drive on icy snow. By the time I reach Alisa's driveway, I stop once I see her dad's truck parked. Shit. I really need them to have this heater, but I don't want to cause issues.

Taking a deep breath, I move toward the house deciding that Alisa's warmth and well-being are more important than a potential grounding. I park and climb onto the porch. Knocking on the door scares me a little, but I keep telling myself it'll be okay.

A man, taller than me with a medium build, answers. His dark hair is short and the stubble around his chin and face is graying. Alisa's father looks so much older than I recall. This is the man my mother had an affair with.

"Can I help you?" his blue eyes narrow at me like he recognizes me but can't remember.

My mouth stops working, but I pull it together. "Mr. Hopewell, I'm Ben, an old friend of Alisa's."

Recognition registers on his face. "Ben Lamar."

"Yes, sir."

He extends his hand and I shake it. "Good game Friday."

Wasn't expecting that. "Thanks." Doesn't he know who I am?

"Gonna win that state championship?"

I give a small chuckle, because it's the same old man talk I get everywhere I go. As if this town depends on basketball. "That's the plan."

"Good. What can I do you for?"

"Actually, I came by to drop off this heater for you and Alisa." I know it sounds like I'm calling out his inability to provide heat. I need to make up something. "Power's been going out around here, so I thought I'd see if you and Alisa needed it."

"Basketball star and charitable. You don't see that often in kids these days. Your parents did well with you."

He really has no idea. Was my mom just a one-night stand? "I'll be sure to tell them."

"Well, thank you for the heater. We really appreciate it."

"Of course. Let me know if you need anything."

"I will. Thanks."

"Hope to see you at games."

He nods and retreats inside. I leave, wishing I could see Alisa again. Mr. Hopewell doesn't seem to know or care who I am. Was Mom wrong? Was she telling the truth? Was it really someone else and she doesn't remember?

Shaking my head, I drive home hating how all these things make me look at Mom in a bad light. Forgive. She always taught me forgiveness.

But it's tricky.

alisa

I'm scared to leave my bedroom. I can't believe Ben came to the door when I asked him not to. Why did he do that? Was he purposefully trying to get me into trouble?

"Alisa," Daddy calls me into the living room.

Biting my lip, I try swallowing the lump in my throat as I make my way. "Yes."

"Ben Lamar came by. Brought this." He holds up the heater. "What kind of sob story did you tell him?"

"None."

He raises his eyebrows. "Don't lie to me."

"I told him nothing."

"He seems to think we need a heater. The only reason he'd think that is if you told him I can't afford the kerosene. Did you tell him why we couldn't afford it? Because you decided to keep all the money yourself?" He moves closer and I stiffen. "Why are you telling others about our problems?"

"I'm not. I swear."

His hand meets my face with a hard smack. "Why are you lying to me?"

He removes his belt and strikes me on the shoulder. I fall to the floor and lose count of the whippings. "Our business is ours. Don't ever make them pity us." He kicks me in the leg and bends down to my tear-stained face. "And don't ever fucking lie to me again. Get up and get yourself cleaned. I don't want to see you for the rest of the night."

I stumble to my feet and disappear inside my room, hiding in the bathroom. My shoulder, back, arms all throb and sting from the belt. I clench my teeth and reach for my scissors. They've become so dull. I need to find something sharper.

Why did Ben do that? Did he do it on purpose? Is all this just a game to him? Playing with me? It makes sense. I fell right into his trap. It's my fault I let him come over. And now he knows my secret. The whole school will know.

I jump when I hear the front porch door slam closed. Then the rumbling of Daddy's truck roars down the driveway. The wind is harsh as it blows, seemingly so hard it'll take the house with it. I hear every creak, and the plastic on the windows crinkles. It's dark outside. And so cold, I shiver. I realize I've been in the bathroom the whole time. Something tickles down my arm and when I look down, I watch the line of blood slowly roll over my skin.

I've made such a mess of things. I'm not Mom, and I can't fill her shoes. It's hard taking care of Daddy. I'm not good at it, and I don't know what to do anymore.

ben

It's only been about a few hours or so, but I miss Alisa already. What I would give to spend another night with her. As I slowly drive back home, I'm focused on ways to convince Mr. Hopewell to let me date Alisa. But first, I have to convince my own parents. That's going to be pretty difficult. But that isn't the only issue.

As I pull into my driveway, my heart leaps against my chest. Seeing Courtney's car on the curb worries me and ruined my mood. I'm not expecting her. There's still snow all over the ground, but the roads are clear. I'm surprised Courtney came over in it. Removing my jacket and extra layers, I head upstairs forcing myself to face the music.

Nudging my bedroom door open, I spot Courtney curled up on my bed. I silently curse myself for telling her about the back door always being unlocked.

"It's about time you got here," she says, sitting up. "Where were you? And where are your parents and Hayden?"

"Hayden's at her friend's, my parents went out of town but are stuck."

"So it's just us?" She grins as she slides off the bed. Moving toward me, her lips curl into a sexy smile and she wraps her arms around my neck. Courtney's warm, and she smells like strawberries.

Taking her hands, I remove them from me.

Her face twists in confusion, then she frowns. "I miss you."

I grip the back of my head, dreading every second. "Why are you here?"

"I'm sorry if I ever hurt you, but you don't make it easy. But we can work on it."

"No, Courtney. It's over."

Anger flickers in her eyes. "Is this about that trailer trash girl?"

I clench my teeth, knowing she's only trying to get a rise out of me. "First of all, she's not trailer trash. Second, you and I are not good for each other, and you know it. We never work."

"So you're going behind my back with this bitch? Don't play stupid with me. Suddenly, this girl pops up, and you decide you don't love me anymore? Who is she? What makes her so special?"

"Courtney, this isn't about Alisa. So leave her out of it." I silently kick myself for saying her name.

"Alisa? You're dumping me for *her*? This whole time it wasn't about Zach liking her. It was about you?"

My hands fly to my head. "Will you for once listen to me? You and I are not good for each other. If we were, you wouldn't have slept with Tyler."

"Omigod. Are you still upset over that? It happened months ago. I make one mistake and you rub it in my face all the time. You aren't perfect either."

"Do you realize what that did to me? I don't think you have ever understood how much you hurt me."

"Oh, grow up, Ben. It's not like we're married."

"Wow. Spoken like someone who cares. You make me feel like shit, and I don't deserve it."

She scoffs. "You're the one always making me feel like crap. I haven't done anything."

I let out a frustrated sigh, hating that she got me to argue with her. We sit for a few minutes, quiet, both of us breathing hard. I want to punch something, but I just focus on my breathing. I don't understand why she fights so hard against me when I know she doesn't love me. What's in it for her? Does she just want some pawn to boss around forever? Because I won't be that guy. Or is it because she thinks I look good on her arm? Am I her way out of this town?

"You know how hard it is at home, and you know you're the only one who helps me through it. I don't understand why you're doing this. You never loved me, did you?"

"At one point in time I did. I can't be that person for you anymore. Why'd you come over?"

When she looks up with tears in her eyes, there's something else there. Fear? I've seldom ever seen fear in her eyes. She lets out a breath. "I'm pregnant."

My stomach tightens like she just punched me hard. The room spins, and I see little dots of flashing light swarm around my head. I take a deep breath. "What?"

"You heard me. You knocked me up."

alisa

I slowly open my eyes, wanting to throw the alarm clock across the room. I barely slept, and my body is sore. My room is freezing so I dress as fast as I can to keep warm. A rush of anger wells up in my chest as my gaze sweeps across the coat and accessories Ben gave me. I snatch them up, and sling my backpack over my shoulder, ignoring the pain.

Once I get to school, I see him with Courtney. She's touching him with a warm smile on her face. I knew it was all a lie but seeing it in front of me hurts. My heart twists.

Biting my lip, I march toward Ben, throwing the coat in his face.

"Alisa—"

"What is *she* doing with Hayden's coat?" Courtney asks, her eyes wide.

"Nothing." I start to walk away, but she pushes me, igniting anger inside me.

Turning around, I swing clumsily but miss.

Her hand slips to my throat and she squeezes. "Stay away from him." Her blue eyes glare into mine. I want to punch her.

"Courtney, stop!" Ben pulls her off me, and I fall. "Leave her alone."

"No," she yells, clawing her way to get to me. Ben takes her down the hall, leaving me on the floor with an audience.

I knew it would happen, and I shouldn't be surprised. I hate being at home. I hate being at school. I have nowhere to go.

Zach comes up to me and helps me to my feet. "Are you okay?"

I want to cry, but I don't. I nod instead.

"She's a damn psycho, and I'm sorry she has it out for you. I don't know what's going on. I thought they broke up."

I shrug. "Ben lied. I gotta get to class," I tell him and walk away. I had one of the most amazing weekends of my life, but it meant nothing to Ben. I deserve this. All I do is hurt people. That's why they leave. I feel so alone now.

Once I walk inside the classroom, someone trips me and I fall, spilling my books in front of me. People laugh, but I quickly gather my books and take my seat.

After class, I make my way toward my locker, trying to ignore the whispers, but they fill my head.

Worthless.

Slut.

Homewrecker.

It doesn't end.

I make my way to the bathroom, needing solace. I go to the stall on the end and take out the razor I stole from Daddy's box cutter. I make one cut and hear the door open. I need to be alone. When it's clear the person isn't leaving, I shove the razor in my pocket and leave the stall. Courtney leans against the wall next to the door, arms folded across her chest with a glare. Waiting for me.

"I thought I told you to keep your skanky hands off my boyfriend."

I swallow hard. "Nothing happened."

She laughs. "Are you sure? Because you throwing that coat at him this morning says otherwise."

The bell rings and I'm late for class. "I need to go."

"You know what's funny about this situation? Is that you actually fell for such a prank."

I knew it. "What?"

"Oh, you don't know?"

"Know what?"

Pity washes over her face. "I guess I can understand why you fell for it. Ben is a dreamy guy, and he can be very persuasive. But you have to admit it's unlikely he would actually like someone like you."

"What are you talking about?"

"Omigod, you're so precious. So naïve. Ben never liked you. He was playing with you."

I knew it. And he made me believe it.

"Ben and I are together, and we're getting married."

Married? I nod and move around her to the door.

"I'm sorry. I thought it would be best to hear it from a friend instead of him. He likes playing pranks on girls."

"So you're okay with your boyfriend kissing other girls?"

She pushes me. "He would *never* kiss you."

"He did."

She towers over me. "You are so pathetic that you actually conjure up crazy ideas. You live in such a ridiculous fantasy world." She laughs. "You can't handle the fact that he played you. What makes you think he actually likes *you*?"

I'm tired of feeling small and being teased. I want to run away. I open the door and step out, but she catches my arm.

With a sadistic grin plastered to her face, she grips my arm tight. "You're nothing to him."

"Let go."

Courtney glances down and sees blood through my sleeve. She gives a fake laugh, then without warning, jerks my sleeve up, revealing my scars. She gasps, then recovers with a laugh. "You can't even kill yourself right. Keep working on it. You'll get there."

Everyone sees the scars. They see the poor freak crying in the hall. My eyes meet hers, and all I see is red. Tackling her we fall to the ground. She quickly has the upper hand. I yank her hair, trying pushing her off me while the crowd cheers.

Next thing I know, someone pulls her off and picks me up off the ground. A teacher. She sends us both to the principal's office as dread hits deep in my stomach. What have I done?

"What happened?" Mr. Rutledge asks.

"She flipped out and attacked me," Courtney cries.

"Is this true?"

I nod, unable to make eye contact. I taste blood on my lip, knowing it's probably swollen.

"She's completely off her rocker, sir."

"Courtney," he warns. "What made you attack Courtney?"

She said I should kill myself. "Nothing."

"See?"

"Courtney please wait outside."

Huffing, she leaves the room.

"Did she say something to you?" Mr. Rutledge asks.

Yes. I shake my head.

"Fighting results in suspensions, Alisa," he tells me sternly.

I nod again, choking back the tears. I messed up. I'm such a failure.

"I will have to inform your father."

Looking up, I meet his eyes. My heart drops to my stomach like an anchor in the ocean. It pulls me down, making my knees weak. He can't call Daddy. Daddy will never forgive me for this. I clear my throat. "Um, I've learned my lesson. I promise, no more fights."

He frowns, the pity reaching his dark eyes. "I'm sorry, but it's policy. Since you admitted to attacking Courtney, I have to suspend you for a week."

Tears burn at the back of my eyes.

"Is everything okay? I've had a couple of teachers mention you."

But you never said anything to me.

"They said your grades started slipping a few weeks ago. Do you need any help?"

No one can help me.

"Alisa, are you okay?"

Help me. I want out of this misery. "Everything is fine. I wish everyone would stop asking me."

"Just remember we're here to talk and listen."

Except you don't.

Maybe I can rush home fast enough to delete the message. Biting my lip, I don't hear anything else he says, just the pounding of my heartbeat.

ben

Word in this school travels fast. Faster than damn lightning. I overheard someone saying Alisa attacked Courtney. I can't even fathom what Courtney said to her. I ask the teacher for a bathroom pass, and she finally grants it to me. Out in the hall, I race toward the office. Maybe I can catch Alisa. I should check on Courtney, given her fragile state, but I can't bring myself to do it. I already hate myself for leaving Alisa this morning, but I didn't want Courtney to hurt her.

When I reach the office, I almost run over Alisa. Tears fill her eyes, and it breaks my heart. I fucked up everything with her.

"Alisa…"

"Leave me alone."

"Alisa, please let me explain."

"Explain what, Ben? Did this weekend mean anything to you?"

"Of course, it did."

"You told me you broke up with her."

"I did, but it's complicated."

She wipes her tears. "I knew all of this was a prank. I fell for it. You got me. Go be happy with Courtney."

"Prank? This wasn't a prank." She starts to turn, and I grab her arm, but she flinches and jerks away from me.

"Don't pretend you don't know what I'm talking about. I don't want to hear it."

Pain cuts my heart, and I know I can't be with the girl I love. I know I hurt her, and I don't deserve her. I screwed up like I always do.

The further she walks away from me, the more I hate myself. I know Courtney did something to Alisa and it pisses me off even more. I don't know how to fix any of it. But I have to try.

alisa

I reach the parking lot, terrified of going home.

"Alisa, please talk to me." His voice makes my knees weak, but I can't face him. The wind slices through me, and I wrap my arms around myself hating how cold it is and how I can never stay warm "Where are you going?"

"I got suspended, Ben. Because of her. Because I can't control myself."

He shakes his head. "You didn't do anything."

Yes, I did. "It doesn't matter."

"It should."

I shrug and turn around.

"I gave you this jacket to keep warm."

"I don't need your charity."

"Will you just take the damn jacket? I hate seeing you freezing all the time."

He touches my shoulder, and I wince. Twisting around to face him, I bite my lip from the tears. Ben hands me the jacket, and I take it, wanting to be warm.

"Thanks."

"What happened to your lip? Did Courtney do that?"

I don't even know anymore. "Nothing. What do you want?"

He grabs the back of his head. "I know you didn't do anything to Courtney. I'll fix it."

"Fix what, Ben? You can't fix everything. Don't worry about me. Worry about your girlfriend."

"Fuck!"

When I look up, I see tears well in his eyes.

"What am I going to do?"

"Are you trying to figure out how to keep us both?"

"I broke up with Courtney, before you and I spent the weekend together." His voice is shaky. "It's over. She showed up at my house to talk. She's pregnant. I'm having a kid, Alisa."

Oh. Wow. I don't even know what to say. Or think. I can't imagine how he's feeling or what he's going through. What's going to happen? Nausea grips me like a vice. The one thing I thought would be here to keep me sane is now just a memory. His confession confirms the fact that we will never be together.

But it doesn't matter because once I get home, there won't be much for me ever. This suspension will be on my record. No cooking school will ever accept me. No one will.

"I can't do this," he says. "She's ten weeks."

Wow. "Why'd she keep this from you?"

"I don't know. I don't know what to do. I don't want her. I was ready to finally be with you. The one I'm meant to be with."

I take his hand, unsure if that's what he wants. No matter what, he's still my friend. Maybe I'm being too nice.

He looks up, a tear slides down his face. I wrap my arms around him. He lets out a sigh. "Alisa, you are not, nor have you ever been a prank. I know that's just Courtney getting inside your head. Please don't trust her. She hates you because I love you. I'm so sorry about all of this. I don't deserve you at all. You deserve so much more."

"It's okay, Ben. We'll get through this."

He leans against a car beside me, exhaustion wearing on his face. "Did you guys stay warm last night?"

No. "Yeah."

"I'm really sorry if I got you in trouble. I just can't stand the thought of you freezing. I guess I need to look for a job. Pretty sure my parents will disown me."

"They won't."

"I'm so sorry. I don't want this to change us. I love you and I want to be with you. I just need some time."

"Okay."

He squeezes my hand. "I'll understand if you don't want to be with me."

"I do, but maybe you need to let your mind settle before you make any decisions. I'll be here as long as you want. But maybe I should keep my distance." The pain stabs me again.

"Let me take you home."

"You shouldn't leave school. You have a game tonight."

"I know. I don't care, Alisa. I just…I can't do it tonight."

I nod and let him take me home. We don't talk at all on the way. I can't believe Courtney's pregnant. And I fought with her. What if I hurt her baby? Hers and Ben's baby. My stomach twists at that, and twists again hoping that by some miracle Daddy isn't home.

"Mailbox?" Ben asks.

"Yeah."

He pulls his car next to it and puts it in park. It's like we both know this is it. This is how our story ends. It was too good to be true.

Ben faces me and gazes into my eyes. He leans over and kisses me. I know it's a goodbye kiss, and I let it overtake me. I record to memory the soft way his lips mesh with mine and the gentle way he touches my face. Always gentle.

When he pulls back, he frowns and kisses my forehead. "I love you."

"I love you." I bite my lip to keep from crying.

Getting out of Ben's car, I carry what's left of my broken heart down the long driveway to face my father.

ben

I hate leaving Alisa. It makes my skin crawl that I was irresponsible and got Courtney pregnant. I don't want to drag Alisa down with me. She deserves so much more. I've lost her again, and there's nothing I can do to stop it. I did this, and there isn't any fixing it now.

My mind is in a million different places, and I need to talk to someone. After dropping her off, I start driving with no destination in mind. Images of me holding a kid; being with Courtney; me turning into Dad; It all taunts me.

I find myself in my driveway, staring at the basketball goal. I love basketball. It's helped me in ways I never thought it could. It relieves stress. It's who I am. I need it. But if I never got into basketball, I never would have known Courtney. None of this shit would be happening. I'd still be friends with Sarah. And maybe Alisa and I would be together without all this mess.

I go inside and get on the computer. No one's home, thankfully, and if they ask why I'm there, I can always feign sickness. Though Dad will ride my ass about skipping and the game.

I need something to occupy my mind.

Sarah emailed me again, and I begin my reply. By the time I realize it, I've written a novel to her. I let everything out. All about Alisa, aside from the cutting, about Courtney, the pregnancy. Our parents. All of the madness. I hit send and let out a long breath.

A few minutes later, she sends an instant message.

ravengirl97: OMG

basketball_guy24: yeah

ravengirl97: ur mom and her dad?

basketball_guy24: yeah

ravengirl97: shit. i really don't know what to say

basketball_guy24: yeah

ravengirl97: courtney's a bitch. how far along is she?

basketball_guy24: 10 weeks.

ravengirl97: any symptoms?

basketball_guy24: other than crazy?no. not really

ravengirl97: of course not. bc she's perfect

basketball_guy24: i don't know what to do

ravengirl97: i'm sorry. u can't abandon she devil or the kid

basketball_guy24: I know

ravengirl97: i guess just lay low for now

basketball_guy24: yeah

ravengirl97: so Alisa got suspended? bc courtney's a bitch?

basketball_guy24: i don't know why. she didn't do anything. how could they believe Courtney over Alisa?

ravengirl97: ur really asking that? bc Courtney is perfect and a cheerleader and she can get away with whatever. she's manipulative. why do you think you got back together with her? she gets whatever she wants.

I sigh. Sarah's right, and I hate it.

ravengirl97: i wish Alisa would call. i miss her.

basketball_guy24: i know. pretty sure she's gonna get grounded

ravengirl97: or worse

I can't ask what she means by that because Courtney calls my name from downstairs. I really should lock the backdoor. Looking at the time, I see that it's after three. I tell Sarah I'll talk to her later and shut down the computer.

"Omigod Ben, are you okay?" Courtney asks as she walks in my room.

"I'm fine."

"We have a game tonight. Why are you home?"

"I'm not playing tonight."

"What?"

"Why are you here?"

She looks annoyed. "I just thought I'd come check on you. Wasn't like you were the one who got attacked." She moves to my bed and lays on her stomach. "Ben, it was horrible. She just went off on me."

"Should you be laying like that?"

She furrows her eyebrows and rolls her eyes. "Oh. I can until I start showing." She turns over and invites me to lay with her. I used to love nothing more than holding Courtney, but all I can think about is Alisa and being with her. Having her in my arms made everything right. It made me feel whole, and it tears me apart that I can't be with her. Because I fucked up. Again. I fucked up the one thing that matters to me.

"She is totally crazy, Ben."

I doubt she went off on Courtney. I should be more sympathetic since she is carrying my child. This is my problem, too. I made my bed. My stomach clenches, and I feel exhausted.

Rubbing my eyes, I worry over how to tell my family. I doubt Courtney's told hers. Otherwise, I would've heard it from my parents.

When I glance down, I catch her rubbing her stomach, and it causes an ache to stir inside me. I haven't even really spoken to her about the baby. Even just thinking that doesn't sound right.

"Are you scared?" I ask.

"No. Why would I be?"

Her answer surprises me. "We're only sixteen, Courtney. Don't you want to go to college? Or finish high school?"

"Why does any of that matter when we're going to be together for the rest of our lives? We're gonna have a family. Besides, our parents will help every step of the way."

I can't believe her, but at the same time, it doesn't surprise me. She has never had to take care of herself. Her parents have always done and paid for everything. "You really think your parents are going to be okay with this?"

"Ben, no matter what I do, my parents are never okay with it. You know this. I'm not the golden child. Me being pregnant in high school is fitting."

"Your parents love you, and you know you're meant for more."

"I have nothing going for me. My parents remind me all the time of what a disappointment I am to them. Maybe now they'll see that I have some purpose in life."

"They just want what's best for you." I have to believe that. Even I believe that my parents want the best for me. Isn't it like that for all parents and kids? Shouldn't it be like that?

"No, they don't."

"Pretty sure Dad will kick me out when he finds out."

Courtney groans. "Whatever. Don't be so dramatic. Your dad would never do that. But if he does, go live with your mom whenever they finally separate."

Ouch.

"They love you no matter what. And my parents will help."

"Do they know?"

"No."

"Raising a kid is a lot of work and takes a lot of money."

"I know this," she snaps.

"And you're okay with living off our parents? If they even let us?"

She sits up and faces me. "What's your deal, Ben? Do you not want to have a baby?"

"Shh. Keep your voice down." I turn on the radio in case one of my parents comes home. "Courtney, I'm not ready to be a father."

"Should've thought about that before we slept together."

"You should've remembered to take your pill."

"Oh, so it's my fault?"

"It's both of our faults."

"So just because I'm pregnant means your life is over?"

"That isn't what I said."

"You implied it. This is our life now, Ben. Don't be a loser and abandon me."

"I'm not going to," I say, defeated. My pager beeps. Hope grips my chest that it's Alisa, but my heart deflates. Zach. I unwrap Courtney from me and get up.

"Who is it?" Courtney asks in an accusatory voice.

"Zach."

"What does he want?"

"I don't know."

"What is wrong with you? Would you stop pacing? You're giving me whiplash."

I didn't realize I was pacing, but I need something to calm my nerves. The front door slams.

"Benjamin!" Dad yells.

"You should go." I'm almost relieved that he came home yelling at me since it gives me a reason to make Courtney leave. The tension in this house is ridiculous and someone has to go.

"He can't yell at you while I'm here."

"Courtney, come on. You don't need to be here."

She groans and gets off the bed. We walk downstairs together.

"Hi, Mr. Lamar," Courtney says.

"Ben, it may be best she leaves."

"She's leaving now. I'll call you later," I say as I walk her out.

"It's gotten really bad here, hasn't it?"

"It's okay. I'll talk to you later."

Closing the door, I meet Dad in the kitchen. Better get this over with.

alisa

Walking down the long gravel road to my house feels even longer once I see Daddy's truck. I take deep breaths, not knowing what to expect. For once, I wish our phone was cut off, but Daddy just paid the bill.

When I reach the door to the porch, my heart shatters and breathing becomes difficult. Clutching my chest in hopes of calming myself, I step up onto the porch. Tears cloud my eyes as I turn the knob to the house with a shaky hand. Once open, I walk in as Daddy presses play on the answering machine. A bulge lodges itself in my throat as I bite my lip.

"Mr. Hopewell, your daughter, Alisa, got into a fight today and is now suspended for the remainder of the week."

Daddy's hands clench into fists, and I know what's to come. I deserve it.

He turns around. He's wearing his uniform pants and a white t-shirt. "What the fuck is this about?" His voice is calm, but I hear the anger.

"I-I—"

"Stop stuttering and tell me."

"I pushed a girl. I didn't mean it."

"No matter what I do, you don't listen. You are an unruly child. Why do you do these things?"

I don't have an answer for him. "I'm sorry, Daddy. It won't happen again."

"Damn right it won't. Go to your room."

Nodding quickly, I rush toward it, but he grasps my hair, pulling me back and hit me in the face.

Whiteness blinds me as I feel liquid in my mouth.

"Get your worthless self cleaned up. When I get home tonight, we're finishing this."

Tears roll down my cheek as I nod. Slowly, my vision comes back.

Daddy sighs. "I wouldn't have to hit you if you just behaved. Do you understand?"

"Yes, sir."

He sighs again. "I'm going go to work. Have something for dinner."

"Yes, sir."

Daddy leaves, and I force myself to my bathroom. Staring at my reflection, disgust rises inside me. My lip is swollen, and blood slowly trickles down. I'm a failure. I can never do anything right. I'm a sorry excuse for a human. I pull open the drawer, grab a razor, and lift my sleeve. As soon as the blade touches my arm, I breathe a sigh of relief. Anger at myself comes through the blade. Why can't I be good? It's all Daddy asks me to do, and I can't do it.

After the bleeding stops, and I clean the wound, I clean up around the house, ignoring my throbbing bottom lip. I cook a simple dinner. My heart isn't in it. I messed up and made Daddy mad.

By the time I finish the chores, I skip eating and run a bath.

I want to talk to Ben to see how he's doing. I want to hear his voice. I know it's wrong, and I know he could be with Courtney. Staring at the phone, the tears roll down my cheeks. I can't call him. He needs space. Time. I have to let go of him. For good.

ben

"Ben!" Dad yells as soon as I walk back inside.

I make my way to meet him in the kitchen. His tie is loosened, and he looks stressed. His job isn't easy, but it isn't the only thing in his life. Part of me wonders if Dad being a workaholic is why Mom cheated. He's never here, and when he is, it's usually to lecture.

"What are you doing home?" he asks.

"I wasn't feeling good."

He sighs. "You have a game tonight. Your skipping will prevent you from playing. I'll call Coach Turner and talk to him."

"Not everything is about basketball, Dad."

"What's gotten into you? Why have you been rebelling against your mom and me?"

Is he serious? "You really don't get it, do you?"

"Ben, I don't have time for games."

"She cheated on you, Dad. And you walk around like it's okay. I'm in love with Alisa, but I can't be with her." *Shit*. I let her name escape.

"Alisa? Jack Hopewell's daughter?" His face turns red, and I see the vein in his forehead protrude.

I don't care. "Yeah. Alisa. She's the only thing keeping me sane."

"Yeah. Until she manipulates you into having a kid."

A sickening feeling settles in the pit of my stomach. Is that what he thinks happened to him? They all think Alisa's the bad one, but they don't see that it's them. And Courtney.

"Ben, you're young. You have a whole life ahead of you. Personally, I think you need to forget about the girls and just focus on basketball because that is the only thing that's going to get you somewhere."

Good to know he doesn't think I can get anywhere with my brain.

"Is that what you wish you had done?" I ask.

"With how things are now, looking back, yeah I wish I had. And if you're smart, you'll do the same thing. I don't want to see you skipping anymore, especially on game days. That's the dumbest thing you can do."

"Doesn't matter that I got sick?"

He meets my eyes, with a clenched jaw. "Brush it off. Are you a man or a weak child?" He shakes his head. "You choose your own path, but if you keep following this ridiculous nonsense, you're going to end up like that girl's father. Broke and a cheater and alcoholic."

"I grew up with Alisa. Her dad may not be perfect, but at least he's trying to get his life together."

Dad raises an eyebrow. "I never took you to be naïve. Must have gotten that from your mom. The guy has always been an alcoholic, and if you think living in poverty is getting your life together, you've got another thing coming."

"Why are you and Mom so judgmental? Aren't you supposed to care about your city and its people?"

"The only reason that girl likes you is because you have money and you're going places. I assure you, you sleep with her, she'll figure out some way to get herself pregnant. Just think about that next time you think about her."

Clenching my teeth, I grip the bar stool, wanting to throw it across the room. "You don't know her. She's not like that at all." He's got it all wrong. Alisa would never do that. He's got to be talking about Courtney because that's exactly what happened. That's why she's still with me. Because her family life is terrible, and she's struggling in school. I'm her way out.

Dad scoffs. "Stop being stupid, boy. Go back to school and play the game."

"No." I don't want to play tonight.

"What did you say to me?"

"You think you have all the answers, don't you? What's best for me? What's best for this family. But you don't. You or Mom don't have a clue. I said I'm not playing tonight."

"This girl worth losing everything over?"

"This has nothing to do with Alisa. You have no clue about anything."

Dad moves closer to me, grips my shirt in his fist and slams me against the wall. "You better shut your fucking mouth because you don't have any idea what's going on."

"It's one game. Pretty sure they'll do fine without me."

"Hey!" Mom yells, and we both turn our head toward her. "What is going on?"

Dad releases me, but I know he's not done getting out whatever it is he needs to.

"Go upstairs," she tells me, but I'm not leaving her alone with him.

I stand there and cross my arms.

"Go," she demands. "I'll be fine."

I've never seen my dad hit her or even come close. It's usually just me, but he hasn't done that in years. He's stressed out, and I get that, because I feel like hitting something.

Fuck. Is this going to be me in a few years? Shaking my head, my nausea returns, and I go back upstairs.

My parents start warring with each other. Because of me. I did this. I thought things were going to be better. Things would be back on track with them.

But I was wrong. I've been wrong about so many things, it's hard to know if anything I ever do is right. This isn't how I wanted life to be, but we don't ever exactly get that choice. Alisa flashes in my mind. All I keep imagining is her cutting herself, and it kills me that I can't be there to help. To save her from whatever demons she faces.

A knock on my door startles me, and I sit up from my bed. Mom enters. Her eyes are red, and she looks awful.

"I'm sorry," I tell her as shame settles inside me.

She shakes her head and closes the door. "Ben, none of this is your fault. And I'm sorry if you were led to believe that. Your father shouldn't have gotten out of hand."

"I shouldn't have told him about Alisa."

Mom takes a deep breath and sinks down onto the bed next to me. "Ben, I haven't been fair to you at all. I'm not perfect, nor am I a great mother."

"What? Mom?"

"I got scared. You have such an amazing future ahead of you, and it was wrong of me to push Courtney onto you. I know she hurt you deep, and I never meant to make you feel worse. I thought Courtney could change and make you happy, but that isn't the case. You're miserable. You're stressed all the time. Moody. And I know it isn't all because of what's happening at home."

How could she have noticed all that? Is that what Courtney told her? "Then why were you pushing us to get back together?"

"Because your father hated, hates me for what I did. It ruined us. I didn't want you to hate her. It was a mistake, and I guess I projected myself into the situation. I wanted you to forgive her, because I wanted your father to forgive me. I know it doesn't make sense, and it was very wrong of me. I am so sorry, Ben. For everything."

I put my arm around her and pull her close. "It's okay."

"No, it isn't okay. I've been seeing a therapist, and I've been blaming everyone else but me for my mistakes."

"Mom, I'm sure Dad didn't help. If you two were so miserable that it led you astray, then he's just as much at fault as you."

She shakes her head. "If that's something Courtney told you, she's wrong. Cheating is never okay. If you're unhappy in a relationship and you've done everything you can to salvage it, then there's nothing else you can do. You have to let it go."

Is she talking about her and Dad or Courtney and me?

"Ben, you deserve to be happy. You deserve to do whatever makes you happy, and to be with whomever makes you happy. If Alisa is that person, you should be with her."

What? Why is she telling me this now? Does she know Courtney's pregnant? Is that why she's saying this? "Why are you saying this to me now?"

"Because I'm realizing how terrible I've been, and how unsupportive I've been for you. And Hayden. It's your choice, and it's always been your choice. I'm not involving myself in your relationships."

"Have you talked to Courtney?"

"No. I took her under my wing in a way because I felt bad, and I felt like she and I were similar. But I have my own daughter that I have been unfair to."

I don't know what to say or how to act. Mom has completely turned a new leaf. Is that what she's been doing when she's been out of town?

Mom takes my hand. "Ben, your father and I are getting a divorce. Hayden and I will be staying with Aunt Valerie."

That's an hour away. "How is she going to school? Am I not coming?"

"For right now, it's best if you stay with your father. He needs you."

Fat chance. "You didn't hear him earlier?"

"I did and talked to him. Your father is hurting, though he'll never admit it. This will only be temporary."

Until it's slightly not temporary. "Are you and Hayden moving to Birmingham now? You're going to leave me here?"

"Ben, of course, I want you to be with us, and that is your decision. But you have a life here. Scouts will come watch you play here; you've built a legacy."

"I can transfer." I have no doubt Courtney wouldn't mind leaving this town either. But I'd never see Alisa. She would be all alone.

"I know. Just don't make any rash decisions. I need to find a place and get settled first."

"Why can't you stay here?" I don't want her to leave. Or Hayden.

She looks at me like I know the answer. And I do.

I need to run. I need to get out of here, and once Mom leaves my room, I clamber down the stairs like I can't get out of the house fast enough.

As I run, the cold air hits my lungs. I know I can't run away from any of this, but just tonight I can. I'm almost tempted to run to Alisa's, but I don't. By the time I return home, it's quiet. Doors are closed and for the time being, it's peaceful. Dad's car isn't here. I wonder where he went. Probably to some hotel for the night.

I reach my bedroom door, and Hayden opens hers. She crosses the hallway and wraps her arms around me. I hug her back, hating the bulge that forms in my throat. I don't know what to say to my sister to comfort her. I won't say goodbye to her. All of this feels too surreal. This can't be really happening.

But it is.

alisa

When I wake the next morning, I leave a note for Daddy telling him I'm going to work. Might as well since I'm suspended. On the way, I walk next to the nearby park. The same one Sarah and I hung out in. It's cold and windy as I watch a few ducks float across the pond. One of them grooms itself and dips its head under the water a few times. It's such a simple thing, yet I'm mesmerized by it. The duck joins its flock, its family, and they float away. I miss having a family.

Toward the end of my shift, Ben comes through my line. I love seeing him, and the way his hazel eyes light up when he sees me, except tonight, a horrified expression washes over his face.

"Alisa, what happened to your eye?"

I clear my throat. "I tripped and fell. Hit the coffee table." I look away from his gaze.

"Damn. Are you okay?"

"Yeah. Fine."

"Can we talk when you get off?"

"S-sure. I get off in a few minutes actually." I ring up a Coke for him and give him his change.

"I'll meet you outside."

What does he want to talk about? Something's wrong. I'm so nervous that it takes me two times to count my till.

Grabbing the coat he let me borrow, I meet him outside.

"Hey," he says. The sound of his voice ignites my heartbeat, and my throat tightens. Why is this so hard?

"Hi."

He looks exhausted and defeated. I hate seeing him like this. I can't imagine what he's going through, but I wish I could comfort him.

"Are you okay?" he asks. "How much trouble are you in?"

"I'm okay. I'm grounded."

"I'm really sorry."

"It wasn't your fault. Are you okay?"

He releases a long sigh and pauses. "I don't know. Everything is messed up." Ben begins to unload everything. His parent's divorce. His mom and sister moving. The pregnancy with Courtney. How he wants to be with me but can't. I listen and can't help but ache for him. I know what it's like to live with fighting parents and how uncomfortable and painful it can be. My parents never divorced, but my mom's death sent Daddy over the edge, and he's the worst he's ever been.

"I'm sorry. I didn't mean to go off like that."

"It's okay. You can talk to me anytime."

"Talking to you helps so much."

Hearing that is uplifting, but sad at the same time. We don't always get what we want. "You help me, too. You know we shouldn't be talking."

"My mom wants me to be happy."

"What?"

"She's been going to therapy and told me that if I want to be with you, then I should."

An ache twists inside me. He's having a baby with someone else.

"Perfect fucking timing. But if I hadn't treated you the way I did, or if I had realized how I was being manipulated by Courtney…"

"Ben, you can't focus on the what ifs in life. I know it's easy to do."

We're quiet for a moment.

"I know you're grounded, but any chance you could come over?"

"Now?"

"Yes. I have a surprise for you."

"I…I don't think I should."

"Look, I'm going to support Courtney and our kid, but I can't be in a relationship with her like that. I want you."

"Ben."

He holds up his hands. "I know. It sounds more messed up than it did in my head. Sorry. There's so much shit going on in my head, but you are the only thing keeping me sane. I want to do something for you. As a thank you for everything you've done for me. We can even go to the library."

"What is it?"

"It'll be worth it."

My heart pounds as I agree. He lets me in the passenger seat, and within a few minutes we're at the library. I don't understand what's going on.

We walk toward the row of computers, and he sits at one. Pulling out a computer chair, he invites me to sit. After a few mouse clicks and punching of keys, he moves to the side, inviting me to sit in front of the computer.

I do and look at him.

"Talk to her." He points to the screen and when I look, it's a chat window.

"W-who is—"

"Sarah."

I'm so overcome with emotion that I burst into tears.

"Oh, uh, I—"

I hug Ben tightly, then spend the next hour chatting with Sarah. I've wanted to call her over the past several weeks, but I've been too scared.

When we walk out into the cold night, I turn to him. "Thank you."

"Of course."

"I love you," I say, and he looks as if he might cry. Instead, he gathers me into his arms and holds me. I rest my head on his chest.

"I love you."

I don't know how long we stay like this, but I want it to last forever.

"Ben."

"I know." He pulls away. "I don't want to lose you again."

"I'm not worth all this."

"Stop saying that. You are worth so much. You're beautiful and you have a beautiful heart. I love you, Alisa."

But I'm not.

"Come on." He opens the door and I slide inside, not wanting to go home. Not wanting any of this to end.

Once he starts the engine, a slow song plays. It has a sad, nostalgic rhythm and I let the song take over. He takes my hand and squeezes it.

ben

Dad and I carry out the last two boxes and put them in the back of the UHAUL that Mom rented. It's really happening. She and Hayden are staying with Aunt Viv in Birmingham until they can find a place.

I'm trying so hard to keep it all in. Stoic, just like Mom.

"Be careful," Dad says with a strained voice.

Is this really what they want? Why can't they work through it?

"I will." Mom nods. "I'll call when we get there." She hugs me. I'm like a robot.

"Are you sure you don't need help unloading?" I ask.

She gives a tight smile. "It's okay. You have a game tonight."

It's not that important.

Hayden doesn't say a word when I hug her. She wraps her arms around me so tight that I almost lose it in the driveway. I'd never admit it to her, but I'm going to miss her. Am I really choosing basketball over my family? Is that the right choice? Should I move with them? I'll be going away to college anyway in a year, I remind myself. Still. This is different.

Then another wave of pain hits me. Courtney's pregnant. Neither one of us will be going to college. I've always been so careful, except for the one time I wasn't.

The house feels empty now. What I wouldn't give to hear Hayden listening to her crappy music; or Mom banging around in the kitchen; or even the two of them bickering.

"Dammit Ben! Where's your head at?" Zach yells at me after I had the ball stolen from me for the fourth time.

Not in the game. My fadeaway has been weak all night. I sank one layup, and that's it for the game. We're down thirty points. Alisa and Courtney and our baby and my family are swimming in my head.

The whistle blows, and I join my team near the bench. Sweat is dripping down my face, and my head is pounding. I haven't been practicing like I should. I haven't been doing a lot of anything.

"Ben, you're out," Coach Turner says.

"What?"

"Hazen, you're in." Scott stands removing his warmup jacket.

"You're kidding right? We can come back from this. Just give me a chance."

"Ben, sit down!" Coach yells. I've never been thrown out of a game. But I've also never missed one either.

Clenching my teeth, I throw my towel down. I can't believe how just a few days ago I was on top of the world. And a week later, my life has done a complete 180. I can't wait to get home to hear Dad talk about my lack of playing tonight. I'm surprised he hasn't rushed down on the court to yell at Coach. Probably missed the whole thing because he had a call to take.

At half time, we're in the locker room completely defeated. Coach comes in screaming.

"Ben, what the hell are you thinking out there?"

"Just a bad night," I say.

"A bad night? You haven't made one complete pass. You can't even sink the ball in the basket at all. You're playing like you've never touched a damn ball."

I stand from the bench. "I don't need this. You won't play me? Then I'm out."

"You get back here."

When I keep walking toward the door, I hear Zach and some of the other guys call my name, but I ignore them.

"You walk out that door, don't step foot in here again."

I don't care. I've reached my boiling point. Shoving the door open, I leave basketball.

The night is as dark as my life as I make my way to my car. I don't know where I'm headed. Definitely not home.

"Ben, are you okay?" Courtney yells after me. I know she must be freezing in her cheerleading outfit, even though she's wearing long sleeves.

I sigh. "No, I'm not."

"I'm sorry your parents are making your life hell for you, but everything's okay. We have each other." She takes my hand and brings it to her stomach. "And little Ben. Or little Courtney."

It feels like a knife is twisting inside my chest. No matter how much I try to avoid it, it's there. I'm going to be a father. Defeated, I lean against my car.

"Why don't we go to the party tonight? Forget everything. Just have fun."

"I'm really not in the mood to party. And you're pregnant."

She lets out a loud groan. "God, Ben, you're never in the mood for anything anymore. Maybe you need help. Come on. It'll be our last hurrah."

Spoken true words by someone who loves me. Besides, last party I went to ended with a kid in Courtney's stomach.

"No."

She lets out a disgusted sigh.

"Ben!" I see Dad charging out of the doors toward me. I can't take his yelling.

"Call me later," Courtney says and jogs back inside the building.

I open my car door. "Ben, wait."

I stop. He doesn't sound angry.

He reaches my car, breathless. "I know things at home haven't been easy, but you can't walk away from this."

"Why does it even matter?"

"Because you can do something with your life. You've worked hard. Don't let our stuff mess this up for you. You deserve this."

What the hell is going on with my parents? They're suddenly supportive. "I can't go back in there tonight."

Dad nods. "It's okay. I'll talk to Turner. Look, Ben..." He grips the back of his neck. "I'm sorry for what we've put you and Hayden through. I...started seeing a therapist."

"Oh."

"I'm sorry your mom and I couldn't make things work."

"Okay." I don't know how to respond.

"I'll be at home with some dinner. If you feel like joining me. I don't know."

I have never seen my dad so lost. I don't know if I'm supposed to comfort him or what. I'm not sure dinner's supposed to fix everything, but maybe it's a start. Maybe we are more alike than I thought. We've both been hurt and make mistakes and we don't always react in the best way. We aren't perfect.

Monday morning arrives way too soon. I usually love the weekends, but lately not so much. My heart does a little flip when I see Alisa in the hall. Our eyes meet, and I want so much to go to her, but I don't. I don't want to cause her anymore pain. I don't want to keep reeling her in, only to let her go.

"Hey, Ben," a girl says. I turn and meet Kim's eyes.

"What do you want?"

"I heard what happened with your parents. Janie's pretty broken up that Hayden left."

"So am I. What do you want?"

"Look, I'm sorry. Courtney was my friend, but I can't do it anymore. I'm tired of it all."

"Great." I slam my locker. "Anything else?"

"Uh…so…Courtney got messed up at Friday's party. Pretty bad. She hooked up with Tyler."

"What?" Red flashes across my face. I clench my teeth.

"I also don't think she's pregnant."

"Why do you think that?"

"I was at the store with her and Rebecca the other day and she bought stuff."

Female stuff is what she means. "Are you serious?" Rage wells inside me. I had my doubts, but I ignored them. Deep down I thought maybe this was some ridiculous attempt to keep me, but I never could believe Courtney could be *that* vicious.

"What's with the come-to-Jesus moment?" I ask.

"She's a bitch and making you and Alisa miserable. I'm tired of her trying to boss me around. I gave in because I didn't wanna be everyone making fun of me, but it's wrong."

"Thanks. I guess."

The bell rings. The halls clear quickly. I'll catch Courtney eventually. She can't hide from me forever. I'm definitely not in the mood to learn about math. I'm too pissed off.

After the second class, I am determined to find her. When I see a group gathering around a set of lockers, I cringe. Somehow, I know Courtney's up to something. Alisa flees down the hall, and I see Courtney laughing with her friends. Except Kim. Anger knocks me in my stomach. As I approach closer, I feel sick. Alisa's locker is vandalized with words. *Slut. Cutter. Freak. Whore.*

I get in Courtney's face. "What is your problem?"

She gives a fake innocent look. "Why do you think this was me?"

I know we have yet another audience to our fight, but instead of Courtney making me feel like shit, the truth is coming to light.

"Because I know damn well it was you. You spread those rumors about her sleeping around, too. You went too far."

She shrugs. "Don't you think *she* went too far?"

I clench my teeth. "She never got so drunk, while pregnant, and slept around on me."

Gasps are like surround sound, and for the first time Courtney looks embarrassed.

"What are you even talking about?"

"Stop lying. I'm over all of this. You were never pregnant, were you?"

She says nothing. I shake my head. I can't believe she lied to me. This whole time.

"I'm in love with Alisa, Courtney. Not you."

That sobers her up. She looks at me in complete shock. "You're joking."

"No. And you can leave Alisa alone. She doesn't deserve any of this. You don't know what either of us have been through because you never cared enough. No one's going to pity you. Your parents think you aren't as good as your sister because you do stupid shit like this. Grow up."

I walk away, finally freeing myself from the chains of Courtney Andrews.

alisa

Seeing my locker with all those words on it hurts. It shouldn't bother me. I should be used to it. And it's true. When I rush to the bathroom, I frantically search for my razor, but I can't find it. I want to punch something. The urge is growing. Standing in the stall, trying to catch my breath, I'm on the verge of tears, but I don't want to cry. I don't want anyone knowing I've shed a single tear because of them. I have to get out of here.

Bolting from the bathroom, I see the crowd still gathered around my locker. When I overhear Ben tell Courtney and everyone else, he's in love with me, I halt. Hearing that does something to me. My pulse quickens, and I feel…*good*. It's almost like when Mom and I would cook. That feeling I got that we were happy, and everything was okay.

Did I hear him right? Hesitantly, I turn around, and when Ben sees me, he walks toward me with purpose. Once he reaches me, his lips press against mine in a yearning way. It's the best kiss I've ever had. Everything is spinning, and my heart won't slow its beat. He takes my face in his hands, and I'm on fire. It's one of the best feelings. It's freeing. Exhilarating. I feel so high. Warmth spreads throughout me, and I know I'm safe.

He draws back a little. "I love you."

I can feel my face stretch into a smile. I love him. I've always loved him. But he's having a baby with someone else. I pull away, and that feeling fades. I hate how one second, I'm on top of the world, and the next, it's gone.

The bell rings, and the halls begin to clear.

"Why did you do that?" I shake my head. "I need to go." I turn for the door.

"Alisa, wait—"

But I'm out the door. It's cold and the rain is pouring. I move under the ledge close to the building. The one Sarah and Damon spent time smoking under.

"Hey. Are you okay?" Ben asks once he spots me.

I nod, not looking at him.

"What's wrong?"

"Ben." I bite my lip. "I appreciate what you did today. But I know this can't work. You really need to focus on Courtney and your baby."

"She lied to me."

"What?" I look up, meeting his hazel eyes.

"I thought you heard all of that. Courtney lied about being pregnant."

I gasp. "Why would she do that?" Tears cloud my eyes.

"To control me. It's all part of her manipulation. She wants what she wants, and she'll do anything to get it."

I lean against the brick wall. My knees are weak, and I almost burst into tears.

Ben wraps his arms around me and holds me tight. I love the way he smells and the feel of his arms. "I will be good to you if you'll let me. I want to try because I hate being away from you. It almost killed me when you left years ago and fate or whatever has stepped in and brought you back. I want this to work."

"I do, too." His words sound perfect, yet I don't know how to take it. "I'm not good enough."

He cradles my head in his hands, pinning my eyes with an intense gaze "Stop saying that. You're more than good enough, and I want to show you. We can take our time. It's you, Alisa. It's always been you. You're my everything."

My heart hammers wildly in my chest. He makes me feel. I'm scared, but I trust him. Wrapping my arms around him, I kiss him. It's just me, Ben, the rain. And this intense high whizzing throughout me.

"Why don't we go to the fair tonight?" he asks, once we part. "I need to do something fun and being with you is all I want.

I chuckle. "Ben, it's raining."

His lips turn up into a grin. "The storm is supposed to end this afternoon."

I'm still grounded, but I want to have fun, even if I'm probably going to pay for it later. Just one night. "Okay."

His lips press against mine, and the only sounds are my heartbeat in my ear and the spattering of rain hitting the concrete.

It's the strangest thing. I've been on an emotional roller coaster ever since I've come back. But this feels right. I know nothing will happen with Ben at my side. I love this feeling, and I never want it to end. This is what happiness feels like.

ben

Seeing Alisa let go is amazing. I love watching her laugh. I haven't seen her like this since we were kids. For all the heartache and pain, she's been through, it's refreshing to know she still has that amazing light and fearlessness inside her. I haven't seen it in so long.

"What is it?" she asks.

"Nothing."

"Why are you looking at me?"

"I love seeing you smile. You look beautiful."

We ride the Ferris wheel. She clutches my hand the entire time. The teacups make us nauseous. The carousal makes us laugh because of how ridiculous it is. But we enjoy being kids and being carefree. I win a small panda bear in a ring toss and give it to her.

When I drop her off at home, I kiss her, gently at first, but it becomes heated within seconds. I can't help myself with her. My hand slips underneath her shirt and I graze her bare skin. Her lips are incredibly soft, and her low moans drive me crazy. I love the way she runs her hands through my hair.

We part, breathing hard, and even though I can't see in the dark, I bet her cheeks are a beautiful pink. I hold her for a little while longer until she has to go inside.

I definitely need a cold shower.

When I get home, it's quiet, thankfully. Things are far from good again, but at least with Alisa by my side, I know I can get through it all. She helps me so much.

After my shower, I call her. We talk about our incredible night. Basketball. Cooking. My parents' divorce. Her dad's girlfriend. Talking to her makes me feel better. I can tell her anything and she doesn't yell or judge me. She's always so kind to me and says the sweetest things. I know I don't deserve her, but I will do everything I can to make her happy.

Days drift by like some insanely amazing dream. I keep pinching myself because I can't believe it isn't a dream. I've managed to get back on my game with basketball and school. Alisa and I hang out as much as we can, in between her working and school. She seems happy, less shy, and she promised that she quit cutting. I haven't noticed her sneaking off or anything. She says things at home are better since Diane is around, and she makes her dad happy. I know it can't be easy for either of them without her mom. I remember her kindness, and as I look at her picture, I see how Alisa looks so much like her.

"She's beautiful, like you," I say.

The familiar pink color rises to her cheeks, and I can't help but love her reaction. "Thanks," she mumbles.

I chuckle. "Since you're off tonight, wanna go see a movie? That new scary movie is out. Supposed to be good."

"Which one?"

"Scream."

"Okay."

"If you get too scared, I'll comfort you."

She chuckles. "I think you were the one afraid of scary movies. Remember when we watched Pet Sematary with Sarah?"

"Okay, admittedly that movie is creepy. And we were nine when that came out."

"Yeah, it gave me nightmares, but Mom calmed me." Her smile vanishes, and she looks away. "I'll get my coat."

I pull her to me and hold her. It's all I can do. I don't know what it's like to lose a parent. It's bad enough that Mom has moved out. I don't know what I'd do if I lost either of mine. It's hard enough not seeing my mom every day, but I still get to talk to her.

"Let's go." She takes my hand.

Once we reach the porch door, she freezes.

A car tears down the driveway, crunching over the gravel and slinging it everywhere. Whoever's driving doesn't seem to care about the gravel hurting the car.

I hear Alisa curse under her breath. "You have to go Ben."

Shit. It's her father, and I've gotten her in trouble. "I'll explain—"

"No. Just go." She pushes me, but it's too late. The old yellow car comes to an abrupt stop as dust from the gravel road floats in the air. The engine cuts off. The door groans as it opens, and a woman steps out. Her short dirty blond hair is messed up, and her skin is so tan. She's dressed in a shirt that shows too much cleavage, and her nametag is in an awkward place. Diane looks young. I wonder how old she is. Her brown eyes rove up and down me as she smokes a cigarette. She smiles.

Gross.

"Hi," she says in thick Southern accent. "Who's your friend?"

"I'm Ben. I…came over to give Alisa her homework assignment and to take her to work."

"Well, I'm Diane." Her hand reaches out, and I shake it. "I'm gonna be Alisa's new mom." She flashes her left hand, and a large diamond catches my eye.

Not the way I'd introduce myself, but okay. "Oh. That's-Congrat—"

"He proposed to you?" Alisa asks, her voice sounds a million miles away.

"Yes. We're gonna be a happy family, aren't we?" Her lips stretch into a large smile as she holds out her arms. "Come give your new mama a hug."

Alisa hesitantly lets the woman hug her.

How could her dad afford that? He can't even afford heat. None of this feels right. I don't like the uneasiness that resides in my stomach.

"I have to go to work."

"Did you cook mine and your daddy's dinner?"

"Yes, ma'am."

"Oh honey. Call me 'Mom.'"

I have never wanted to hurt a woman, but I want to slap this one. How dare she ask Alisa that? Who is this lady? I have to get Alisa out of here.

"We should get you to work." I take Alisa's hand. "Nice to meet you."

"You, too, cutie. Don't be a stranger, now."

Gross.

As soon as we get into the car, I turn the ignition and haul down the driveway.

"Are you okay?"

She nods, but I can see her hands shake. "Yeah. Are you ready to go see the movie?" Her voice falters.

"Alisa," I hesitate. "Maybe we shouldn't." I take her hand and squeeze it.

"It doesn't matter."

"Do you think she'll tell your dad that I was here?"

"No. I don't know." I don't know what she's thinking, but I know she's hurt.

"She shouldn't have said that. That was shitty."

"It-it's okay. She makes my dad happy."

"Okay, that's great, but what about you? She completely sounds like she's trying to erase your mom."

"My mom's dead, Ben. She's not coming back. She wants to be my mom."

What kind of messed up thinking is that? Was that something Diane told her? What is going on?

"Let's go see the movie. Please."

I take a deep breath. "Are you sure?"

"Yes."

She's determined, and stubborn. I don't want to push it, but I want her to enjoy herself, especially if she's about to get grounded again. But I still don't feel good about it. But I get it if she wants to get her mind off things. And if I can help, so be it.

"That was scary," Alisa says as we walk out of the theatre and to my car.

"Did you like it?"

"Yeah. I love scary movies. I love how they reimagined the whole slasher movie."

"Isn't as good as Halloween."

"Well, that's a classic."

I drive us back to her house, or rather the mailbox, and like usual at the end of our dates, we sit quietly listening to the radio. One of my favorite Smashing Pumpkins songs, "Luna" plays. Their *Siamese Dream* CD has been on rotation for weeks, and no matter how many times I think I should be tired of it, I'm not.

"I really like this song," she says. "Will you make me a mixed tape and give it to me tomorrow?"

"Of course. What all do you want on it?"

"Surprise me."

I smile. "You know making mixed tapes takes time, and there's a science to it."

She raises an eyebrow.

"I'm serious. You can't just throw random songs on a tape. It has to flow. It has to match the mood or theme."

"I didn't realize so much went into it."

"Of course. It's like writing a letter to someone, and in my case, a love letter."

I know she blushes because she peers out the window. She bites her lip and for a second, I swear I see her chin quiver. "I should go."

My most hated part of our nights. "Will you need a ride in the morning?"

Alisa shakes her head. "I'll see you tomorrow."

"I'll be there waiting with your tape."

We kiss for a long time, and like always, neither one of us wants to let each other go. But we do, and I watch her walk down the long, dark driveway.

alisa

Diane is still there when I get home. Which I guess she's going to be living here now. How could Daddy afford that ring? Then a stabbing pain hits me. He used my savings to buy her a ring. My chance of getting out of here is now wrapped around her finger. My new mother. I know she wants me to call her 'Mom,' but I can't.

No matter how many times I walk inside the house expecting there to be heat, I'm always disappointed when it's cold and drafty.

"Where have you been?" she asks when I close the door behind me. The raw stench of whiskey surrounds her. Cigarette smoke lingers in the air. It just sits there, like Diane, lazy and bored. It's hard to breathe, and I can't help but cough.

Did she forget? "I was at work."

"Alisa, honey. I went to the store, and they said you were off."

Damn. I swallow hard.

She takes my hand, squeezing it. "Look, I don't mind you dating. But we need to set some ground rules."

She's okay with me dating? "Okay."

"First of all, you have to be honest with me."

"Okay." I can do that.

"I was worried about you, and I know your daddy worries, too. We just have to know where you are at all times."

"But…Daddy won't let me date."

She grins. "You let me worry about him. Now, the second thing is, if I'm gonna be your mama, you have to call me that."

I can't. She isn't my mother. I open my mouth to respond, but I see something familiar around her neck, and fire ignites inside me. Whatever patience I once had is gone. It's like she's trying to become my mother. She's wearing my mother's necklace. "Take that off."

"What'd you say to me?"

Staring into her brown eyes, I clench my teeth. "Take off the necklace."

She gasps. "Alisa, that isn't nice."

"It was my mother's."

Diane sighs. "We've been over this many times. Your mother is dead. I'm putting it to good use."

It's too much. I'm not ready to let go of my mom. I'm not ready to call this lady 'mom.' I push her and reach for the necklace, tearing it from her neck.

She gasps. "How could you? I have been nothing but nice to you. But you hate me. You're always so mean and rude. I don't know what else to do to make you like me." Tears well in her eyes. "Just go to your room."

The anger is too much. I grab the razor, needing solace. I promised Ben I would stop, but I need it. I need it now. And I hate myself that I do.

The slamming of a car door wakes me. Confusion sets in for a moment, but when I remember that Diane caught Ben and me, a bulge lands in my throat. "Oh no, oh no," I repeat over and over.

The sound of my father's boots clumping across the porch forces my heart to beat too fast. I can't catch my breath. I close my eyes, and everything is dizzy.

Daddy opens the door, sets his keys in the dish next to the door. I hear Diane's voice muffled through the thin walls. She starts to cry.

Gripping the bed sheets, I wait.

"Alisa," he calls for me in a calm voice.

I stumble to my door, opening it with a shaky hand. I use the door frame to the living room for support. "Yes."

"Come here."

I swallow hard and move closer. Diane stands beside him.

"Where did you go tonight."

"I went to work."

"You better not lie to me."

I swallow again, but I can't dislodge the bulge in my throat. "I-I went to work. I promise."

"Why was there a boy here?"

"He was bringing my homework. It was Ben," I say, hoping his name will help.

Diane holds up Ben's jacket, and my heart sinks. "He left this behind because he was hurryin' to put his pants back on."

"What? No! She's lying!"

He moves closer. I look away from his heated glare and bite my lip. I can smell alcohol on his breath. He sways subtly. I know he's been drinking for some time.

"You callin' Diane a liar?"

"She threatened me with a knife. Look what she did to my arm!" Diane lifts her arm, and there's a small cut across the top. Why is she doing this?

"What the hell is wrong with you?" He shakes his head removing his belt.

Nothing I say can save me from this. Whatever he does, he's going to do. "I'm sorry," I cry. "I'm sorry I'm a failure! But you cheated on Mom." It slips out.

"What did you say?" Something flickers in his eyes. Shame? Pain?

It's true? How could he do that to Mom?

"How dare you. Your apologies mean nothing. All you do is hurt people. You beat up some girl at school. You're whoring around, and you're attacking Diane!"

My chin quivers. "No. That's not what's happening." Tears pour down my face.

His belt comes down, and I block my face. It hits my arm and back hard. I fall, clenching my teeth from the pain.

"I don't know what the fuck is going on with you, but you're gonna learn to behave." He jerks me up and drags me toward the front door. Daddy opens the door and pulls me outside. The wind hits me like a bag of ice on my skin. My teeth chatter as he pulls me outside, past the porch door. I lose my balance, but he still drags me. His boots shuffle through the dead grass. I tremble as we head toward the shed. Is he going to keep me there?

"No, Daddy." I try to fight against him, but his grip is solid.

"You wanna know what it's like on your own? You continue to lie to me. You don't care about nothing. This will keep you where you belong until you learn to behave."

"No, please! Daddy, it's cold!"

"Shut up!" He stumbles as he tosses me into the small, white shed. "Stay in there until you figure shit out," he slurs his words.

As he closes the door, I grab the handle. "Please! I can do better."

Daddy swings open the door with force, pushing me into the wooden table behind me, and I slip to the floor. He slams the door and locks it. I watch through the tiny window on the side as he walks away. I could use some of his tools to smash the window open, but I don't. Maybe it's for a couple of hours. It's so dark inside. So cold.

I pull my knees up to my chest, trying to ignore the cold. The bright moon shines through the shed a little. It darkens as clouds slowly drift across. I close my eyes and think of my mom. It hits me that it's been eight months since she died. I have no doubt that Daddy blames me. She asked for her pain medication, and I gave it to her. It was enough to put her to sleep and never wake up. I need my mom and I miss her. I miss how she comforted me. I miss cooking with her. She wouldn't be proud of me if she knew what I have been doing the last several months. She would be disappointed. She would disown me. I blindly search the shed for scissors or a razor. I release a sigh of relief when I find a razor.

ben

A nagging feeling stays with me all day. Alisa didn't show up at school yesterday or today, and when I try calling, the line is dead. I've been biding my time until her father leaves for work, so I can check on her. She acted weird last night, and I know she's probably very grounded because of me, and it sickens me. No matter what, I seem to always be hurting her.

I'm a fucking mess because of all of this. I need to see her. I need to know she's okay. I've never felt like this with any other girl. Never.

Hesitating at the edge of her long driveway, I decide to creep down it. Alisa's old car is the only one out front and the house looks dark. I take a deep breath and park. I don't want to get her into more trouble, but maybe I can explain to her dad that it's important. I knock on the door, and no one answers. I call her name, but nothing.

Is she ignoring me? If she's no longer allowed to see me, can't she tell me? My chest aches as that nervous feeling comes back. I step off the porch, and wander to the back of the house. I'm not one for breaking and entering, but maybe there's a back door that's unlocked. It's incredibly black out here, and I see a dark shed. Pulling open the screen to the back door, I try, but it's locked.

I hear metal clank against a floor, like someone dropped something. Staring at the shed, I know that's where the noise came from. Something doesn't feel right. Moving toward the shed, I look around, hoping no one's going to come out of the darkness and attack me. I swear it feels like a freaking scary movie. I reach the shed, but it's locked.

"Alisa?" I roll my eyes. There's probably some crazy animal in here knocking shit off a shelf. Shaking my head, I start walking away, but the small window catches my eye. I peer inside, but I can't make out anything. Something's moving inside though and I jump.

"Ben?"

My stomach sinks. Is she trapped? "Alisa? Shit! Where's the key?" I want to break the window, but it's too small for either of us to fit through.

"I don't have it. It's okay. My dad will be back soon."

She's damn crazy if she thinks I'm just going to walk away and leave her in there. "Hold on." I race to my car and grab the tire iron and a flashlight and run back to the shed. I slam the tire iron onto the knob, breaking the door open.

Dropping the tire iron, I rush up to her and flip on the flashlight. "Are you okay?" When the light shines on her, I completely freeze. Her eye is black, her skin is pale and sallow. She's freezing when I grab her and pull her toward me. Her entire body trembles. "What happened?"

"C-c-clumsy. The wind…it knocked the door closed. It happens all the t-t-time."

I remove my jacket and wrap it around her. I don't buy her story. Something's wrong. "How long have you been in here?"

"Not long."

Lie. "Come on. I need to take you to the hospital." When I try to move, she doesn't budge. It's like her feet are cemented to the ground. For someone so fragile and small, she is definitely strong.

"No. I'm fine."

"Alisa…how did you get the shiner?"

"I tripped."

Another lie.

"Why are you here?" She pulls away from me, inviting the cold between us.

"I came looking for you."

Alisa holds herself even with my jacket. "About what?"

"Can we go inside where it's warm?"

Biting her lip, she glances at me for a second.

"Or my car?"

"Okay."

I open the passenger door for her and take a deep breath before I slide in on my side. Turning on the ignition, I flip the heat to full blast. I contemplate taking her to the hospital, but knowing her, she'd throw herself out of the car. But she needs to go.

"Alisa, what's going on?" I already know, but I'm scared to say the words because they're so incomprehensible.

She looks like she's about to fall apart.

"Can I please take you to the hospital? Or at least my house?"

She shakes her head and nods at the same time. Just as fast as tears roll down her cheeks, she wipes them away.

When I gather her into my arms, she flinches and cries out.

"What? What is it?"

"I…I just hurt myself."

I know he hurt her. How could he do this? This man already fucked with my family. How could he hurt his daughter? "What happened?"

"Nothing. I was being clumsy. I'm sorry. I—"

"Alisa, tell me. I promise you can trust me."

She won't speak, but I pull her into an embrace as carefully as I can. Clumsy. I've seen her with bruises on her arms, her face, her legs. I've seen the deep cuts on her stomach. She's incredibly afraid of her father.

I kiss her forehead. "I'm taking you to my house."

She nods.

I hate seeing her in so much pain. I don't know what to do. I have to talk to her, because I'd rather she hate me forever than her end up dead.

Putting the car in gear, I leave the darkness of the countryside. When we get to my house, I bring her upstairs.

"Are you hungry?"

She shakes her head.

"Are you still cold?"

She shakes her head.

"Do you want to sleep?"

The way she looks up at me causes my heart falter. Exhaustion wears on her face. Bags cling underneath her eyes. Her hair still has dirt and leaves in it. She looks awful, and I can't stand it. How the fuck did she wind up in that shed? Did her dad put her there? The thought pisses me off, and I want to fucking show him how it feels, but I have to set my anger aside for the time being.

"Do you want a shower?"

She shakes her head again.

I sit next to her on the bed and invite her to lie down next to me. I wrap a blanket around her. She trembles for a while before she finally falls asleep. I don't let go of her at all through the night. Dad hardly checks on me, so I know we'll be undisturbed. I kiss her forehead and pull her closer, hating the harrowing images that cross my mind all night.

It isn't until noon the next day that she finally wakes up. I don't know what hell she's been through. She looks exhausted and worn down. Like her soul has been taken out of her. And that fearlessness…is once again gone.

I make breakfast for her and try to get her to eat as much as she can. She does, but it isn't a lot.

"How are you feeling?" I ask, but I know it's a dumb question. I just want to get her talking.

"I'm okay. Thank you for letting me stay last night."

"Of course. Stay as long as you need."

She shakes her head. "I know you want me to say something, but I can't. Ben, you need to forget about me."

I let out a sigh. "Alisa, stop doing that. Stop pushing me away because I'm not going anywhere."

"You should. I don't deserve you."

"You do. You deserve better. Why do you feel that way?" I'm trying so hard not to get angry, but I have a feeling that bastard has told her she's not good enough. Or worse. "What if you spoke to a counselor?"

"About what?"

I have to tread lightly. Choose my words carefully. "I know you're dealing with stuff at home. It just seems like it's worsened."

"Diane doesn't like me. She blames me for things I don't do."

"What about your father?"

"What about him? He's doing the best he can."

I sigh internally. I love, yet hate, her stubbornness. "Did he do that to your eye? The bruises all over you?"

She lowers her head so that her hair hides her eye.

"He's been hitting you."

Alisa looks up. "What? Ben, I don't want to talk about this anymore."

"Please tell me. I can help."

"Help with what? He disciplines me, okay? Stop making this into a big thing."

I clench my teeth, wanting to hit something. How can she be like this? I don't understand. I know I'm going to lose her if I keep it up, but she needs to be safe. "Hitting you in the face is not disciplining. It's abuse and you need to tell someone."

She shakes her head. "There's nothing to tell."

"Trust me, it's not nothing."

"Ben, stop. Just…let it go."

I know I overstepped boundaries, but I don't care. She has to know she's not alone. I take her hand, holding it tightly. "I'm here for you. You don't have to hide from me."

"I'm not hiding," she says through clenched teeth.

"I have to tell someone."

Tears fill her eyes as she snatches her hand from mine. She gets up from the table and bolts out the door. I chase after her, catching her arm. The fear in her eyes speaks volumes, and I release her. "I'm sorry. I'm not trying to freak you out or hurt you. I'm doing this because I love you. Please don't leave, Alisa. You have to know I can't sit by and do nothing."

"Nothing happens. Just leave it alone."

"Alisa…"

"What do you want from me? I know I'm not good enough. It's my fault my mom died, which caused my dad's relapse. I promised her that I'd take care of him, but I can't. I failed at it."

"It wasn't your fault. None of it is. Why do you think that?"

"Because. She asked." Alisa breaks down. "She asked for her pain medication. And I gave it to her even though she already took a lot." The pain is too much for her to handle and she sinks to her knees. I rush to her, pulling her to me. "I did what she asked. She made me promise to take care of him."

"Alisa, it isn't your fault. Your father should be the one taking care of you, not the other way around."

"Take me home."

"Please, Alisa. You can't keep living like this. We have to tell someone."

"No! Things are fine. Everything is fine." But even as she says the words, I know she doesn't believe them.

"You know it's not okay that he hits you."

She starts breathing hard. I need to do something to calm her before she goes into a full-blown panic attack.

"It's okay. I'm right here. I promise we'll get help. We can call the police or talk to a counselor."

Alisa clutches her chest.

I pull her to me, holding her close. "It's okay," I say.

When she's calm, she pulls back a little.

"You have to talk to someone."

Alisa cries, and I hold her. I had my suspicions, but I couldn't believe them. Why would any parent do this to their child? How could they? This poor girl deserves the world, and I have to do the only thing I know to help her. I have to tell someone.

ben

As I approach the door to the counselor's office the next morning, my throat feels like someone's squeezing the hell out of it. I don't want to be here, yet I do.

"Come inside, Ben. I won't bite," Mrs. Tanner says.

Hesitantly, I cross the threshold.

Her short brown hair is perfectly straight, and she's dressed in a white button-down shirt. She removes her glasses. Her green eyes look tired. "What can I help you with?"

I clear my throat, which is suddenly dry. "I need help."

"Okay. With what?"

Sensing the severity of what I need to say, she gets up and closes the door. She hands me a small bottle of water and returns to her seat. I chug the entire thing and take a deep breath before sitting across from her.

"I don't really know how to talk about this or how to start."

She nods. "It's okay. Take your time."

Wiping the sweat from my hands on my jeans, I look up. I am never this nervous. "I have…my girlfriend…" Fuck.

It feels like tiny ants are crawling all over my skin. Nausea claws at my insides. "I think she's being abused by her father."

Her eyes widen and she leans forward on the desk. "Why do you think that?"

I take another breath. "She comes to school with bruises on her arms. I've seen her with black eyes. Swollen lip." I swallow hard. "Yesterday, I found her locked in a shed. She says she's just clumsy, but she's very afraid of her father."

"These are very severe accusations. Has she admitted the abuse?"

"She hasn't denied it. She…she also cuts herself."

"I'm really sorry to hear about your girlfriend. You did the right thing."

"I don't know how to help, but I can't sit by and let it continue. I love her."

"We can call child services, and they will check on the situation."

"What will happen to her?"

"If it turns out to be true, she will be sent to foster care."

Fuck.

I've heard horror stories of foster homes. Some are pretty messed up, similar to hers. I will hate myself even more if she winds up in another abusive home. Maybe by some miracle, Dad will let her stay with us. "Will she know it was me?"

"No. Your name will be protected. If you need time to decide to tell me who it is, I understand. This isn't an easy decision."

It's not. But I can't wait. What if her dad hits her so bad, she ends up in the hospital? Or worse? What if she ends up in foster care with a terrible alcoholic again? I have to save her. She has to know how she deserves so much more than this. I take a deep breath, hating what I'm about to do. I only want her to be safe. Free from all the pain she's endured. I want her to grow and become a happy, carefree woman. She deserves that and more. But no matter my intentions, I know this will end any relationship I have with her.

I swallow hard. "Her name is Alisa Hopewell."

alisa

The sound of the cold rain hitting the window is almost hypnotic. I don't want to move. I just want to stay in the same spot. I came home after a couple of days, and Daddy apologized and brought me a stuffed pig. He told me I needed to shape up. From now on, I'm only going to focus on school and work. I won't talk back. I won't be reckless anymore. I can be the perfect daughter.

The door opens to my room, and Diane comes in with a laundry bag. "Wash this by tonight."

"Wash it yourself," I mumble, surprising myself. Where did that come from?

"Alisa! Don't talk to me that way."

"What the hell is going on in here?" Daddy storms into the room.

"She talked back to me."

I swallow hard as Daddy stares at me. He seizes my arm, squeezing it so hard it starts throbbing. Just as he raises his fist, something outside the window catches his eyes. When

I turn around, I see a police car and another vehicle come down the driveway. Terror crawls up to my heart encasing it in a strange hold as both cars slow, pulling up next to the house.

Daddy releases me as two officers get out of one car and a woman gets out of the other. They start walking toward the porch, and Daddy hurries to the door.

Diane stays behind, throwing me a glare in my direction. "What did you do?"

"Nothing."

I swallow hard as Daddy opens the door. I strain to hear what they're saying.

"Good afternoon," Daddy greets them.

"Hi. My name is Patty Sardone. I'm with Child Protective Services. This is Officer Davis and Officer Grimes."

"Nice to meet you," he says. "Would you like some coffee?"

"No, thank you. We're here because there have been reports of abuse. We need to investigate."

My breath hitches as Diane grips my arm so hard, I know there will be bruises later. She glares at me, and I know I'm going to get in trouble. My heart is racing, and Diane shoves me into the bathroom. She closes the door and I'm hidden in the dark, holding my breath. I can't hear anything they're saying, but I quietly open the bathroom door and ease out when I see that she's gone. The bedroom door is cracked, and I move closer.

"Is Alisa here?"

"No," Diane immediately says. "She's at work. But Jack would never hurt anyone. He's the sweetest man."

"Are you Alisa's mom?"

"No," Daddy snaps. "She's my fiancé. And I don't abuse my daughter."

My heart is pounding so hard it's throbbing in my ears.

"We need to check the premises," Officer Davis says.

My breath hitches, and I need to hide. Why would Ben do this to me? Why would he take my father away?

The police officer opens the door to the bedroom, and I freeze. "Alisa?" His blue eyes pin me, but I manage to look away.

Swallowing hard, I slowly nod.

"We're just here to ask questions," he says. "My name is Officer Davis. Do you feel safe talking to me in here?"

"Yes."

He closes the door to my bedroom but doesn't come any closer. For some reason, I'm not scared. His eyes are kind and even though his hands rest on his belt that holds a gun and a baton, I'm not afraid of him. He's tall and his hat almost brushes against the low ceiling.

"How is school going?"

"Fine." Why are they here? What do they want to know?

"Grades good? Friends?"

Heat creeps up my cheeks. "My-my grades haven't been good. My best friend recently moved away. Her mom died."

"I'm sorry to hear that. Do you have a boyfriend?"

"Yes." But he's the one who told.

"How is that going?"

"Fine."

"Can you tell me what abuse means to you?"

I swallow hard. "What?"

"What happened to your eye?" the officer asks.

I roll my eyes. "I slipped and fell into the coffee table."

He studies me for a moment. "It's okay to tell the truth. Most kids don't realize it. Does your father hit you?"

"No."

"Do you know why a person would report it?"

"I get picked on at school a lot. Some kid was playing a prank."

I bite my lip and refuse to meet his eyes. I want them all gone, and I never want to see them again. Why would Ben do this to me?

I cross my arms in front of my chest. "Is that it? Have you got what you needed?"

"Alisa, I was abused as a child and teenager. It took a long time for me to realize that it wasn't normal. Or right. You deserve to be safe and in a better environment."

"I'm sorry that happened to you. But I'm fine."

He nods with a smirk. "I was the same way. I know something's going on. For one, your father is already intoxicated, as is his fiancée. She lied about your whereabouts. You deserve better, Alisa. You can get out of this and live without fear."

"He's my father."

"Yeah. He is. And he shouldn't be treating you so poorly. If you ever need someone to talk to, call me." He scribbles something on the back of a card and hands it to me. "That's my home number."

I nod.

His hand is on the door, and I could tell him everything. I could tell him how fearful I am of coming home. How I never get anything right. How I constantly have to walk on eggshells. How everything is my fault, and I'm never good enough. But I can't force the words to come out of my mouth.

"One more thing," he says as he turns toward me. "This isn't your fault, and you deserve better."

He opens the door and after a few minutes, they leave. I'm frozen in the middle of my room, listening to the rain pour harder against the window. And I wait for the storm to come.

ben

Usually Smashing Pumpkins is enough to calm me down. But tonight, I'm nervous. I have been for days. I haven't seen or heard from Alisa since she left my house. I hate it. I don't know if I made the right decision. Dad says it was, and it was the first time he and I had a conversation worthwhile. A real father-son talk. He offered to do something, but I told him I didn't need anyone else involved. With Alisa, we have to tread lightly.

My door opens, and Dad enters. "Ben, Alisa is downstairs. She won't come inside, but she's soaking wet and looks terrible."

Fuck.

I haul ass down the stairs, throwing open the door. I rush up to her, wanting to gather her in my arms, but she presses her hand against my chest. It's pouring fucking cold rain out here. She shifts, and the porch light shines on her face. Her eye is swollen. I clench my teeth hating the churning feeling in my stomach. What have I done?

"Are you okay? Your eye—"

"How could you do this to me?" she yells.

"I had to—"

"They sent police officers to my house!" Her voice is full of venom.

"Did they take your dad away?"

"No. I told them someone was pranking me."

My stomach sinks. "What? Why would you—"

"What happened to friendship? What happened to you always being there? What happened to me being able to trust you?" Tears mix with the rain as we're both completely soaked. "You lied, Ben!"

"I had to do this to save you."

"I don't need saving. You don't get it. They'll take me away." She gives in to the tears and lets me put my arms around her.

"I know, but you can't stay there."

"They'll take me away from you."

My heart falls. She's putting up with this because of me? I feel sick and I hold her closer. "What? Alisa, you can't stay there. I love you so much, but you can't live this way."

"You don't get it. My life is about to change forever in a matter of minutes. I will never see my father again. Or you. I hope you're happy." She wriggles out of my arms.

"Alisa—"

"I'm leaving."

"Where are you going?"

"Don't call. Don't write me."

I'm going to vomit. "Where are you going? Please don't run away. We can fix this. I can help you."

"If you love me at all, don't contact me." She turns around and leaves in the pouring rain, taking my heart with her. Again.

alisa

The police station is full of several shady looking people in handcuffs. I don't want to do this. I feel sick. My throat is dry. I'm cold and shivering from the rain. It feels like worms are crawling around in my stomach.

Officer Davis comes up to me. He offers a blanket and his hand. "It's okay, Alisa."

When he pulls me into a room, I tell him everything through thick tears. I'm shaking, and I don't know if I'm doing the right thing. When I'm finished, I excuse myself to the bathroom. Racing to the nearest stall, I heave until there is nothing left.

Oh no. What have I done? They'll take Daddy away, then where will I go?

This isn't happening. How can I live with someone I don't know? Will they be like Daddy?

There's a knock on the door, and it startles me.

"Alisa? Are you okay?"

I never know how to answer that. I betrayed my father and mother. She made me promise to take care of him, but I didn't. I was selfish.

"Alisa?"

"I'm fine."

"We need to go."

Taking a deep breath, I unlatch the stall door and face the officer.

"Do you have a bag?"

I shake my head.

"Would you like to go back and get anything?"

I know Daddy won't be home for a few more hours.

We return to my house and, almost within an instant, I want to forget and take back everything I've said about Daddy. He's just doing his best. The tears collect in my throat. But I say nothing.

When I get inside, I try not to think about the eeriness of it. It feels colder. Darker. Creepier.

Grabbing as many clothes as I can, and Mr. Zebra and the red bear Ben gave me, I scan the bathroom for anything I missed, and once I spot my drawer, I clench my teeth, needing my scissors. I need them now more than ever.

"Alisa, are you ready?" Officer Davis asks.

Clearing my throat, I nod, leaving my scissors behind.

epilogue

After boiling chickpeas, run them over cold water to remove the skins. I've only done this once before, and it was oddly satisfying. Each time I found a chickpea with skin on it, a small part of me celebrated. I guess the idea of shedding skin resonates with me.

Maybe because that's what I did essentially. At least, I feel like I'm in new skin.

A lot can happen in a short amount of time. After I gathered clothes from my house that night four months ago, I was in a home for children for the first few nights. It was scary, and I didn't sleep. Those first few weeks were hard. I missed Ben. Sarah. And I missed my father.

Officer Davis came back with his brother and his brother's wife, and next thing I knew, I was in some strange house with the couple and their seven-year-old son an hour away from Daddy. And Ben. It's in a suburb of the city, and it's completely different than Vinemont. There are more grocery stores and shopping malls than I ever knew existed.

Why they wanted me is beyond me. I've been here for a few weeks, and so far, it's…quiet. I'm not sure if I'll ever get used to that. Dan and Kaitlyn keep the heat on all the time. There's always food and electricity. I feel safe here. I sleep every night, but I still have nightmares. Some are of Daddy finding me. I wake in terror, and Kaitlyn is always there comforting me.

Their son, Paul, is sweet. Really smart. Kaitlyn is a middle school teacher and has never once asked me to call her 'mom.' Dan is a doctor home every evening. It isn't like in the movies or TV shows where they're constantly working. He's not always working unless he has to deliver a baby. They seem nice. And Officer Davis, or Uncle Reid as Paul calls him, visits often to see how I'm doing. I guess he convinced them to take me. They've put me in therapy, but I don't really know what to talk about. They also know my secret and try to help. I really try to stop, but it's hard sometimes.

It's weird that they know everything about me. They tend to tread lightly around me, like I'm going to snap. I know Dan and Reid were abused, so maybe I'm supposed to be treated like a wounded animal. Paul acts normal. He says he likes me and wants to keep me. He asks me to read to him sometimes before bed, and I do. It surprisingly brings me comfort.

I rinse the chickpeas and remember the last time I cooked Greek. I was at Ben's house, and we kissed for the first time. I miss him. The last thing I said to him wasn't how I wanted it to go. I've thought about writing a letter, but I don't know where to begin. I've been talking to Sarah almost every day now. We talk on the phone, chat online. She tries to convince me to call Ben, but I can't.

"What's on your mind?" Kaitlyn asks as she grabs a water bottle from the fridge.

"Nothing," I say. It's an automatic response, but I know she won't accept it. "Sorry. Um…I was thinking about my friend."

"What about them?" She meets my eyes.

I can feel my cheeks burn. "Just how much I miss him."

"What's his name?"

"Ben."

"How long has it been since you spoke to him?"

"December."

"Wow. You should call him."

"What?"

"Unless you don't want to."

"No, I just…" I place the chickpeas in the food processor. "I don't even know what to say. I wasn't very nice to him the last time we spoke."

"Who is he?"

"He was my boyfriend. We grew up together."

"Ah. If he really cares about you, he'll still wanna talk to you. Does Sarah know him?"

"Yes."

"What does she say?"

"She thinks I should call him."

Dan walks in, grabbing a coke from the fridge. No matter how many times I witness it, I still think of Daddy getting a beer. "Call who?"

"Alisa had a boyfriend."

"Boyfriend, huh?" He leans against the sink and cracks open the can. "Is he nice?"

I can feel myself smile. "Yes. He's the one who—" I stop myself. "He helped me."

Dan nods. His hair is balding at the top and wrinkles crowd his eyes. "Well then. I look forward to meeting him. He better not be an Alabama fan."

"Oh, Daniel." Kaitlyn laughs as she playfully pats his shoulder.

"What are you making?" Dan asks.

"Hummus."

He taps his round belly. "You are going to make me fat."

"Hummus is healthy though," I tell him.

"In moderation, I'm sure." He kisses the top of my head and leaves the room.

"Mama, I washed my hands so I could help," Paul says as he brushes by his father. He holds up his hands, showing her.

"I see that. Alisa's gonna cook Greek tonight. Lots of veggies."

Paul makes a disgusted face. "But you'll make them taste good?"

"Of course," I tell him.

Kaitlyn helps me cook grilled chicken pitas. We sit down at the table to eat dinner as a family, like every night. We talk about our days. No one argues. No one yells. Afterward, Dan and Paul clean up, and I retreat upstairs to my room to finish my homework. I don't work anymore. Dan and Kaitlyn want me to focus on school and help me with my assignments.

My room walls are decorated with band posters. The Cure. Nirvana. Tori Amos. Bush. I get to listen to music any time I want. At least, once my homework is done.

The phone rings and I answer.

"Hey," Sarah says.

"Hey."

"Uncle Todd said Damon and I can come up for spring break."

I gasp. "Really?"

"Yes."

"I can't believe it. I miss you so much."

"I know, man. I miss you, too. Maybe…we'll get to see Ben, too."

I roll my eyes.

"Yeah. I heard that. Still haven't called him, have you?"

"No."

She groans. "Will you just call him already?"

"I don't know what to say to him."

"Doesn't matter."

"I don't remember his number."

Sarah lets out a loud laugh. "That's a good one. He misses you. He talks about you all the time."

"Fine."

She gasps. "Are you going to call him? Because I'm chatting with him online now. I can tell him."

She is relentless. "Okay." Nerves move around inside my stomach as if little worms were taking up residence.

"I'm taking credit for this reunion. Call me after."

She hangs up, and I stare at the phone. I still remember his number, but I'm scared.

With a shaky hand, I pick up the receiver and dial the number. I feel a little faint as I bite my lip.

"Hello?" he answers, and my heart swells.

"Hi Ben."

"Alisa? Oh my god. How are you?" I can hear excitement and worry in his voice.

"I'm good."

He releases a sigh of relief. "It's so good to hear from you. You sound amazing."

"Thanks."

There's a pause.

"You know Sarah is online constantly asking how this is going?" he asks.

"She's a bit invested in this, isn't she?"

He laughs. "A little. I closed the chat though. She can wait."

"How have you been?"

"I've been good. We won the state championship."

I smile. "I saw. I'm proud of you."

"Thanks. I'm proud of you, too."

"Me?"

"Of course. You're very brave."

"Thanks. Look, I wanted to thank you for what you did. You saved me."

"You saved yourself, Alisa. I just kinda nudged you."

"You showed me that I'm worthy and deserving. You showed me love and challenged me."

"You did the same for me."

It's like we are two lost souls that found solace in each other. We are both deserving and we are both good enough for love. In all forms. Including loving ourselves.

"I still have that mixed tape for you," he says.

"Really?"

"Yeah. I'd really like to give it to you."

My face burns, and I'm so glad he can't see it. "Okay."

"I'm actually visiting my mom and Hayden this weekend. I could come by."

"How do you know where I live?" I already know the answer.

"Sarah. You're actually about ten minutes from Mom. And every time I've been down there, I've wanted to visit you."

"I miss you." My quivering chin catches me off guard.

"I miss you, too. Do you want to have dinner Friday?"

Heat fills me. "Yes."

"Awesome. Want to hear a song from the tape? It'll be like a teaser."

"Sure."

A few seconds pass, and I hear a Smashing Pumpkins song. I only know because Billy Corgan's voice is very recognizable. It's a slow song, and as it progresses, my pulse edges higher and higher. By the end of the song, Billy Corgan's crooning about being in love.

"The song reminds me of you."

I smile.

Excitement runs through my veins once I hang up the phone a couple of hours later. Whatever happens, happens. I don't want to lose him again, though. And I think our paths were meant to cross again so we could save each other.

Losing my mother was the worst thing that ever happened, and it started a domino effect of my life turning upside down. But in the best way possible. Everything happens for a reason, and if I hadn't gone through what I did, I may not be here.

I don't know if I will ever see my father again. I feel a strange ache when I think of him. I couldn't save him from himself, and neither could Mom. Only he can do that. I hope that he becomes a better person for whomever will cross his path. I've not spoken to him, and I'm not sure I want to.

I've come to realize I was cutting myself to show others that I was in pain. I never wanted to ask for help. I wanted them to ask. But now if I ever have the urge to hurt myself, I make myself talk. There are people who love me and who are here for me.

I was always Daddy's little girl, but somewhere along the way, I gave up that title. I did everything for him, and it was never enough. Now, I do things for myself, and I am good enough.

the end

playlist

Fade Into You – Mazzy Star

Pictures of You – The Cure

Luna – Smashing Pumpkins

Black – Pearl Jam

One Headlight – The Wallflowers

If You Could Only See – Tonic

Silent All These Years – Tori Amos

Black-Dove (January) – Tori Amos

Nutshell – Alice in Chains

Today – Smashing Pumpkins

Hurt – Nine Inch Nails

I'm Kissing You – Des'ree

Time After Time – Cyndi Lauper

My Skin – Natalie Merchant

Wild Horses – The Sundays

Porcelain – Better Than Ezra

Upside Down – Tori Amos

Comedown – Bush

Bullet With Butterfly Wings – Smashing Pumpkins

Dumb – Nirvana

The Day I Tried to Live – Soundgarden

You Learn – Alanis Morissette

resources

If you or someone you know is in need of help in terms of self-mutilation, abuse, or any mental condition, the links below can help. Please know you are not alone. You matter.

National Alliance on Mental Illness | 800.950.NAMI
text "NAMI" to 741741 | https://www.nami.org/home

National Domestic Violence Hotline | 800.799.7233
 https://www.thehotline.org/

National Suicide Prevention Lifeline | 800.273.8255
https://suicidepreventionlifeline.org/

SAMHSA's National Helpline | 800.662.4357
https://www.samhsa.gov

acknowledgements

I first wrote this story in 1996, and at that time there weren't many books that portrayed abuse or mental conditions. I put this away for the longest time, but it kept coming up in my head. I wanted to rewrite it and keep it set in the 90s. Writing with the same music I grew up with was so nostalgic and therapeutic for me in so many ways. After so many years and so many rewrites, here she is, and I'm so proud of this novel.

I want to thank all of my readers and fans. Your patience, understanding, support, and love over the years has helped propel me to keep this dream alive. You are truly amazing.

There are so many people who helped me through this process and helped me in life that I want to thank. My editor, Lindsey Alexander. Without you I wouldn't have been able to bring these characters to life and realize what was missing. Thank you for believing in me and in this story.

My cover designer, Lauren Perrin, who blew me away with her amazing skills.

To my bestie boo, Laura Trujillo. Even though you hate my buts, your friendship means the world to me, and I don't know what I would do without you. Thank you for your honesty and for helping me with this journey.

Angie Rivera, I don't know what I'd do without you either. Driving 17 hours to see me for my birthday is one of the best gifts I've ever received. You truly are amazing and have the kindest most genuine soul.

Jennifer Watts, your unconditional love and friendship has gotten me through all the years.

Nicole Hoffmann thanks for helping me through times when I get stuck in stories. Keep up the glitter, girl.

Thank you, Stephanie Wooddell for all the makeup and health advice and for cheering me on all the time. I promise I won't make you wear a flower crown.

Sarah Rutledge, Gina Morgan Moody, and Caitlin Denman, for all your excitement and continuous support and friendship over the years.

Thank you to my amazing family of friends – Strummer's Army. You are a great group of ladies that I admire and appreciate your support. I don't know what I'd do without you all and all the advice, furbaby pictures, laughter, and dick glitter.

To all the musicians for creating scenes in my head and getting the right emotion and for helping me through life.

And of course, to my family for cheering me on. I love all of you. Your support truly means the world to me.

Finally, thank you to my fiancé, Brandon for never questioning my dreams; for always wanting to give me the best life possible; for believing in me; for always being there; for making my coffee every morning. I love you.

about the author

Carrigan Richards is the young adult author of critically acclaimed *Pieces of Me,* a contemporary romance, the *Elemental Enchanters Series,* a paranormal romance series, and *January Dreams Series,* a romantic mystery series. She lives in Atlanta, Georgia.

When she's not writing (which is rare), she's spending time with her fiancé, family, and friends, listening to music, playing with her furdog, Eli, or cheering on her Atlanta Braves. Carrigan loves hearing from readers. Follow her on Twitter, Instagram, TikTok, look for her on Facebook or follow her blog at www.carriganrichards.com.

www.ingramcontent.com/pod-product-compliance
Lightning Source LLC
Chambersburg PA
CBHW010605310726
48969CB00010B/2573